The Mobile Library

THE DELEGATES' CHOICE

Ian Sansom

W F HOWES LTD

This large print edition published in 2009 by
W F Howes Ltd
Unit 4, Rearsby Business Park, Gaddesby Lane,
Rearsby, Leicester LE7 4YH

1 3 5 7 9 10 8 6 4 2

First published in the United Kingdom in 2008
by Harper Perennial

A CIP catalogue record for this book is available
from the British Library

ISBN 978 1 40742 976 2

Typeset by Palimpsest Book Production Limited,
Grangemouth, Stirlingshire
Printed and bound in Great Britain
by MPG Books Ltd, Bodmin, Cornwall

FSC
Mixed Sources
Product group from well-managed
forests and other controlled sources
Cert no. SGS-COC-2953
www.fsc.org
© 1996 Forest Stewardship Council

The Delegates' Choice

ALSO BY IAN SANSOM
FROM CLIPPER LARGE PRINT

The Mobile Library: Mr Dixon Disappears
The Mobile Library: The Case of the
Missing Books

For the Group

CHAPTER 1

'I resign,' said Israel.

'Aye,' said Ted.

'I do,' said Israel.

'Good,' said Ted.

'I've made up my mind. I'm resigning,' said Israel. 'Today.'

'Right you are,' said Ted.

'I've absolutely had enough.'

'Uh-huh.'

'Of the whole thing. This place! The—'

'People,' said Ted.

'Exactly!' said Israel. 'The people! Exactly! The people, they drive me—'

'Crazy,' said Ted.

'Exactly! You took the words right out of my mouth.'

'Aye, well, you might've mentioned it before,' said Ted.

'Well, this is it. I'm up to—'

'High dough,' said Ted.

'What?' said Israel.

'You're up to high dough with it.'

'No,' said Israel. 'No. I don't even know what it

means, *up to high dough with it*. What the hell's that supposed to mean?'

'It's an expression.'

'Ah, right yes. It would be. Anyway, I'm up to . . . here with it.'

'Good.'

'I'm going to hand in my resignation to Linda.'

'Excellent,' said Ted.

'Before the meeting today.'

'First class,' said Ted.

'Before she has a chance to trick me out of it again.'

'Away you go then.'

'I am *so* gone already. I am out of here. I tell you, you are not going to see me for dust. I'm moving on.'

'Mmm.'

'I'm going! Look!'

'Ach, well, it's been a pleasure, sure. We're all going to miss you.'

'Yes,' said Israel.

'Good,' said Ted.

'So,' said Israel.

'You've time for a wee cup of coffee at Zelda's first, mind? For auld time's sake?'

'No!' said Israel. 'I need to strike while the—'

'And a wee scone, but?'

Israel looked at his watch.

'Meeting's not till three,' said Ted.

'What day is it?' said Israel.

'Wednesday.'

'What's the scone on Wednesdays?'

'Date and almond,' said Ted, consulting his mental daily special scone-timetable.

Israel huffed. 'All right,' he said. 'But *then* we need to get there early. I am definitely, *definitely* resigning.'

They'd had this conversation before, around about mid-week, and once a week, for several months now, Israel Armstrong BA (Hons) and Ted Carson – the Starsky and Hutch, the Morse and the Lewis, the Thomson and Thompson, the Don Quixote and Sancho Panza, the Dante, the Virgil, the Cagney, the Lacey, the Deleuze and Guattari, the Mork and the Mindy of the mobile library world.

Israel had been living in Tumdrum for long enough – more than six months! – to find the routine not just getting to him, but actually having got to him; the self-same rainy days which slowly and silently became weeks and then months, and which seemed gradually to be slowing, and slowing, and slowing, almost but not quite to a complete and utter stop, so that it felt to Israel as though he'd been stuck in Tumdrum on the mobile library not just for months, but for years, indeed for *decades* almost. Israel felt trapped; stuck; in complete and utter stasis. He felt incapacitated. He felt like he was in a never-ending episode of *24*, or a play by Samuel Beckett.

'This is like *Krapp's Last Tape*,' he told Ted, once they were settled in Zelda's and Minnie was bringing them coffee.

'Is it?' said Ted.

'Are ye being rude about my coffee?' said Minnie.

'No,' said Israel. 'I'm just talking about a play.'

'Ooh!' said Minnie.

'Beckett?' said Israel.

'Beckett?' said Minnie. 'He was a Portora boy, wasn't he?'

'What?' said Israel.

'In Enniskillen there,' said Minnie. 'The school, sure. That's where he went to school, wasn't it?'

'I don't know,' said Israel. 'Samuel Beckett?'

'Sure he did,' said Minnie. 'What was that play he did?'

'*Waiting for Godot*?' said Israel.

'Was it?' said Minnie. 'It wasn't *Educating Rita*?'

'*Riverdance*,' said Ted. 'Most popular Irish show of all time.'

'That's not a play,' said Israel wearily.

'Aye, you're a theatre critic now, are ye?'

'Och,' said Minnie. 'And who was the other fella?'

'What?' said Israel.

'That went to school there, at Portora?'

'No, you've got me,' said Israel. 'No idea.'

'Ach, sure ye know. The homosexualist.'

'You've lost me, Minnie, sorry.'

'Wrote the plays. "A handbag!" That one.'

'Oscar Wilde?'

'He's yer man!' said Minnie. 'He was another Portora boy, wasn't he, Ted?'

4

Ted was busy emptying the third of his traditional three sachets of sugar into his coffee. 'Aye.'

'Zelda's nephew went there,' said Minnie. 'The ones in Fermanagh there.'

'Right,' said Israel. 'Anyway . . .'

'I'll check with her.'

'Fine,' said Israel.

'And your scones are just coming,' said Minnie.

'That's grand,' said Ted, producing a packet of cigarettes.

'Uh-uh,' said Minnie, wagging her finger. 'We've gone no smoking.'

'Ye have not?' said Ted.

'We have indeed.'

'Since when?'

'The weekend, just.'

'Ach,' said Ted. 'That's the political correctness.'

'I know,' said Minnie. 'It's what people want though, these days.'

'You'll lose custom, but.'

'Aye.'

'Nanny state,' said Ted, obediently putting away his cigarettes and lighter.

'Smoking kills,' said Israel.

'Aye, and so do a lot of other things,' said Ted darkly.

'It is a shame, really,' said Minnie. 'Sure, everybody used to smoke.'

Israel stared at the yellowing walls of the café as Ted and Minnie reminisced about the great smokers of the past: Humphrey Bogart, Lauren

Bacall, Bette Davis, Winston Churchill, Fidel Castro.

'Beagles,' said Israel.

'What?' said Minnie.

'And Sherlock Holmes,' added Israel.

'Aye,' said Ted.

'Was he not a druggie?' said Minnie.

'Sam Spade,' said Israel.

'Never heard of him,' said Minnie.

Sometimes Israel wished he was a gentleman detective, far away from here, with a cocaine and morphine habit, and a slightly less intelligent confidant to admire his genius. Or like Sam Spade, the blond Satan, pounding the hard streets of San Francisco, entangling with knock-out redheads and outwitting the Fat Man. Instead, here he was in Zelda's, listening to Ted and Minnie and looking up at old Christian Aid and Trócaire posters, and the dog-eared notices for the Citizens Advice Bureau, and the wilting pot plants, and the lone long-broken computer in the corner with the Blu-Tacked sign above it proclaiming the café Tumdrum's Internet hot-spot, 'The First and Still the Best', and the big laminated sign over by the door featuring a man sitting slumped with his head in his hands, advertising the Samaritans: 'Suicidal? Depressed?'

Well, actually . . .

He sipped at his coffee and took a couple of Nurofen. The coffee was as bad as ever. All coffee in Tumdrum came weak, and milky, and lukewarm, as though having recently passed through someone else, or a cow. Maybe he should take up smoking, late in life, as an act of flamboyance and rebellion: a smoke was a smoke, after all, but with a coffee you couldn't always be sure. The coffee in Tumdrum was more like slurry run-off. He missed proper coffee, Israel – a nice espresso at Bar Italia just off Old Compton Street, that was one of the things he missed about London, and the coffee at Grodzinski's, round the corner from his mum's. He missed his friends, also, of course; and his books; and the cinema; a nice slice of lemon drizzle cake in the café at the Curzon Soho; and the theatre; and the galleries; and the restaurants; it was the little things; nothing much; just all the thriving cultural activities of one of the world's great capital cities . . .

'Just remind me,' he said to Ted, once Minnie had gone off for the scones. 'Why do we come here?'

'It's the only place there is,' said Ted.

'Yes,' said Israel, amazed. 'I know, but . . . it's, like . . .' He took another sip of his coffee. 'They don't even serve proper coffee.'

'I think the machine's broken,' said Ted.

'The machine's always broken.'

'Mmm.'

'It's that sort of chicory stuff, isn't it,' said Israel, licking his lips, trying to figure out what it was, the unpleasant burnt taste and the feral, sicky smell, like something someone had just brought up. 'That's what it is. I think it's that . . . what do you call it?'

'What?'

'Ersatz coffee.'

'I don't know what you're talking about,' said Ted. 'I had a cappuccino once in Belfast.'

'What?'

'They have coffee bars down there everywhere now. It's like the Continent.'

'Oh, God,' said Israel.

'What?' said Ted.

'No,' said Israel, shaking his head. 'No.'

'No what?'

'No. Just no. It's no good, I can't drink this,' said Israel, drinking his coffee.

He was thinking now about Gloria: whenever he started thinking about London his thoughts turned quickly to Gloria.

Gloria was the Eros in Israel's Piccadilly Circus, the Serpentine in his Hyde Park, the St Paul's in his City, the Brick Lane of his East End . . . her dark hair cascading down over her shoulders, her piercing brown eyes, his hand in hers, their bodies entwined . . .

'Scones!' said Minnie, interrupting Israel before the point of no return, and placing a couple of enormous steaming chunks of hot scone down on the plastic gingham-look tablecloth.

'I was wrong,' she said.

'Sorry?' said Israel. 'Wrong? About what?'

'It's not Zelda's nephew at Portora.'

'Right.'

'It's her other nephew.'

'Uh-huh.'

'Zelda's other brother's boy – Niall, the fella who's the computer-whizz?'

'Right,' said Israel.

What? Who? Niall? The nephew? The other nephew? Why on earth did people in Tumdrum go on like characters in Russian novels, insisting on talking about their friends and family members as if you'd known them for years, when of course you hadn't, you had no idea who the hell they were talking about, unless you'd lived here your whole life, which Israel hadn't. Did Israel speak to people in Tumdrum endlessly and incessantly about *his* family and friends? Did he ever mention *his* sisters, or his cousins, including the successful ones, or his mother's neighbours Mr and Mrs Krimholz, or the butcher, the baker and the candlestick makers of his own lovely little patch of north London? No, he did not. People in Tumdrum seemed to assume that the mere fact of living there instantly made you a local, as though you absorbed local knowledge of complex hereditary diseases and bloodlines by osmosis. I mean, how was he supposed to keep up with the progress of your mother's sister's urinary tract infection when he'd never even met your mother? It was a physical impossibility: he'd have had to be telepathic, and a qualified medical practitioner, and, also, he'd have to care, and he didn't. He was not bothered. Am I bothered? *Est-ce que je suis bovvered?* Israel slathered a piece of scone with butter.

'Was that the fella who used to go out with Zelda's cousin's husband's sister?' said Ted.

'Ugh!' said Israel.

'What?' said Ted.

'That's yer man,' said Minnie.

'Who?' said Israel. 'Who? Who are you talking about now?'

'You know,' said Minnie. 'The big fella. They used to live down there at Lough Island Reevy, in Down.'

'Hello?' said Israel. 'Excuse me! I don't know what you're talking about. Some of us were not born around here you know.'

'No, pet,' said Minnie pityingly, moving off to another table. 'Never mind.'

'God,' said Israel.

'Don't,' said Ted, wagging a finger.

'What?'

'You know what.'

'Oh, God.'

'I'll not tell ye again,' said Ted, who was a very vehement anti-blasphemer, unless he was doing the blaspheming.

'Sorry,' said Israel. 'I'm going to have to bite the bullet, though,' he continued, picking up his scone, trying to decide where to start.

'Uh-huh,' said Ted, who'd already started on his own. 'She's a fair junt of scone, but, isn't she? And nice and warm.'

'No, I mean with the job. I'm definitely going to resign.'

'Mmm.'

'Even if it means going back to working in the Bargain Bookstore.'

'Good man ye are.'

'In Thurrock.'

'Uh-huh.'

'In Essex,' said Israel, convincing himself. 'I still have plenty of friends there.'

'Mmm.'

'A man has to have his self-respect,' said Israel.

'Or what does he have?' said Ted, finishing a mouthful.

'Exactly!' said Israel. 'Take this morning.'

'Why?' said Ted.

'Because,' said Israel.

'It wasnae a bad morning,' said Ted.

'Wasn't bad!' said Israel, using the scone gavel-like on the table; the crust did not give. 'You see! That's it!'

'What's it?'

'That's the problem.'

'Is it? The scone?'

'No! This morning *wasn't bad*, you said?'

'Aye.'

'*Wasn't bad?*'

'Aye.'

'*Wasn't bad?*'

'Yer right.'

'No, it wasn't bad! It was *terrible*!'

11

'Ach,' said Ted, picking a date out of his scone.

'You're just inured to it, Ted.'

'Ee-what?'

'Inured. It's . . . Anyway, I'm young and you're . . .'

'What?'

'Older.'

'Aye.'

'And look at us! We're nothing more than errand boys!'

'I don't know about that,' said Ted.

'I've got a degree from Oxford you know,' said Israel.

'Uh-huh,' said Ted, picking at his scone. 'Oxford Brookes, wasn't it you said?'

'Which is *in* Oxford,' said Israel. 'I don't know if you've been there?'

'Can't say I have,' said Ted. 'No.'

'No!' said Israel triumphantly. 'Well then. I am a highly educated librarian. I shouldn't be – *we* shouldn't be – just doing errands for people.'

'We're not just doing errands for people.'

'Yes, we are!'

'We're a service,' said Ted.

'A library service,' said Israel. 'A *library* service. Not a Tesco home delivery service! Picking up people's groceries is not the kind of service I had in mind when I got into this job,' said Israel. 'It's ridiculous.'

'It's not ridiculous.'

'It is!' said Israel. 'Honestly. This morning . . .'

First stop of the day, up round the coast, and first in, a man in his seventies, not one of their regulars.

'D'ye have the *Impartial Recorder*?'

'Sorry?' said Israel.

'The paper? D'ye have the paper?'

'No. No. I'm afraid not.'

'The *Tele* then?'

'No. Sorry. We don't have any papers.'

'You don't sell any papers?'

'No. Sorry.'

'You sell books then?'

'No, no, we don't sell books either.'

'D'ye not?'

'No.'

'Why not?'

'We're a library.'

'Ach, aye. Second-hand books then.'

'Erm . . . Well, yes. Sort-of, I suppose.'

'By the yard, or by the pound?'

'Sorry?'

'I saw a thing about it on the telly once. Books by the yard. Or the dozen. I don't know. I can't rightly remember.'

'Right. Well, we don't actually sell books here at all. You have to *join* a library. Like you do a video shop or . . . something. I need to see a utility bill, something with your name and address on it, and then I can—'

'I'd not be showing you that, indeed; that'd be under the Freedom of Information Act, wouldn't it? I don't know who ye are. Are ye the police?'

'No. I'm not the police.'

'You could be anybody.'

'Yes, true. I could, of course, be . . . anybody. I am *in fact* the librarian though. Here. In the . . . mobile library. Where we . . . are.'

'You're a funny-lookin' librarian.'

'Yes, well, sorry, I . . .'

'D'ye sell milk?'

'No.'

'Bread?'

'No.'

'A pan loaf just?'

'No!'

'Ach. We used to have Paddy Weekly – he was great, so he was – but he was driven out by the supermarkets, ye know.'

'Yes.'

'We've to get to Ballycastle for shopping these days.'

'Right.'

'I prefer the shopping in Coleraine, meself.'

'Uh-huh.'

'I can get me feet done and me hair cut – there's a wee girl who comes round the Fold – but if I give ye a wee list ye couldn't do me a few messages once a week, could ye?'

It just wasn't right.

'It's just not right,' said Israel, picking absent-mindedly at his scone. 'You know, the longer I spend working as librarian, the more I'm questioning my vocation.'

'Uh-huh,' said Ted, whose own scone was rapidly diminishing in size, down from bowling-ball size to tennis-ball size; maybe a little larger.

'No!' said Israel, correcting himself. 'Not just my vocation in fact. The very ground of my being.'

'Would ye like a top-up of coffee?' said Minnie, who was doing the rounds.

'Yes, thanks,' said Israel.

'Still on Beckett then?' she said, pouring Israel another cup of the café's so-called coffee.

'Questioning the very ground of his being,' said Ted.

'Oh,' said Minnie. 'I think I'll leave you to it then.'

As a child back home in north London, Israel had always imagined that a life communing with books might be a life communing with the great minds and lives of the great thinkers of the past, those who had formed the culture and heritage of the world, and that it might perhaps be his role to share these riches with others. In fact, in reality, as a mobile librarian on the perpetually damp north coast of the north of the north of Northern Ireland, Israel seemed to spend most of his time communing with the great minds and lives and thinkers who had produced Haynes car manuals, and *Some Stuff I Remember About Visiting my Granny on her Farm in the Country, Before I Was Horribly Mentally, Physically and Sexually Abused by my Uncles and Married Three Unsuitable Husbands and Became an Alcoholic and Lost*

Everything and Lived in a Bedsit in Quite a Nasty Part of a City Before Meeting my Current Husband Who is Rich, and Wonderful, and Then Moving Back to the Country, Which is Ironic When You Think About It: The Sequel, and *Shape Up or Ship Out! The Official US Navy Seals Diet*, and *How to Become a Babillionaire – Tomorrow!*, and pastel-covered Irish, English and American chick-lit by the tonne, the half-tonne, the bushel, and the hot steaming shovel-load.

'Ach, come on,' said Ted. 'It's not that bad. You're exeggeratin'.'

'I'm what?'

'Exeggeratin'.'

'Exaggerating?'

'Aye.'

'I'm not! What about that other old man in this morning?'

'Who? Which other old man?'

'The old man in the baseball cap, that was dripping with rain.'

'When?'

'When it was raining?'

'Ach, aye.'

Their second stop, up further round the coast. A lay-by. The rain had come on – even though it was June. June! Pounding with rain in June! Jesus Christ!

Old Man in Baseball Cap, Dripping with Rain: 'Ye've some books here, boy.'

Israel (restrainedly): 'Yes. Yes. It's a library.'

Old Man in Baseball Cap, Dripping with Rain: 'Aye.'

Israel (doing his best to be helpful): 'And can I help you at all?'

Old Man in Baseball Cap, Dripping with Rain: 'No. I'm only in for to be out of the rain.'

Israel: 'Right. OK. That's fine. Happy to be of—'

Old Man in Baseball Cap, Dripping with Rain: 'Mind, would ye have any books about . . .'

Israel: 'About? What?'

Old Man in Baseball Cap, Dripping with Rain (indicating width between finger and thumb): 'About this thick?'

Israel: 'Er. Well, possibly. Any subject in particular you're after?'

Old Man in Baseball Cap, Dripping with Rain: 'I don't mind about the subject.'

Israel: 'Right. So, anything really, as long as it's . . .'

Old Man in Baseball Cap, Dripping with Rain (indicating his required width again): 'This thick.'

Israel: 'I see. What's that, then? About two, three centimetres?'

Old Man in Baseball Cap, Dripping with Rain: 'Quarter-inch.'

Israel, scanning the shelves: 'OK. Erm. I don't know, Carol Shields, have you read any of her? She's very popular.'

Old Man in Baseball Cap, Dripping with Rain: 'How thick's she?'

Israel: 'Erm.'

Old Man in Baseball Cap, Dripping with Rain (taking book from Israel): 'She'll do rightly.'

Israel: 'Do you have a ticket with you?'

Old Man in Baseball Cap, Dripping with Rain: 'No. I've not a ticket. The wife does, but.'

Israel: 'I'd need to see the ticket really. I could always hold it over for you.'

Old Man in Baseball Cap, Dripping with Rain (glancing outside): 'Ach, no. I'll not bother. We've family over at the weekend. I thought it might be the thing for to fix the table – there's a wee wobble where we had the floor tiled.'

Israel: 'Right.'

Old Man in Baseball Cap, Dripping with Rain: 'I'll get an offcut a wood, sure. It's only because you were insisting that I was askin'.'

Israel: 'OK, right.'

Old Man in Baseball Cap, Dripping with Rain: 'Rain's off.'

Israel: 'Good.'

Old Man in Baseball Cap, Dripping with Rain exits.

Israel: 'Sorry we couldn't be of more help!'

'Sure, there was no harm in him,' said Ted.

'No!' said Israel. 'No! You're right. There may have been no harm in *him*, but he did harm to *me*! To my mental health! I am a highly trained professional.'

Ted coughed.

'I am though,' continued Israel. '*We* are. And we should be treated with respect.'

Israel had imagined that a librarian in a small town might be regarded as a kind of cultural ambassador, an adept, like a country priest guiding his grateful parishioners into the mysteries of the holy realms of the book. In fact most library users in and around Tumdrum and District seemed to regard a librarian as nothing more than a glorified shop assistant, and the mobile library as a kind of large motorised shopping trolley. There were only so many small errands that Israel could perform in a day without beginning to feel like a grocer's assistant, and there was only so much sugar, tea, biscuits, potatoes, newspapers, betting slips and hand-rolling tobacco that the mobile library could carry before they would have to start abandoning the books altogether and go over entirely to carrying dry goods and comestibles. If they ripped out the issues desk and put in a deli counter and got a licence for selling drink, Israel and Ted could probably have made a fortune: your breaded ham, a bottle of Bushmills, and the latest Oprah or Richard and Judy Book Club Recommends, available together at last from a veritable touring one-stop shop; they'd be babillionaires by Christmas.

'You're getting carried away now,' said Ted.

'I am not getting carried away!' said Israel.

Israel glanced around the café at all the old familiar faces. 'Look!' he said

'What?' said Ted.

'Sshh! Behind you!' said Israel.

'What?' said Ted, turning round.

'No! Don't turn around!'

'Why?'

'It's her.'

'Who?'

'Mrs Onions.'

'Aye,' said Ted. 'What's wrong with her, sure?'

'Oh, God, Ted. She's another one.'

'Another one of what?'

'Another one who's cracking me up!'

That was the third stop.

Mrs Onions: 'D'ye have any books with those sort of suedey covers?'

Israel: 'Erm. No, no, I'm afraid not. We're right out of the . . . suede-covered books at the moment, I think.'

Mrs Onions: 'You've plenty of other sorts of books.'

Israel: 'Yes. We do. That's true.'

Mrs Onions: 'I could take one of those. But I like the old suede covers, ye see. My granny used to have one, when she lived on the farm down in the Mournes. The butter, honestly, beautiful it was.'

Israel: 'Uh-huh.'

Mrs Onions: 'Will ye be getting any in?'

Israel: 'It's possible, yes, that we will be getting in some suede-covered books in the future. I could certainly—'

Mrs Onions: 'Ach, I'll not bother for the moment. I've shopping to get here.'

Israel: 'Good. Well, it's lovely to . . .'

And there was more! Much, much more, every day: the man who'd come in and take out any books that he deemed were unChristian, and then claim that he'd lost them; the woman who used Sellotape as a bookmark; the creepy man with the moustache who was continually ordering gynae-cology textbooks on inter-library loan. It was too much. Israel still found it hard to believe that he'd ended up here in the first place, and the longer he stayed the less he believed it, the more he felt like merely a vestigial presence in his own life, a kind of living, breathing Chagall, floating just above and outside the world, staring down at himself as librarian, as though this weren't really him at all, not really his life, as if he were merely observing Tumdrum's nether-world of inanities and bizarre and meaningless human exchanges. The longer he stayed in Tumdrum the more he could feel himself slowly withdrawing from the human world, becoming a mere onlooker, a monitor of human absurdities.

He took another bite of his scone.

'I feel like a Chagall,' he said.

'He says he feels like a Chagall,' said Ted to Minnie, who'd arrived with offers of another top-up of coffee.

'He'd need to get himself smarted up first,' said Minnie, winking; Israel was wearing corduroy trousers, his patched-up old brown brogues, and one of his landlady George's brother Brownie's old T-shirts, which read, unhelpfully, 'Smack My Bitch Up'.

'What?' said Israel.

'But anyway,' said Minnie. 'We'll not have that sort of dirty talk in here, thank you, gents.'

'I can't go on, Ted,' said Israel.

'No?' said Ted, reaching forward and taking Israel's other half of scone.

'Not the scone!' said Israel. 'I mean . . . *this*. Life! Here, give that back, it's mine!'

'Say please,' said Ted.

'Just give me the bloody scone!'

'Steady now,' said Ted, handing back the scone. 'Temper, temper.'

'Och, you're like an old married couple, the pair of you,' said Minnie.

'Oh, God,' said Israel, groaning.

'Language,' said Ted.

'Coffee?' said Minnie.

'No. I don't think so,' said Israel, checking his watch. 'Oh, shit! Ted!'

'Language!' said Minnie.

'Sorry, Minnie.'

'Ted!'

'What?'

'We're late for the meeting!'

'Aye,' said Ted. 'Behind like the cow's tail.'

'What?'

'You'll have to hand in your resignation after.'

'He's resigning?' said Minnie.

'Again,' said Ted.

'Yes!' said Israel. 'That's right. I am. I'm handing in my resignation today. I was just distracted there for a moment.'

Ted winked at Minnie as they got up to leave.

'See you next week then?' said Minnie.

'I very much doubt it!' said Israel. 'Bye! Come on, Ted, quick, let's go.'

And with that, Israel Armstrong went to resign, again, from his job as mobile librarian for Tumdrum and District on the windswept north coast of the north of the north of Northern Ireland.

CHAPTER 2

'**S**orry, Linda,' he said when they arrived. It was his customary greeting; he liked to get in his apologies in advance. 'Sorry, everyone.'

'Ah, Mr Armstrong and Mr Carson,' said Linda. 'Punctual as ever.'

'Yes. Sorry.'

'You are aware that the last Wednesday of every month at three o'clock *is* the Mobile Library Steering Committee?'

'Yes,' said Israel.

'Always has been.'

'Uh-huh.'

'And always will be,' said Linda.

'Right.'

'For ever and ever, Amen,' said Ted.

'And yet you, gentlemen,' continued Linda, ignoring Ted, 'somehow always manage to be late?'

'Yes. Erm. Anyway, you're looking well, Linda,' said Israel, trying to change the subject.

'Don't try to change the subject, Mr Armstrong,' said Linda. 'This is not a fashion show.'

'No. Sorry.'

'Honestly!' said Linda, playing up to the – very appreciative – rest of the committee. 'You put a bit of lipstick on, and they can't think about anything else. Typical man!'

'Sorry,' said Israel, sliding down lower and lower in his seat.

'You're all the same.'

'Sorry. We had some trouble . . . with the van.'

They hadn't had trouble with the van, actually, but they often did have trouble with the van, so it wasn't a lie in the proper sense of the word; it wasn't as if Israel were making it up because, really, the van was nothing but trouble. The van was an old Bedford, and Ted's pride and joy – rescued, hidden and restored by him at a time when Tumdrum and District Council were scaling down their library provision, and resurrected and brought back into service only six months ago when Israel had arrived and taken on the role of mobile librarian. The van wasn't merely a vehicle to Ted; it wasn't just any old van; it wasn't, to be honest, even a van in particular; the van was the epitome, the essence, the prime example of mobile library vans in general. To Ted, his van represented pure undiluted mobile library-*ness*. It was the Platonic van; the ur-van; the über-van; it was a totem and a symbol. And you can't argue with symbols: symbols just are. Thus, in Ted's mind, there was absolutely nothing – not a thing – wrong with the mobile library van. The corrosion in the engine, and the mould and mildew in the cabin, and the occasional seizure of the clutch, and some problems with the brake callipers, and the cables, and the wiring looms, and the oil filter, and the spark-plugs, and the battery – these were simply aspects of the van's pure vanness, a part of its very being, its complete and utter rusty red-and-cream-liveried perfection.

'So,' the chairman of the Mobile Library Steering Committee, a man called Ron, an archetypically bald and grey-suited councillor, was saying, 'Here we all are then.' Ron specialised in making gnomic utterances and looking wise. 'All together, once again.'

Also on the committee was Eileen, another councillor, a middle-aged woman with short dyed blonde hair who always wore bright red lipstick with jackets of contrasting colours – today, an almost luminous green – which made her look like the last squeezings of a tube of cheap toothpaste. Eileen was a great believer in Booker Prize-winning novels. Booker Prize-winning novels, according to Eileen, were the key not merely to improving standards of literary taste among the adults in Tumdrum and District, but were in fact a panacea for all sorts of social ills. Booker Prize-winning novels, according to Eileen, were penicillin, aspirin, paracetamol and snake oil, all in one, in black and white, and in between hard covers. Eileen believed passionately in what you might call the trickle-down theory of literature; according to her, the reading of Booker Prize-winning novels by

Tumdrum's library-borrowing elite would lead inevitably and inexorably to the raising of social and cultural values among the populace at large. Even a mere passing acquaintance with someone who had read, say, Ian McEwan or Salman Rushdie could potentially save a local young person from a meaningless and empty life of cruising around town in a souped-up hot hatch and binge-drinking at weekends, and might very possibly lead them instead into joining a book group, and drinking Chardonnay, and learning to appreciate the finer points of the very best of metropolitan and middle-brow fiction.

Israel did not like Eileen, and Eileen did not like him.

'Can't we just get lots of copies of the Booker Prize-winning novels?' Eileen would opine, all year round. Her clothes and her slightly manic cheeriness always gave the Mobile Library Steering Committee meetings a sense of evening occasion – like a Booker Prize awards night dinner, indeed – as though she might at any moment stand up at a podium, raise a glass of champagne, and offer a toast, 'To Literature!' Other members of the committee could often be heard to groan when she spoke.

The other committee members were two moon-faced men whose names Israel could never remember, and who both required endless recaps and reiterations and reminders of the minutest detail of the mobile library's activities, most of which, when recapped, they found profoundly unsatisfactory. Both of them wore glasses and were bald. Israel called them Chi-Chi and Chang-Chang.

And then of course there was Linda Wei, Israel's boss. His line-manager. His nemesis. The person who – apart from his landlady, George, and Ted, and most of the other inhabitants of this godforsaken town – had made Israel's stay in Northern Ireland as unpleasant and as difficult and as miserable as possible. Linda it was who, when Israel complained about his working conditions, would put her fingers in her ears and sing, 'I can't hear you! I can't hear you!' Linda it was who had introduced performance-related pay – for librarians! What were they supposed to do? Force books on people? Offer them money-back guarantees and loyalty cards? – and who had doubled the number of runs that Israel and Ted were expected to complete in a week, and at the same cut the stock back to the bare bones of celebrity autobiographies, bestsellers and self-help manuals. And now Linda it was to whom Israel was about to hand in his resignation. Sweet, sweet, sweet revenge. He was composing in his mind the words he was going to use.

'It is with great regret that I have to inform you that . . .'?

No, that wasn't right.

'I have to tell you now that I have discharged my last . . .'?

No.

'You are probably all aware of the reasons why I have chosen to renounce . . .'?

No.

'I have found it impossible to carry the heavy burden of responsibility . . .'?

'Hasta la vista, baby!'?

That was about the best he could come up with.

He was looking forward to it. A grand exit and then up, up and away from Tumdrum. Over to England. To London! The bright lights. The streets paved with gold. And never to return. This place was bad for him – psychically bad. It was doing him damage. He could feel it: he was calcifying inside; he could feel himself losing synaptic connections on a daily basis. He was de-evolving. He needed to beat a retreat, start over, and get his old life back.

He couldn't wait for the meeting to be finished. He wasn't good in meetings; he was meeting-phobic.

'Anyway, as I was saying,' Ron was saying, 'before we were interrupted. Meltdown. Total. Meltdown.'

Israel tried to follow the conversation for a few minutes, and failed. He and Ted seemed to have arrived at the Mobile Library Steering Committee in the middle of a hotly contested debate about the pros and cons of installing an on-board microwave oven in the van. This seemed unlikely, but Israel checked the agenda:

6) Microwave ovens
To note that the Council is to consider the use of microwave ovens in all public areas, including mobile learning centres.

This proposed innovation had developed into a passionate debate about the Health and Safety implications of combining hot food and drink and members of the public. Ron believed that there were indeed major Health and Safety implications, there having already been unconfirmed reports, from some councils which had introduced microwaves and drinks machines into community halls, of some less forward-thinking members of the public using non-microwavable plastic beakers in the microwaves.

'Meltdown!' Ron kept saying. 'A very high risk of meltdown.'

It was generally agreed that the risk of meltdown needed to be further looked into. The issue was therefore referred to the Mobile Library Steering Committee Health and Safety Sub-Committee – Israel and Linda – for further discussion. Israel wouldn't mind a microwave in the van: he could maybe get pies from the Trusty Crusty for his lunch.

They moved on to the next point on the agenda.

7) Sexual and racial harassment – appointment of advisers
To note that Council policy on sexual and racial harassment now requires two members

of staff (one male, one female) from each
library to act as advisers. These advisers to be
appointed annually by each library.

'We need to appoint advisers,' said Ron.

'I'll advise,' said Linda.

'Good. Thank you, Linda. So now we need a male,' said Ron.

Ted was looking at the floor.

Israel was pretending he couldn't hear.

'Israel?' said Ron.

'Yes?' said Israel.

'Sexual and racial harassment?'

'Yes. Terrible,' said Israel.

'Would you mind?' said Ron. 'With Linda?'

'Erm.'

'Sexual and racial harassment with Linda?' said Ted, mostly to himself.

'Yes,' said Ron.

'Sure,' said Israel.

'What's that on your T-shirt?' said Eileen. '"Smack My Bitch Up"?'

'Yeesss,' said Israel. 'It's just a phrase.'

There was a lot of other stuff: stuff about budgets; and footfalls; and deadlines for this, and deadlines for that; and Israel soon lost interest and pretty soon after that he also lost the will to live. While Linda was speaking about rolling out wi-fi connections across the county, Israel sat staring down at the thinly veneered pale wood surface of the table around which they were all sitting, like miniaturised modern-day medieval knights discussing their forthcoming crusade against the Infidel, or Mafia bosses running a failing cold-storage and meat-packing plant, and for a moment he imagined that they were a parachute display team and that the table was in fact nothing but a big inverted bag of air held by a gathering of cords and they were all about to drop down thousands of feet, out of the blue sky, down to earth . . . Which, indeed, promptly they did.

'Mr Armstrong?' Linda was saying. 'Hello? Mr Armstrong? Earth calling Armstrong? Excuse us?'

He was doodling. His agenda looked like a greyscale photocopy of an early Jackson Pollock, pre-*Full Fathom Five*. At the last Mobile Library Steering Committee meeting Linda had proposed a motion banning all doodling, claiming that it was an act of passive aggression, perpetrated almost wholly by males, but the motion was voted down – Ron was a secret doodler, as were Chi-Chi and Chang-Chang. Linda had also been pressing for a Mobile Library Steering Committee team-building weekend away – with orienteering, and white-water rafting, and abseiling – which absolutely nobody else at all thought was a good idea. No one wanted bonding; quite the opposite. She'd also been pressuring Ted and Israel to sign up for a 'PR and Power Presentation Skills' course running over in Derry; they had, so far, successfully resisted.

She was basically completely crazy, Linda, as far as Israel could tell, and she'd got even crazier since splitting up with her husband and coming out as a lesbian, which made her Tumdrum's only Chinese Catholic lesbian single parent, as far as Israel was aware, and as much as he disliked Linda – and he really disliked her a lot – you had to respect her for that. There'd been a leaving-do recently for a retiring librarian down in Rathkeltair, and they'd all gone out to a Chinese restaurant which had a karaoke, and once everyone had done their 'Country Road's and 'Imagine's and 'A Whiter Shade of Pale's, Linda insisted on getting up, Baileys in hand, and singing – unaccompanied, because there was no backing track – an old music-hall song, 'Nobody Loves A Fairy When She's Forty', encoring with 'Two Lovely Black Eyes' and 'The Man Who Broke the Bank at Monte Carlo'.

Really, you couldn't help but like Linda.

'Armstrong!' Linda was saying. 'Pay attention!'

At least, you couldn't help but like her in theory.

As always, the major issue facing the Mobile Library Steering Committee had been tucked away deep into the agenda.

'So, gentlemen. Now the good news.'

'Item 9,' said Eileen.

Ted looked at Item 9.

'Oh, my God,' said Israel. 'Ted?'

'What?' said Ted.

'Oh. My. God!'

'What?'

'Item 9.'

'What about it?'

'Look at it.'

Ted peered at the agenda. 'Aye.'

Israel read it out: '"Replacement of mobile learning centre vehicle."'

'What?' said Ted.

'Your van, gentlemen,' said Linda, with some pride, 'is going to be replaced.'

'What?' repeated Ted.

'The van, Mr Carson, we've found the money through some Lottery funding and a new development grant.'

'No way!' said Israel.

'Way,' said Linda.

'We can't get rid of the van,' said Ted. 'There's nothing wrong with the van.'

'Now, now, Mr Carson,' said Linda.

'That van is perfect,' said Ted.

'Except for the steering,' said Israel.

'It's a wee bit sloppy, just,' said Ted.

'Corrosion in the engine,' added Israel.

'Well? New engine,' said Ted.

'Clutch,' said Israel.

'Needs replacing just.'

'Brakes.'

'Yes, yes, we get the picture, thank you, gentlemen,' said Linda. 'Well, Mr Carson?'

Ted was silent.

'When do we get the new one then?' said Israel. 'What's it going to be like? What colour is it going to be?'

'Well, actually, gentlemen,' said Linda, with a further flourish, 'we would like you to go and choose.'

'What?' said Israel. 'You are joking!'

'No. We are not joking, Mr Armstrong. We're sending you to the Mobile Meet, so you can meet up with some of the manufacturers and—'

'The what?'

'The Mobile Meet,' said Linda, 'is organised by the Chartered Institute of Information and Library Professionals. It's an annual event where mobile librarians can meet and swap experiences and discuss the latest technology. It's a prestige event.'

'Right,' said Israel.

'It's in England,' said Linda.

'No!' said Israel.

'Yes,' said Linda.

'You're joking!'

'No. We are not joking. Again,' said Linda.

'That's fantastic! You're sending us over?'

'Yes,' said Linda.

'Like on a business trip?' said Israel.

'I suppose,' said Linda.

'Wow!' said Israel. 'All expenses paid?'

'Well—' began Linda.

'Whereabouts?' said Israel. He could barely contain his excitement.

'Somewhere down in Wiltshire?' said Linda. She pronounced it Wilt Shire.

'Wiltshire? Great! God! Where's that?'

'Stonehenge?' said Ron. 'Somewhere round there.'

'How close to London?' said Israel.

'M3,' said Ron. 'M4?'

'Is that close by?'

'Not far, I don't think,' said Ron. 'I went with the wife once to Salisbury. Years ago. Visiting some friends of ours over there. That was nice.'

'Oh, yeah!' said Israel, punching the air. 'Oh, yeah! Oh, yeah! Oh, yeah! Oh, yeah! Oh, yeah!'

'What?'

'This is brilliant. Linda, I can't thank you enough. This is fantastic! It's the best day of my life.'

'Right, well, thank you, Mr Armstrong.'

Ted had been rather quiet.

'Mr Carson?' said Linda.

'You can't replace the van,' said Ted. 'She's irreplaceable.'

'No one and nothing is irreplaceable, Ted, I'm afraid,' said Ron. 'Us old warhorses included.'

'We've had that van nearly thirty years,' said Ted.

'Exactly,' said Linda.

'What about a refurbishment?' said Ted.

'We've looked into the price of a refurbishment and it's not economical, I'm afraid,' said Linda.

'When did ye look into a refurbishment?'

'We've looked into a refurbishment.'

'Not with me you haven't.'

'No, we had some consultants look into it.'

'You had consultants looking at my van?'

36

'It's not actually your van, Mr Carson. It's the—'

'It only needs a bit of work.'

'New engine?' said Linda, referring to a list. 'Bodywork. Chassis.'

'Well?' said Ted.

'She'd hardly be the same vehicle, would she, Ted?' said Ron.

'Like the philosopher's hammer,' said Israel.

'What's he going on about?' said one of the nameless councillors.

'No idea,' said the other.

'We're looking at a number of possible suppliers at the moment,' said Linda. 'Mostly specialist coach builders – they do hospitality units, mobile police stations.'

'Wow!' said Israel. 'Ted! We could have our own hospitality area, and a VIP lounge.'

'Here are the brochures, gents,' said Linda, handing over some thick glossy booklets. 'If you'd like to be having a look at those.'

'Fantastic,' said Israel.

'You will of course be fully consulted about the exact specifications.'

'Ted! Look at this! What about a mini-bar, eh, Ted?'

Ted's eyes were glazed.

'We could have a toilet and everything. Remember that time you were caught short and . . . Ted?'

'I think you'll agree the standard of craftsmanship on this sort of vehicle is quite different to your own—' began Linda.

'What?' said Ted.

'Efforts, Ted. Which have been much appreci-ated, may I just say.'

'I want it minuted that I'm very unhappy with this,' said Ted.

'Right,' said Linda. 'I really don't think there's any need for that.'

'I want it in the records!' said Ted.

'Well, that's fine, if you insist.'

'This'll be fantastic, Ted,' said Israel. 'Listen—'

'I'll tell you what, I'll listen to you when you've learned to wipe your arse,' said Ted.

'Right. Thanks.'

'Come on now, Ted, there's no need for that sort of language now, is there? There's ladies present,' said Ron.

'Women, thank you,' said Linda. 'This is the twenty-first century. Anyway, maybe you two . . . gentlemen . . . can talk it over between yourselves? And let me know whether we can go ahead with our plans and book your tickets over to England?'

CHAPTER 3

The meeting had ended, as was traditional at Mobile Library Steering Committee meetings, amidst argument, dissolution and general disarray – 'Don't forget the Booker Prize longlist, announced in August!' cried Eileen. 'That's August!'; 'PR!' Ron was saying. 'New van! Great PR!'; and 'Some reports of discrepancies in cataloguing!' Linda was reminding Ted and Israel; and 'What?' said Chi-Chi; and 'What?' said Chang-Chang – and then it was the long drive home in the van with Ted silent and sulking and Israel flicking through the fat, plush brochures and the programme for the Mobile Meet, the UK's, quote, Premier Mobile Library Event. Unquote.

It was an uncomfortable, damp, sweaty summer's evening; tempers were frayed; temperatures high; and Israel knew that he was going to have to do something pretty special to persuade Ted to go with him over to England. This was his opportunity to ensure himself a free trip back home: the prospect of leaving Tumdrum was the best thing that had happened to him since arriving.

'There's some really good stuff on at this Mobile Meet thing,' he said casually.

'Huh,' said Ted.

'Look. A Guide to Electronic Self-issue,' said Israel.

'Bullshit,' said Ted.

'Supplier-Select Book-Buying For Beginners,' said Israel.

'Bullshit.'

'Bibliotherapy,' said Israel.

'What?'

'Bibliotherapy,' repeated Israel.

'Bullshit.'

'Honestly, some of this stuff looks really good,' said Israel. 'I think it'll be really interesting.'

'That's because you're a ragin' eejit, like the rest of them.'

'Thank you.'

'My pleasure. Hirstle o' blinkin' eejits, the whole lot of youse.'

'What' all of idiots?'

'Ach, read a fuckin' dictionary, Israel, will ye? I'm not in the mood.'

'Right. Ted,' said Israel soothingly, 'not being funny, but you really shouldn't take this personally.'

'I shouldn't take it personally?'

'No. The whole van thing, you know. You need to see it as an opportunity rather than a threat.'

Israel could sense Ted's neck and back – his whole body – stiffening in the van beside him, which was not a good sign. Ted was like a dog:

he gave clear warnings before attacking. Israel's softly-softly, soothing approach was clearly not working; he'd rubbed him up the wrong way.

'An opportunity!' said Ted, his shaven head glistening, his slightly shiny short-sleeved shirt shining, and his big hairy forearms tensing and tensing again. 'An opportunity! The van I've tended like me own wean for the past . . . God only knows how many years, and they're planning to throw on the scrap heap? And I should view that as an opportunity?'

'Yes, no, I mean, just . . . You know, all good things must . . . and what have you—'

'Ach!'

'Plus,' said Israel, trying an entirely other approach. 'Yes! Plus! You could think of it as a nice holiday, you know. We're going to get to go over to England, relax, choose a new van. It'll be great fun.'

'Fun?'

'Yes.'

'You are actually stupit, aren't ye?'

Israel thought fast. 'We could have air conditioning in the new van,' he said, wiping the sweat dramatically from his brow. 'You know how hot it gets in here sometimes. And with the rain, in the summer. You were complaining about it only yesterday. Dehumidification.'

'We don't need dehumimidifaction.'

'For the . . . books, though.'

Maybe a clerkly appeal, an appeal to worthiness,

to the ancient and high-minded principles of librarianship?

'We can't think of ourselves always, Ted. We're librarians. We have to think of the good of the books. You know, that's our first responsibility, as librarians, to the books, rather than to the van.'

'To the books?'

'That's right. To the books. And . . .'

God, what else would appeal to Ted?

'Our responsibility to the clients.'

'The clients?'

'Yes,' said Israel, without conviction.

'Are ye having me on?'

'No,' said Israel. Clearly an appeal to their responsibility to readers wouldn't work. It wouldn't have worked with him either.

'You're not even half interested though?' said Israel tentatively. 'I mean, they're giving us carte blanche, Ted. We could go for the full works. Anything we want. You know, like a mobile Internet café. "Would you like an espresso with your Catherine Cookson, madam?" We could have our own blog! Honestly, it'd be amazing.'

'No,' said Ted. 'It wouldn't be amazing.'

'Why?'

'Because we're not getting a new bloody van!'

'Language, Ted.'

'Don't talk to me about my language, ye fuckin' eejit!'

'Sorry,' said Israel.

'Thank you,' said Ted.

42

'We are getting a new van, though,' said Israel determinedly.

'We're not getting a new van,' said Ted, more determinedly. 'We are not going to England, we're not going to some daftie wee librarian conference—'

'The Mobile Meet,' corrected Israel.

'And we're not getting a new van.'

'But—'

'They'll not get rid of this van,' said Ted. 'If they want to get rid of this van they'll have to get rid of me first.'

'Don't say that, Ted.'

'The van's staying.'

'Ted!'

'And so am I. Here! In Norn Iron. And we are not getting a new van.'

'We are, Ted,' said Israel.

'We're not.'

'We are.'

'We're not. I'm telling you now,' said Ted, turning across to look at Israel, and gripping the steering wheel so tight that Israel thought he might actually choke it and throttle the whole vehicle. 'Again. We. Are. Not. Getting. A. New. Van! We're not going anywhere. We're staying put! D'ye understand me?' When Ted raised his voice it was like someone hitting you around the ears.

'Please?' said Israel quietly.

'No!' yelled Ted.

Israel was worried that Ted might have a heart attack or a stroke and they'd end up swerving and crashing and they'd both die, and they'd make the front page of the *Impartial Recorder*: 'Librarians killed in tragic mobile library crash', with a grainy black and white photo. And a few words of tribute from Linda Wei. Which was not the way Israel would have wished to be remembered.

Ted had lost his temper, and Israel had no other means of persuasion. He was reduced to pathetic pleading.

'Please, Ted. A new van? A trip over to England? Seize the day. *Carpe diem* and all that.'

'Aye, and who's he when he's at home?'

'*Carpe diem*? It means—'

'Of course I know what *carpe diem* means, ye fuckin' wee shite!'

Ted punched the steering wheel. Which was never good. It made the whole front of the dashboard wobble.

'Listen!' said Ted. 'Let me make meself perfectly plain. *Do not* patronise me. *Do not* try to talk me round. And *do not* try to appeal to my better nature!'

'No, Ted. No, I wouldn't dream of . . . appealing to your . . .'

That gave Israel an idea. They drove on in silence for a few minutes longer, Israel flicking through the programme of events for the Mobile Meet.

'At the Mobile Meet they have all these competitions, you know.'

'Hmm,' said Ted.

'Driver of the Year.'

44

'Hmm.'

'State of the Art Vehicle.'

'Hmm.'

'Best Livery.'

Israel thought he could just detect a slight interest in Ted's 'hmm's. This could be it. He tried to utilise his advantage. Counter-intuitive was the way to go with Ted; there was no point setting out premises and establishing arguments. There was absolutely no point arguing with Ted, or appealing to his better nature. Cunning – that's what was called for.

'This old thing probably wouldn't stand a chance, of course, at that sort of competition level.'

'Don't ye get started into the van again now.'

'No, no, I'm not. I mean, she just wouldn't, though, would she, realistically, stand a chance of winning a prize at the Mobile Meet? With that, you know, all that competition. Not a chance.'

'Ach, of course she'd stand a chance.'

'I don't think so, Ted. Not up against all those English vans.'

'Ach,' said Ted.

'Not a chance of winning. Not in a million years. If you look at these categories. Concours D'Elégance.'

'What?'

'Concours D'Elégance means, you know, the best-looking van there on the day.'

'Ach, well, if she was there, she'd definitely win that. Best van, no problem.'

'No?' said Israel. 'Do you really think so?'

'Of course she would!'

'Well, I suppose if you pimped her up a bit and—'

'Wee bit of work, no problem,' said Ted. 'Definitely she'd win it. She's a beauty,' said Ted, affectionately stroking the dashboard. 'Aren't you, girl?'

He had found Ted's Achilles heel; his underbelly; his soft spot; his weakness; his fatal Cleopatra. Pride.

'I tell you what,' said Israel. 'Do you want to have a bet on it?'

'A what?' said Ted. 'A bet?'

'Yes, a bet, on you winning the Concours D'Elégance at the Mobile Meet.'

'With you, a bet?' said Ted.

'Yes.'

'Ach,' said Ted. 'I'm good living. I don't gamble.'

'Oh,' said Israel. He knew that in fact Ted did gamble; the week of the Cheltenham Gold Cup he'd talked about nothing else. Israel had had to cover for him every day. Then again, Ted also claimed he didn't drink. And didn't smoke. And he did. And he did.

'I don't gamble,' repeated Ted. 'Unless I know I'm going to win.'

'Ha ha,' said Israel.

Israel could see a glint in Ted's eye.

'A bet,' Ted said to himself. 'The van to win the . . . What did you call it?'

'Concours D'Elégance.'

'Concord De Elephants,' repeated Ted.

'That's it,' said Israel.

'Are ye serious?'

'Yes, absolutely I'm serious.'

Israel could see Ted thinking through the proposition. 'Well?' he said gingerly.

'I tell you what, son,' said Ted, pausing dramatically. Big pause. 'Seeing as you've asked.' Another pause. 'You're on.'

'No. Really? Honestly?'

'Yes,' said Ted.

'Really?' said Israel.

'I said yes.'

'Great!' said Israel. 'How much? A couple of pounds?'

'Couple of pounds!' said Ted, bellowing with laughter. 'Couple of pounds! Ach, ye're a quare geg. No, no, no. No. If I'm going all the way over to the mainland I want to get my money's worth out of you. We'll do it properly. I'll get JP to open up a book on it.'

'JP?'

'The bookie on Main Street. He'll see us right.'

'Erm.'

'Yer bet's definitely on now; ye're not going to back out?'

'No. Definitely. Absolutely,' said Israel. 'Game on.'

'You don't want to change yer mind?'

'Nope.'

'Ye know ye don't back out of a bet, now?'

'Quite.'

Ted reached a hand across. 'Five hundred pounds,' said Ted.

'Five hundred pounds!' said Israel.

'You're right,' said Ted. 'Five hundred's not enough. One thousand says we win the . . . What did you call it?'

'Concours D'Elégance. But I haven't got one thousand pounds, Ted. The van's not worth a thousand pounds.'

'I thought you wanted a bet?'

'I do, but—'

'Aye, right, that's typical, so it is. You're trying to wriggle out of it now.'

'No, I am not trying to wriggle out of it.'

'Ach, you are, so you are. Ye're not prepared to put your money where your mouth is. Typical Englishman.'

'I am not trying to wriggle out of it, Ted.'

'Well, then, are youse in, or are youse out?'

'All right,' said Israel, trying to suppress a grin. 'One thousand pounds says you *won't* win the Concours D'Elégance at this year's Mobile Meet.' He knew his money was safe.

The rest of the journey continued in silence, with Israel elated and exhausted from his negotiations and Ted already planning the few little tweaks and alterations he needed to get the van into top condition. Eventually, Ted pulled up outside the Devines' farm, where Israel was a lodger, and Israel clambered down wearily from the van.

'Hey!' called Ted, as Israel was about to shut the door. 'Did ye not forget something?'

'No,' said Israel, patting his pockets, patting the seat. 'I don't think so.'

'I think you did,' said Ted.

'What? "Thank you" for the lift?'

'No,' said Ted.

'What? The bet?'

'No. The bet's on – we've shaken.'

'Yes,' said Israel. 'And I am a man of my word.'

'Aye. Exactly. And you remember what you were going to do today, Man of Your Word?'

'Erm. No. I don't remember. Should I?'

'You were going to tell her?'

'Tell who?'

'Linda. That you were resigning.'

'Ah, yes. Well . . . things have changed since this afternoon.'

'Have they now?'

'Yes. I feel I have a . . . responsibility to the readers of Tumdrum and District to . . .'

'And it's not because you're getting a free holiday to England?'

'No! Of course not!'

'You shouldn't ever try to kid a kidder,' said Ted.

'What do you mean?'

'I know your game.'

'I don't . . . I'm not playing a game, Ted.'

'Aye.'

'No. I just feel very strongly that my responsibility is to books, and to . . . encouraging the

49

people of the north coast of Northern Ireland to . . . indulge their learned curiosity and to give them unlimited assistance . . . by helping to choose a new mobile library van.'

'Aye, tell the truth and shame the devil, why don't ye?'

'What?'

'I don't care what you think your responsibility is,' said Ted. 'My first responsibility is to the van. One thousand pounds, remember.'

'Fine.'

'Pay for some refurbishments, wouldn't it? You'd better start saving, boy!'

'No, Ted, I don't need to start saving, because alas very soon we shall be in sunny England choosing a brand spanking new top-of-the-range mobile library and we will no longer have need of this . . .' And with that, Israel walked away and slammed the door. '. . . piece of junk,' he muttered under his breath.

Oh, yes!

Ted had been reeled in hook, line and sinker!

Israel Armstrong was going home!

CHAPTER 4

He was packing! Israel Armstrong was packing up and getting ready to go. He had his case out from under the bed, and his little portable radio turned up loud, and he was listening to BBC Radio Ulster, the local station; he'd gone over some time ago, had switched from Radio 4, had made the move away from the national and the international, from big news stories about Bush and Blair and the plight of the Middle East and worldwide pandemics and whither the UN Security Council, to local news stories about men beating each other with base-ball bats in local bars and pubs, and road closures due to mains-laying down in Cullybackey, and good news about the meat-processing plant in Ballymena taking on ten new workers due to expanding European markets and increased orders from Poland for pork. He knew it was a bad sign, but he couldn't help himself; he had grown accustomed to the rhythms and the pitch of local radio, to the shouty-voiced shock-jock first thing in the morning, and the faded country music star at lunchtime who played only Irish country and read out requests for the foot-tappin' welders in Lurgan and all the lovely nurses on the cancer wards down there at the Royal Victoria Hospital, and the mid-morning bloke from Derry who specialised in trading daring double-entendres with his adoring female callers.

Somehow – and how he wished it were not so – Israel could now recognise a tune by Daniel O'Donnell from far distant, and the supersweet sound of Philomena Begley and her band, and he also knew the time the Ulster Bank closed on a Wednesday (three thirty, for staff training), and the times of the high tides (varied according to season), and the best grocer to go to for your soup vege- tables (Hector's) and which one for eggs (Conways). This was not what was supposed to happen. Israel had imagined himself, heading into his late twenties, being able to recommend fine restaurants in Manhattan to his friends, many of whom probably worked for the *New Yorker* magazine, or who were up-and-coming artists with a gallery representing them, and he could have told you what time to go to MOMA and what was happening at the Whitney Museum. Instead, somehow, Israel had ended up knowing what night the Methodists had their ladies' indoor bowling practice (Tuesday) and the Post Office opening hours (Mon-Fri, 9.00 a.m. – 1.00 p.m., 2.00 p.m. – 5.00 p.m.; early closing Wed, 3.30 p.m.; Sat, 10.00 a.m. – 1.00 p.m.).

He turned up the radio louder to drown out the ennui and focused on his packing.

Brownie was back for the summer break from university over in England, so the Devines had moved Israel out of Brownie's room, where he'd been staying, and out of the house and back into the chicken coop in the yard, where he'd first started out when he arrived in Tumdrum. Israel didn't mind, actually, being back in the coop. It was good to get a little breathing space, and to be able to put a bit of distance between himself and George Devine – his landlady with the man's name – and the perpetually Scripture-quoting senior Mr Devine, George and Brownie's grand-father, and he'd done his best with the coop; had put in quite a bit of work doing the place up over the past few weeks. He had a desk in there now, along with the bed, and the Baby Belling and the old sink battened to the wall, and it was a nice desk he'd picked up from the auction down in Rathkeltair (Tippings Auctions, every Thursday, six till ten, in one of the new industrial units out there on the ring road, hundreds and hundreds of people in attendance every week, from as far afield as County Down and Derry, drinking scalding-hot tea and eating fast-fried burgers from Big Benny McAuley's Premier Meats and Snacks van, and bidding like crazy for other people's discarded household items and rubbish, and rusty tools, and amateur watercolours, and telephone seats and tubular bunk beds, and pot-plant stands, and novelty cruet sets, and golf clubs, and boxes overflowing with damp paperback books; Israel loved Tippings; it was like a Middle Eastern bazaar, except without the spices and the ethnic jewellery, and with more men wearing greasy flat caps buying sets of commemorative RUC cap badges). Lovely little roll-top desk it was, although the top didn't actually roll, and a couple of the drawers were jammed shut, and Israel had had to patch up the top with some hardboard; but it did the job.

He also had a table lamp, which had first graced a home some time in the 1970s, by the look of it, and whose yellow plastic shade bore the scars of too many too-high-watted light bulbs; and also a small armchair which had at some time been re-upholstered with someone's curtains, and which had a broken arm; and a couple of old red fire buckets to catch the rain that made it through the coop's mossy asbestos roof; and also he'd rigged up a washing line using some twine and a couple of nails; and he had a walnut-veneer wardrobe crammed in there, with a broken mirror and only one leg missing, to keep his clothes in. To store his books he'd broken apart some old pallets and knocked up some shelving – him, Israel Armstrong, wielding a hammer and nails, and with the blackened thumb and fingernails to prove it – and these pretty sturdy shelves of his were now piled with books on one side of the bed and with jars of tea and coffee on the other, and an old teapot containing all his cutlery, two Duralex glasses and his enamel mug. He'd cut off a bit of an old mouldy scaffolding plank to cover the sink when he needed to prepare his food. The chicken coop wasn't exactly a palace, but nor was it quite the proverbial Augean stable. Israel liked to think of it as an eccentric *World of Interiors* kind of a look – Gloria loved *The World of Interiors*. It was . . . there was probably a phrase for it. Shabby chic, that was it. With the emphasis, admittedly, on the shabby. Super-shabby chic? Shabby shabby chic?

It was shabby.

He squeezed his spare corduroy trousers into his case and went to the farmhouse, to the kitchen to say goodbye to the Devines.

There was only Brownie in, hunched over the table, reading. It was June, but the Rayburn was fired up, as ever. There were flies, but even the flies were resting. Old Mr Devine was a firm believer in fly-paper; the kitchen was festooned with claggy plumes of curling brown tape.

'Israel!' said Brownie, looking up. You could always count on Brownie for a warm welcome.

'Brownie.'

'How are you?'

'I'm doing good, actually,' said Israel. 'Pretty good. What are you reading?'

'Levinas,' said Brownie. Brownie was studying Philosophy at Cambridge.

'Oh, right. Yes.'

'Totality and Infinity?'

'Absolutely, yes,' said Israel.

'Have you read it?'

'Erm. That one? Er. Yes, I think so. I preferred some of his . . . others though, actually—'

'Alterity.'

'Yes, that's a good one.'

'No, that's the idea, translation of the French.'

'Uh-huh,' said Israel dubiously.

'Anyway, how are things on the mobile?' asked Brownie.

'Good! Yes. Excellent,' said Israel. 'Even better now, we're going away for a few days.'

'Oh, really? In the van?'

'Yes. Yeah. Big conference thing over in England.'

'Really?'

'Yeah.'

'Are you giving a paper or . . .'

'No. No. I mean, they did ask me, of course, but I was . . . It's difficult to fit it all in when you're at the . . .'

'Coalface?' said Brownie.

'Exactly. The library is the coalface of contemporary knowledge management.'

'Right,' said Brownie. It was something Israel had read in one of the brochures for the Mobile Meet.

'Anyway. I was wanting to explain to George I wouldn't be around, just so that she—'

'Ah, right. I think she's out with Granda in the vegetable patch if you want to catch them.'

'Great.'

'Good. Well, enjoy the conference.'

'Thanks, you enjoy the . . .'

'Levinas.'

'Yeah. What was it called again?'

'Totality and Infinity.'

'Yeah. Great book. Great book.'

Israel's reading had always been erratic and undisciplined; there were huge chunks missing in his knowledge, while other areas were grossly over-represented; it was like having mental biceps, but no triceps, or glutes, or quads, or forearms; he was a kind of mental hunchback; misproportioned; a freak. Graphic novels, for example, were ten a penny up in Israel's mental attic, along with the novels of E.F. Benson and Barbara Pym – God only knows how they'd got there – piled up uselessly like old trunks full of crumbling paper, together with a whole load of Walter Benjamin, and Early Modernism, and books by Czechs, and the Oedipus Complex, and the Collective Unconscious, and Iris Murdoch, and William Trevor, and Virtual Reality, and Form Follows Function, and Whereof One Cannot Speak Thereof One Must Remain Silent, and *The White Goddess*, and William James, and Commodity Fetishism, and Jorge Luis Borges, and Ruth Rendell, and Jeanette Winterson, and Anthony Powell – Anthony Powell? What was he doing there? Israel had no idea. He had a mind like Tippings Auctions. His actual knowledge of philosophy proper, say, or eighteenth-century literature, or science, anthropology, geology, gardening, or geometry was . . . skimpy, to say the least.

And since arriving in Tumdrum his reading had become even more erratic and undisciplined; he'd had to cut his cloth to suit his sail. Or was it sail to suit his cloth? He was reading more and more of what they stocked in the van, which meant crime fiction, mostly, and books by authors whose work had won prizes or who were in some other way distinguished or remarkable; thus, celebrity biographies and books about people's miserable childhoods. But it wasn't as though he felt he'd lowered his standards. On the contrary. Scott Turow, *Presumed Innocent,* that was a *great* book, much better than most Booker Prize-shortlisted books, in his opinion. And *The Firm,* by John Grisham, that was pretty good too. He'd even started reading Patricia Cornwell from A to Z, but they seemed to go downhill rapidly, and he'd lost interest around about D. Cookery books also he liked: a man cannot survive on scrambled eggs alone. For the journey over to England, Israel was taking with him *A Short History of Tractors in Ukrainian, The Purpose-Driven Life,* and a couple of large-print crime novels. most of the library's crime novels were large print. Israel had discovered a direct correlation between print size and genre: crime fiction, for example, came in big and small sizes, and also in audio, and in hardback, and in several kinds of paperback, and trailing TV tie-ins; literary fiction occasionally came with a different cover relating to a film adaptation. And poetry was just poetry: he'd never come across a book of large-print poems; for poetry you needed eyes like a pilot, with twenty-twenty vision, opposable thumbs, and never-ending patience; on the mobile library they stocked only Seamus Heaney, and derivatives.

To get to the vegetable patch Israel had to pass by the chickens, and he couldn't help but feel a little guilty, having turned them out of their home. George had fixed them up with new runs using some old manure bags over wire netting, but Israel could tell they weren't happy. They eyed him – gimlet chicken-eyed him – suspiciously as he hurried past.

George and old Mr Devine were indeed, as Brownie had suggested, in the vegetable patch, which was close by the main house, protected on one side by fruit trees and on the others by red-brick walls; it was a walled garden; or rather, it had been a walled garden. Like most things around the farm, it had seen better days; one might best now describe it as a half-walled garden.

'George!' Israel called as he entered through what was once a gateway, but which was now merely a clearing through some rubble.

George was kneeling down in among rows of vegetable crops. She ignored Israel, as usual.

'George?'

'What?'

'Could I just—'

'No, thanks. Whatever it is. We're working here.'

'Yes, sure. I see that. I just wanted to—'

'Can you just let me finish here?'

'Yeah, it's just—'

'Please?'

'Sure.'

'If you want to make yerself useful you could be thinning and weeding the onions.'

'Yes, of course. I could . . . I'll just . . .'

'Over there.'

'Where?'

'There.'

He looked around him at vast muddy areas where plants were poking through. He didn't recognise anything. He wasn't sure which were the onions. He went over towards Mr Devine, who was sitting on a wooden bench, a rug across his legs.

'Lovely day,' said Israel.

'It's a bruckle sayson,' said Mr Devine.

'Is it?'

'Aye.'

'Yes, I thought so myself actually,' said Israel. 'Erm.' He pointed towards some green shoots. 'Onions?'

'Cabbages,' said Mr Devine.

Israel pointed again.

'Onions?'

'Cabbages,' said Mr Devine.

'OK.' Israel tried again, pointing at some sort of pointy thing. 'Onions?'

'Cabbages.'

'Is it all cabbages?'

'"Thou shalt not sow thy seed with mingled seed,"' said Mr Devine.

'Yes. Of course. Lovely. Beautiful. And they are . . .' he said, gesturing vaguely towards the rest of the crops.

'Cabbages. Kale. Cabbages. Radish. Potatoes. Chard. Cabbages. Potatoes. Shallots. Cabbages. Onions.'

'Bingo!' said Israel.

Israel got down on his knees. He didn't quite know what to do next. The only thing he'd grown had been mustard and cress, at school, in a plastic cup.

'Thinning?' he shouted enquiringly, over to George.

'Yes, thinning!' George shouted back impatiently.

'Thinning?' he appealed quietly to Mr Devine, having no notion whatsoever what thinning onions might involve.

'"And he shall separate them one from another; as a shepherd divideth his sheep from the goats,"' said Mr Devine.

'Erm.'

'Two inches apart,' said Mr Devine.

'Ah, right, OK,' said Israel. 'Thank you.'

Israel occupied himself not unpleasantly, for about ten minutes, concentrating on the job. It was surprisingly satisfying. For about ten minutes he fondly imagined himself as a smallholder, with cows, and pigs, and a small orchard, and bottling

61

his own tomatoes and mashing his own beer. He could be like Thoreau.

'Ta-daa!' he said, standing up and admiring his handiwork. 'A perfect row of thinned onions!' He stretched out and took in the view. It was idyllic here, really; it was pure pastoral. There were beehives down by the wheat field, and oats, some barley, sheep, the paddock. He took in these sights and breathed deeply, admiring a bunch of huge plants with bright yellow flowers.

'They're lovely-looking flowers,' he said to Mr Devine.

'Aye.'

'What are those flowers?'

'What do they look like?'

'Sorry, I don't know.'

'Ye don't know what a corguette plant looks like?'

'Er . . . Is it a *courgette* plant, by any chance?'

Mr Devine's eyes narrowed.

'And you've some lovely trees there,' said Israel, gesturing towards the fruit trees.

'Plum,' said Mr Devine. 'And pears like a trout's back.'

'Uh-huh.'

'Planted by my father. Cherries. Apple.'

'Good,' said Israel, as though he were a landowner inspecting a tenant farmer's fields. 'Very good,' he said. 'Good for you. Anyway, George,' he said, as George approached. 'I've done the onions.'

'I'm just checking on these early croppers,' she

said, ignoring Israel's onion-thinning achievements, and knelt down by some bushy patches of
green.

'It's finding something early that's floury
enough,' said Mr Devine.

'Uh-huh,' said Israel, faux-knowledgeably. 'It's
quite a crop you have here.'

'Mebbe,' said Mr Devine.

'Yes, you're certainly going to get lots of . . .
cabbages. And . . . potatoes. Have you never
thought of diversifying into . . . I don't know.
Avocados, or artichokes?'

'Ach, wise up, Israel, will ye?' said George, from
in among the foliage.

'Asparagus?' said Israel.

'I refuse to grow anything beginning with "A",'
said George.

'Oh,' said Israel. 'Right.'

'Och, Jesus. I'm joking, ye fool. What do you
want, Israel? Get it over and done with and then
you can be on your way.'

Israel stood up straight as if about to read a
proclamation. 'Well, actually, I've just come to say
goodbye,' he said.

'What did you say?' said George.

'I've come to say goodbye.'

George straightened up slowly from her potato
row and raised an unplucked eyebrow.

'Is this a joke?'

'No. I'm going away, over to England.'

'Well, well, well,' said George, crossing her arms.

'What's that supposed to mean?'

'Just.'

'What?'

'Didn't take you long, did it?'

'To what?'

'Cut and run.'

'I'm not cutting and running.'

'Well, you've been here, what, six months?'

'Nearly eight,' said Mr Devine.

'Eight months,' said George. 'And then you're away? That sounds to me like someone who's cutting and running.'

'Aye, I always thought he was a quitter,' said Mr Devine. '"Because the daughters of Zion are haughty, and walk with stretched forth necks and wanton eyes, walking and mincing as they go, and making a tinkling with their feet—"'

'All right, yes, thank you, Granda,' said George.

'I'm not a quitter, actually,' said Israel.

'Are ye not?'

'No. I'm going to be coming back.'

'He's coming back?' said Mr Devine.

'Are ye coming back, Armstrong?' said George, crossing her arms. 'You don't want to dash our hopes now.'

'Ha ha. Yes, I will be back. It's just a . . . business trip I'm going on.'

'A business trip? Really?'

'Yes.'

'With what, your job as an international financier?'

'No.'

'With the mobile library?'

'Uh-huh.'

Mr Devine started wheezing with laughter.

'A business trip!' said George. 'That right? What is it, an international conference?'

'Well, yes, as it happens.'

'Ach, you're priceless, Israel, so you are.'

'A mobile library conference? Holy God!' said Mr Devine.

'A junket then,' said George.

'Junket? No. It's not a junket. It's the Mobile Meet, which is the UK's premier mobile library conference and—'

'Paid for with our taxes no doubt?' said George.

'"Render unto Caesar,"' said Mr Devine.

'No,' said Israel.

'Not paid for with our taxes then?'

'Well—'

'You're paying to go yourselves then?'

'No. It's—'

'A holiday then, is it?'

'No. It's work. And—'

'Good. How long are you gone for?' said George.

'It'll be—'

'Can we sub-let?' said Mr Devine.

'Sub-let?' said Israel. 'The chicken coop?'

'You've it looking rightly,' said Mr Devine.

'How long?' said George.

'We'll be gone about a week, I think. Few days visiting my family, and then to the Mobile Meet.'

'A whole week?' said George. 'Sure, what are we going to do without ye?'

The conversation had not gone as well as Israel had hoped. He'd half hoped that his departure might excite some small favourable comment and wishes for a good journey and a safe return. He was wrong.

'Is he here for the Twelfth?' asked Mr Devine.

'Are you here for the Twelfth?' asked George.

'Of?' said Israel.

'July,' said George. 'Obviously.'

'Yes. Yes. We'll be back by the twelfth of July.'

'You wouldn't want to miss the Twelfth.'

'Right. No. Anyway,' said Israel. 'You're not . . . considering a holiday yourselves this year?' he asked, trying to be pleasant.

'I've not been on holiday for seventy-eight years,' said Mr Devine, pulling the rug tighter around his knees. 'D'ye not think I could do without one now?'

'Er. Yes. Probably.'

'And some of us have work to do,' said George.

'Yes, quite,' said Israel.

George was already walking away, her back turned from him.

'Goodbye then,' called Israel.

She didn't turn to wave or answer.

Israel walked bitterly back to the chicken coop. He couldn't wait to get away from here, to England, to Gloria, to good coffee, and home.

CHAPTER 5

They very nearly missed the ferry.

Brownie dropped Israel off at Ted's little bungalow out on the main coast road, just by the sign saying 'Try Your Brakes', and along past the little new-build 'Café Bistro', which had never been occupied or let, and which was now proclaiming on a large, ugly estate agent's hoarding its extremely unlikely 'Potential as a Gift Shop'.

Ted's bungalow was sheltered at the foot of a sheer white limestone cliff, its extraordinary vast clear views of the sea – to the left, far out to Rathlin Island and then across to the Mull of Kintyre – blotted out by the perpetual blur of traffic. It could and should have been the perfect little spot, with a bounteous vista, vast and un-interrupted. Instead it was dark and cold, with long, depressing, interrupting views of cars, white vans and lorries; paradise obscured, like Moses allowed a glimpse of the Promised Land, and then cut off by the A2 coast road.

Parked up proud out on the bungalow's weed and gravel forecourt, wedged tight between bins and Ted's neighbours' – the McGaws – little fenced-off area for sheep, and shadowed by the cliff above, yet still somehow shimmering in the late afternoon light, was the mobile library. She looked different.

Ted had absolutely no intention of losing the bet with Israel and had undertaken some essential care and maintenance tasks: he had scraped and cleaned and waxed the van, polishing her and buffing her until her red and cream livery was all ice cream and municipal bright once again, the words 'Mobile Library' and 'The Book Stops Here' picked out gorgeously in a honey gold and crisp forbidding black. The chrome looked chromey, and the headlights clear, and all dirt had been washed from the windows. The van had had a makeover. She looked – and Israel actually thought this for a moment, a weird J.G. Ballard moment – she looked, he thought, the mobile library, she looked *sexy*. She looked absolutely fantastic. She looked flushed, and noble and come-hitherish. She looked good enough to eat. She looked – and again, this is what he thought, he couldn't help it – she looked like Marilyn Monroe.

Israel knew in that instant of recognition, in that perverse, momentary gaze upon the van's pouting, polished, peach-like beauty, that she would win the category for Concours D'Elégance at the Mobile Meet, and that all was lost. He knew that Tumdrum would never get a new mobile library, and that Ted would triumph and would demand

68

his pound of flesh, and that he, Israel, would have to beg for a loan to pay off the bet, would have to beg from Mr Mawhinney, probably, the manager of the Ulster Bank on Main Street in Tumdrum, who borrowed to his limit from the library every week, biographies, mostly, and military history, so perhaps Israel could borrow to his limit from the bank in return? 'I need the money,' he would have to explain, 'because Marilyn Monroe melted the hearts of the mobile library judges at the annual Mobile Meet.' And Mr Mawhinney would say, 'What?' and Israel Armstrong would be ruined and ridiculed by beauty, by this great curvaceous ambulant thing. He'd be condemned to life with Ted on the mobile library for ever. He'd be ruined. He'd lose the duffle coat off his back, and the brogues from his feet, his corduroy trousers; everything.

But, then, on closer inspection it seemed that Israel's dignity and his money were perhaps safe; on closer inspection you could still see the many little rust spots that Ted's primping couldn't cover, and the scuffs and the scrapes and the scratches on the chrome, the little dints on the windscreen, the horrible filthy dirt-brown exhaust. The van was not a movie star; Marilyn was a person. The van was real. Some of the paint-work looked as though it might have been touched up using ordinary household emulsion. And the hand that had painted 'The Book Stops Here' could perhaps have been steadier. Even Ted couldn't work miracles in just a few days. A makeover could not make new.

Buoyed, confused, excited and relieved, Israel rapped loudly and rang at Ted's door.

He was greeted first from inside with the sound of irritable growling from Muhammad, Ted's little Jack Russell terrier, and then with irritable shushings and hushings as Ted quieted the dog, and opened up the door with a scowl. Or at least, not literally with a scowl. Ted opened the door literally with his hand, obviously, *while* scowling, but when Ted scowled it was overwhelming; whatever it was Ted did while scowling became an act of scowl; the scowl became constitutive. He scowled often when they were out on the van, and in meetings with Linda Wei, and often unexpectedly and for no good reason at all in midconversation. Ted's mouth would be saying one thing – 'How can I help you, madam?' or 'Yes, we can get that on inter-library loan' – but his scowl at the same time would be clearly saying something entirely different, something like 'Ach,' usually, or 'Away on,' or 'Go fuck yourself, ye wee runt, ye.' This last was the scowl now facing Israel. He'd only been to Ted's bungalow once before, and Ted clearly wished that Israel wasn't here now. Ted did not believe in franertising – his word – with work colleagues. Franertising was extremely frowned – scowled – upon. Ted held the door open only a crack and Israel could just about see the room behind him, with its drab sofa and the yelping dog.

'Ted,' said Israel.

'That's correct,' said Ted. 'Quiet, Muhammad!'

'Are you ready?'

'No.'

'Oh. You were supposed to be ready.'

'Aye,' said Ted.

'Well, look, hurry up, we need to go, the ferry's at six.'

'Aye.'

'We've not got much time. I can wait outside if you'd rather. But we do need to hurry.'

'Hurry is as hurry does.'

'What?'

'It's just a—'

'Saying, right, fine. Whatever. We need to get going here. Do you want me to load your bags in the van? You're all packed?'

'No.'

'No, you don't want me to load your bags, or no, you're not packed?'

'I'm not packed.'

'What do you mean you're not packed? We've only got a couple of hours before the ship sails.'

'I'm not coming.'

'What?'

'I'm not coming.'

'What do you mean, you're not coming? Of course you're coming.'

'I'm not. Coming.'

'All right, yeah, stop muckin' about now, Ted. We've got to go.'

'I'm not coming.'

'But we've a bet on.'

'I've changed my mind.'

'You said you couldn't change your mind once you'd made a bet.'

'I've changed my mind.'

Well, no.

On this occasion Israel could not afford to have Ted change his mind. He had already had just about enough of Northern Irish intransigence, and stubbornness and self-righteous inconsistency for the past eight months, and now he was pumped and ready to go, and Ted was holding him back.

So, no. No, no, no.

'No,' he said, using his considerable weight to push against the door. 'No. That's it. I'm not having this, Ted.'

Israel stood staring up at Ted's scowl, wedged between the door and some old green cans containing peat. 'You've mucked me about with this enough already,' he said. 'I'm getting on that boat to England this evening whether you like it or not.'

He was trying to squeeze into the bungalow. Muhammad was going crazy. Israel was a bona fide intruder.

'Aye, right, you go on ahead, son,' said Ted, pushing Israel back out of the door, with little effort. 'Because I'm not going. You.' Shove. 'Can.' Shove. 'Go.' Shove. 'Yerself.'

Israel was back out on the doorstep.

'I can't go myself, Ted,' said Israel, furious, pushing back against the door with his shoulder.

'Don't you lean against my flippin' door!' said Ted. 'You'll scratch the paintwork!'

Muhammad was barking himself demented behind Ted's legs.

'Ted. I need you to come with me,' said Israel, sighing, giving up on force and trying calm, quiet negotiation instead.

'Why?'

'Because. I can't drive the van all that way, without some . . . It needs two of us. We're like . . . Butch Cassidy and the—'

'Ach, Israel, wise up.'

'Wise up' was probably Ted's second favourite phrase, after 'Ach', though 'Catch yerself on', 'Ye eejit', and 'What are ye, stupit?' were also extremely popular.

'No, you wise up, Ted, for a change,' said Israel, the words, coming from his own lips, making him feel rather strange, as though suddenly inhabited by another nation and language, an alien within him bursting from his chest. 'We owe this to the people of Tumdrum, to—'

'Ach, Israel, ye want to have to listen to yerself. You're an absolute sickener, d'ye know that? You're as bad as the rest of them.'

'What do you mean, the rest of them?'

'The whole library committee. Ye're a bunch of hypocrites. You've no interest in this mobile library conference thing at all.'

'The Mobile Meet?'

'Aye.'

'Well, actually, as it happens, I am very—'

'You just want an excuse to get over to England.'

'Well, obviously, that too.'

'That's all ye're interested in.'

'No, it's not.'

'Aye, it is.'

'No.'

'Yes.'

'All right, fine,' said Israel, 'if it makes you feel better, Ted. You're right. I don't care at all about the Mobile Meet. I don't care about the new mobile library, or the old mobile library for that matter. I just want to go home. Which means we have to leave in a minute and get on the ferry and go.'

'Well, at least ye're being honest now.'

'Good. And so while we're about it, why don't you be honest?'

'What?'

'If it's honesty time, how about you being honest for a change?'

'What in God's name are ye talkin' about now?'

'I think you're scared of going over to England,' said Israel.

'Of course I'm not scared,' said Ted.

'I think you are scared.'

'Of what?'

'Going over to England. The big wide world out there.'

'I've seen more of the big wide world than ye'll ever see, ye runt.'

'Well, then, what's stopping you?'

'Nothing. Just . . .'

'Well?'

Ted was silent and gazed down at the floor; Muhammad too went quiet.

In all his time working on the mobile library with big Ted Carson, Israel had never known him to drop his gaze. Ted was the kind of person who looked at a problem straight in the eye and waited for it to back down. And if it didn't back down, he punched its lights out.

Israel saw his chance to seize the initiative.

'All right, Ted, listen. We are going. Because, Ted, look. Look at the van, Ted. Ted!' Ted looked up. 'Look. Just look at the van!'

Ted looked across at the clean-scrubbed van.

'I don't want to make you big-headed here, but honestly, you've done an incredible job. It's possible – and I realise I'm talking myself out of a thousand pounds here – it's possible that you might win the Concours D'Elégance. You owe it to yourself, Ted.' Israel was into his stride now. 'Not just that. You owe it to the *van*, Ted. Look at her. She could sit here, loved by you, or you could share her with others, show other people what this little country—'

'Province,' corrected Ted.

'—province is capable of. Do you know what I call her?' said Israel.

'What?' said Ted.

'Marilyn,' said Israel.

'Marilyn?' said Ted.

'Like Marilyn Monroe.'

'My favourite film actress,' said Ted, nodding his head.

'Really?' said Israel. 'There you are then. Let's get Marilyn out on the road and show people what we're made of, shall we?'

Ted took a deep sigh and looked slowly from the van to Israel, and back again from Israel to the van, and out across the obscured vista to the sea, and then he opened the door a crack wider.

'Ach, ye wee bastard. All right. I'll grab me duncher, and the dog. You're going to regret taking on this bet,' he said.

'We'll see,' said Israel, and then, pushing his luck a little too far, 'but you definitely can't bring the dog.'

'I'm bringing the dog.' Ted's face hardened.

'Fine!' said Israel. He didn't like dogs. 'Bring the dog! Fine. But let's just go, can we? We've not got much time.'

'And I need me duncher and some clothes.'

'Your whatter?'

'Me cap, me cap. I'm not going away over to the mainland without me cap.'

And so eventually, somehow, by driving at frighteningly high speed along the winding coast road that Israel had come to love and to loathe, Ted and Israel, and Muhammad the dog, boarded the

Liverpool ferry, and now they stood at the bow of the ship, Ted in his duncher, Israel in his duffle coat, Muhammad in the mobile library stowed safely down below.

Israel was thinking of warm beer, and muffins, and Wensleydale cheese, and Wallace and Gromit, and the music of Elgar, and the Clash, and the Beatles, and Jarvis Cocker, and the white cliffs of Dover, and Big Ben, and the West End, and Stonehenge, and Alton Towers, and the Last Night of the Proms, and Glastonbury, and William Hogarth, and William Blake, and Just William, and Winston Churchill, and the North Circular Road, and Grodzinski's for coffee, and rubbish, and potholes, and a slice of Stilton and a pickled onion and George Orwell. And Gloria, of course. He was almost home to Gloria. G-L-O-R-I-A.

Oh, God. He couldn't wait.

Muhammad, down below, was thinking of bones, and scraps and bouncing balls.

And Ted's thoughts went unrecorded.

And Israel felt the chill wind and the spray on his face and waved goodbye to Northern Ireland. He turned to Ted.

'Goodie!' he said.

'Ach, Jesus,' said Ted.

CHAPTER 6

Israel vomited continually and consistently for most of the journey, although it was dry-vomiting after a while, obviously; retching, voiding, spewing, ructating; stomach turned up and turned overboard; and down, and up, and down again, struck low and lower and down yet again by the ship's gentle toss and heave; beaten down and down in the ship's filthy toilets, down on his knees in other men's yellow filth, clinging to the toilet bowl, face up against white plastic, praying to God for mercy and forgiveness.

Ted spent most of the journey smoking and eating biscuits and sipping tea and worrying about Muhammad.

So it was with great relief to them all when they finally arrived in Liverpool docks and announcements called all passengers to prepare to go back down into the hold and return to the vehicles. Ted stood at the front of the queue, at the top of the steps, and turned solemnly to Israel.

'We're entering your territory now,' he said.

'Well, I don't know about that,' said Israel, extremely queasily.

'England,' said Ted.

'Well, yes, I suppose,' said Israel, swallowing hard.

'So.' Ted took the keys to the van and placed them in Israel's hands.

'No, it's OK,' said Israel, burping. 'I—'

'You're the boss now,' said Ted.

'No, really, Ted. I'd be much happier if—'

'Your country—'

'Needs you?' said Israel.

'I don't know about that,' said Ted. 'But here's the keys anyway.'

When the doors were finally opened to allow passengers down to the hold, Ted strode, Kitchener-like, down the steps to the van. Israel followed gingerly.

He climbed miserably into the driver's seat. He hated driving.

'Ugh! That is disgusting,' he said. 'What's that . . . ?'

Muhammad had left a few little presents for them inside the van.

'Ugh!' repeated Israel. 'Ugh! I think I'm going to be . . . Ugh!' as Ted scraped up what he could from the floor using a spare plastic bag. 'That dog! Is! Ugh!'

'Ach, give over, Israel, will ye? It's only a wee drop of shit, man.'

'A drop! A drop! That's not a drop! It's a . . . ugh! It's a mound! It's like something out of . . . ugh! *Close Encounters of the . . .* Ugh!'

79

'Well, what d'ye expect? He's been shut down here all by hisself.'

'Ugh! Ugh! Ugh! I can't breathe!' said Israel.

'Don't be so stupit,' said Ted.

'I said we shouldn't have brought the dog.'

'Don't refer to him as "the dog",' said Ted. 'He's a name.'

'Ugh! Look. Let me . . . Argh. Can I be honest with you, Ted?'

'No.'

'I—'

'I said no,' said Ted.

'But—'

'What? What part of "No" do ye not understand?'

'It's just . . .' said Israel, holding both hands over his mouth.

'What?'

'I really don't feel very well.'

'Aye.'

'I've got a really bad headache. And I think I might be allergic to dogs.'

'You're not allergic to dogs.'

'But I think I might be though.'

'You're not. You were seasick, ye eejit. You'll be fine.'

'You've not got a hot-water bottle, have you, Ted?'

'Do I look like I've got a feckin' hot-water bottle?'

'No. But—'

'There's your answer then. Now shut up.'

Israel dry-retched while Ted double-bagged the dog shit. There was a great heaving sound as the ferry's doors began winding open at the front of the hold.

'Agh. Ted?' said Israel.

'What?!'

'I really don't think I can drive.'

'It's your—' began Ted.

'Yes, I know. But I really hate driving at the best of—'

'Ach, Israel. You can't hate driving.'

'I do hate driving.'

'You can't hate driving. Nobody hates driving.'

'I do.'

'You don't hate driving.'

'I do! I'm telling you I do!'

'People just drive.'

'Yes, I know, but . . . I've just never really known what you're supposed to do when you're driving.'

'What?'

'No. I mean . . . I never even really liked Dinky Toys.'

'What are ye going on about now?'

The vast doors opened up fully, light flooding into the hold, the steep concrete bank before them. Vehicles all around started revving. The stench of the dog shit was overwhelming. Israel could feel his palms getting sweaty, and a prickling on the back of his neck. He felt nauseous. His head was pounding like someone was in there swinging a hammer and breaking up his mental dresser full of bone china. And he really didn't like driving. He didn't like driving at all. He'd failed his test three times before passing, and eventually he had had to go on a three-day residential course, at a former outward-bound centre in Wales, where he'd been forced to do hill-starts and reversing into a parking space for eight hours a day, and at the end of the course he drove to Hereford to take the test, and failed that too, and in the end he'd only passed when his sister Deborah had started taking him out on the North Circular, to harden him; he wouldn't forget that in a hurry; and neither would she. The memory of it made him feel sick.

'Come on,' said Ted.

Israel put the key in the ignition.

He'd once had a head-on collision with a skip on a wide, empty road during the hours of daylight. And had also accidentally brought down a Belisha beacon on a pedestrian crossing. *And* he'd driven his mother's car into a concrete wall in a multi-storey.

'Hitler,' he mumbled.

'What?' said Ted. 'What?'

'With the Volkswagen, you know. I think that's probably part of my problem with cars.'

'Aye,' said Ted. 'Hitler. I'm sure.'

'*The Italian Job*,' said Israel. 'Did you ever see that?'

'They were Minis,' said Ted.

'I know, but I was just thinking about the meaning of driving.'

'The meaning of driving,' repeated Ted, to Muhammad. 'D'ye hear him?'

'Music. They're really about music, cars,' continued Israel, half-deliriously.

'Is that right?' said Ted.

Israel had listened to a lot of music in cars: he could chart his entire adolescence according to exactly where and when and who he was with in what car when he was listening to, say, Oasis, or Blur's 'Country House', or Pulp's 'Common People', or Portishead, or the Beautiful South. At this moment, however, the most appropriate music would be a doomy Philip Glass film score, or some weepy thing by Arvo Pärt. Israel dry-belched.

'They're machines for listening to music in. Brian Eno said that.'

'Did he now?' said Ted. 'And what would he know?'

'Brian Eno?'

'Aye. What would he know?'

'How d'you mean?' said Israel.

'He. Know? It's a joke, Israel, for pity's sake.'

'Ah, right.'

'Anyhow, it's us,' said Ted. They were next in line to pull away and off and up the ramp and into England.

'You're sure you don't want to—' began Israel.

'Drive!' said Ted.

'Yes,' said Israel. 'Of course.'

He turned the key. The van didn't start.

He glanced across at Ted, who sat impassive,

staring ahead, much as though he were in a film with a doomy Philip Glass score. Muhammad sat in his lap.

'Ted?'

Ted remained silent.

Israel turned the keys in the ignition again.

Israel felt his mouth and throat go dry.

There was an incident on the A40 once, with Gloria. He'd stalled. Couldn't get the car started again. A man had come out of his car and reached in, called Gloria a stupid bitch, and then punched Israel; he'd punched him only lightly, once, but it was in the face. It had hurt.

'Ted?'

'What?'

'She's not starting.'

'Well, try her again.'

'I've tried her again.'

'Well, try her again again.'

Israel could begin to feel the restlessness of the vehicles behind him.

He tried turning the ignition again.

'Turn the ignition and give it a shoggle!' said Ted.

'I am turning the ignition and giving it a . . . shoggle.'

'Ach!' said Ted, placing Muhammad down. 'Are ye totally useless, man? Can ye not do anything right? Let me there.'

Ted stood up, and started pulling Israel out of the driver's seat.

'Out! Come on, out!'

'Ow! Get off! What are you doing?'

'I'm driving. Come on. Shove over. Get out of the seat, ye eejit. You can't even start a bloody vehicle, never mind drive her.'

'It's not my fault!' said Israel, slinking into the passenger seat. 'I don't feel well. It's this stupid van.'

'Don't blame the van. There's nothing wrong with this van.'

'There is.'

'There is not!'

By the time Ted had positioned himself in the driving seat and claimed the wheel, a number of other drivers had started to emerge out of their own vehicles and were approaching the van. There was a sharp tap on the window by Ted's head. Ted rolled down the window – with some slight difficulty. He hadn't got round to fixing the windows.

'Problem, mate?' said a shaven-headed man with a London accent.

'What?' said Ted.

'Problem?'

'No. Why? Have ye a problem?'

'Yeah. I do as it happens. I want to get my van off this ferry and get 'ome.'

'Well,' said Ted, turning the key in the ignition and hoping for the best, 'if you were to stop poking yer nose in here and get back in your vehicle' – and yes! yes! the van started – 'you might be able

85

to.' He loudly revved the van. The man walked away. '*"Problem, mate?"*' said Ted loudly, mimicking the man's accent.

'God,' said Ted, as they drove off the ferry and up the concrete ramp and into the blinding light and Liverpool docks. 'I hate the fucking English.'

'We're not all bad,' said Israel.

'No,' said Ted, casting Israel a pitiful glance. 'Some of youse are worse.'

They drove in a long snaking queue through the docks, past multicoloured containers stacked high one upon the other, and huge lorry trailer-loads and cranes and cargo ships and freighters and they could have been anywhere in the world, until Israel saw a 'Welcome to Liverpool' sign which had been spray-canned to read 'Welcome to poo', and he knew he was back in England.

'Hello, England!' he said.

Muhammad barked in approval.

Israel wound down his window and breathed in the fresh air and he couldn't explain it: it felt like a huge weight lifting from his shoulders. He felt instantly refreshed and renewed, as though he'd slept for a long long time, and awoken with renewed vigour.

'England!' he shouted, through his nausea and over his headache. 'In-ger-lund!'

'All right,' said Ted. 'That's enough now.'

'Do you want me to take over the driving?' offered Israel.

'I thought you hated driving,' said Ted.

86

'Well, you know. Like you say, we're on my manor now.'

'We're what?'

'On my manor.'

'Aye, and ye're one of the Kray twins all of a sudden, are ye?'

'No. Just. Home, I mean. This is my home.'

'Is it?'

'Yes.'

'What? You live in Liverpool?'

'No.'

'So you don't live in Liverpool?'

'No, I don't.'

'So this isn't your home?'

'No! I live in . . . I just mean, England. Oh, never mind. You drive, and I'll . . .' Muhammad looked up at him reproachfully from the floor. 'Just sit quietly here, shall I?'

Just as Israel spoke these words they were waved over towards a set of Portakabins by two armed policemen.

'Ach, no,' said Ted. 'I don't believe it.'

'What?' said Israel. 'What's happening?'

'Just don't say anything,' said Ted, as he swung the van over.

One policeman approached Ted's side of the van. Another approached Israel's. Ted wound down his window.

'Morning, gents,' said Ted's policeman, breathing coffee fumes into the van. 'Any form of identification at all?'

87

'Me?' said Israel, shocked.

'Yes, you,' said Israel's policeman, who'd perhaps had a meal with garlic in it the night before.

The policemen examined the passports. Israel's garlicky policeman seemed satisfied with his. Ted's coffee policeman was not so sure.

'Can we have a word, Mr Carson?'

Ted got out of the van.

Israel started to get out of the van too.

'Ted?'

'You stay there,' said Israel's policeman.

'But—'

'Get in-the van, and stay in the van, sir,' said the policeman.

Israel stayed in the van and waited. And waited. He needed to go to the toilet. He wasn't sure he'd be allowed to go to the toilet. He took some Nurofen. They made him feel sick. You shouldn't take Nurofen on an empty stomach. Israel always took Nurofen on an empty stomach. He'd probably die of a stomach ulcer before he was thirty. Or internal bleeding. Multiple organ failure. Muhammad sat silently, occasionally scratching at himself.

Almost an hour later Ted re-emerged from the Portakabins. He looked ashen-faced. He got in the van.

'Bloody hell!' said Israel. 'Are you all right? What's going on?'

Ted didn't say anything.

'You look like you've seen a ghost,' said Israel.

Again, Ted did not reply.

'I'd almost given up on you there,' said Israel.

Ted started up the engine.

'Hang on,' said Israel, as they moved off through the docks. 'Hang on. What was that all about?'

'Nothing,' said Ted.

'Nothing?' said Israel. 'They don't question someone for an hour for nothing.'

'They do here,' said Ted.

'Really?' said Israel. 'About what? Ted? Is there something you're not telling me?' Ted was always very cagey about discussing his past – he took caginess to new heights, or depths.

'It was a misunderstanding just,' said Ted.

'Probably mistook you for a terrorist, eh?' said Israel. 'Or a drug-runner or something.' The thought of this tickled Israel. 'There's not something you've been meaning to tell me, Ted, is there? You're not a drug-runner, are you?' The thought of Ted as a drug-runner greatly amused Israel.

'Shut up,' said Ted.

'I was only—'

'We're not talking about it any more. All right? So shut up. They made a mistake, and that's it.'

'All right, I was only . . . D'you want me to drive?'

'I'm driving!' said Ted.

'Fine,' said Israel. 'I was only—'

'Which means you're navigating,' said Ted.

'Good,' said Israel. 'No problem.'

'Silently,' said Ted.

'How do you—'

'Just shut up!' said Ted.

'So,' said Israel, after less than a minute. 'Where are we?'

'In Liverpool docks,' said Ted, sighing.

'You know we could get a sat nav system when we get the new van,' said Israel.

'We're not getting a new van,' said Ted.

'No. No. Of course not. So. Directions-wise, we're going to . . . ?'

Ted reached down beneath the driver's seat and felt around and took a book out and handed it over to Israel. It was a large burgundy hardback book with gold embossed lettering on the cover proudly announcing itself as *The AA Illustrated Road Book of England & Wales with Gazetteer, Itineraries, Maps & Town Plans.*

'What's this?' said Israel.

'It's the map.'

'It doesn't look much like a map. It's more like an encyclopaedia.'

'It's all we had in stock.'

Israel opened the book and turned to the title page.

'Erm, Ted. I think this might be a bit outdated.'

'Why?'

'Well, it was published in 1965.'

'I've a map of Ireland was my father's, it's done me rightly.'

'Yes, but, erm, I think there's been quite a bit

of road-building and what have you in England since 1965.'

'Aye, well, there's been a lot of road-building in County Antrim too since 1965, but we never made a fuss about it.'

'OK, well, if you're sure.'

'Aye,' said Ted. 'So?'

They had arrived at the main exit out of the docks.

'Where are we?' said Ted.

'Erm . . .' Israel was flicking through the index looking for Liverpool.

'There's people behind us here,' said Ted. 'Which way?'

'OK, OK. I'm just looking. This doesn't seem to include any motorways or—'

'Do we need to go on the motorways?'

'Well, it's quite a journey.'

Israel kept flicking through the book. There were dozens of exquisite line drawings: Bockleton's lych gate, the lake castle built by Sir Edward Dalyngrigge in 1385, High Wycombe's arcaded town hall, the Jewry Wall in Leicester.

At last, he found Liverpool.

'The cathedral has notable stained glass,' he said. 'And there are a number of good Georgian houses.'

'I need directions,' said Ted. 'Not a fuckin' guided tour!'

There was the sound of the hooting of horns from behind.

'Israel?'

'Yes?'

'Just tell me where in God's name we're supposed to be going here?'

'Right, where are we?' said Israel, starting over again with the book's index.

'In Liverpool! At the docks! Are ye stupit!?'

'Do you know what road?'

'No! We're at a junction. There's people up behind us! What do the signs say?'

'Ah, right, A5036. OK. A5047. A57. Erm . . .'

'Come on! Where do I need to go?'

'Erm. You sure you don't want me to drive and you can—'

'Tell me where to go!'

'I don't know!' said Israel weakly. He had a headache so bad he'd never had a headache like it before. The Nurofen weren't working.

'You're meant to be telling me!'

'Ah. Right. Manchester? Is that south of Liverpool?'

'I don't know,' said Ted. 'You're the Englishman.'

'Liverpool. Manchester. Manchester. Liverpool. Yes, it is, isn't it? I think it is. Manchester. Yes. Definitely. Let's follow the signs for the M62 then, shall we?'

'Right. Thank God.'

Ted pulled out into the heavy stream of traffic, and their journey proper began.

The pair travelled on in haphazard and argumentative fashion for several miles – 'Bear right'; 'I'm trying to bear right'; 'Quick!'; 'I'm going as quick as I can, there's all these lorries up behind me'; 'Road's a bit busier over here on the mainland, eh?'; 'Shut up, Israel' – until at last they safely reached the relative calm of the M62.

'I *think* Manchester's south,' said Israel. 'Should we pull over and ask someone?'

'It's a bit late now, ye fool,' said Ted. 'We're on a motorway.'

'Yes, but we could . . . Maybe we should just check our route with someone.'

'Aye, and what would you be asking them? Excuse me' – Ted adopted here a kind of Cockney-meets-Quentin-Crisp imitation English accent – '*how do I get to London?*'

'Well, yes.'

'What sort of a question is that, ye eejit?'

'How to get to London? What's wrong with that?'

'You sound like Dick blinkin' Whittington, that's what's wrong with it. "*How do I get to London?*" Ye're from London!'

'Yes, but I've never travelled much up north!'

'Holy God, man.'

They drove on for a few moments in silence.

'Are you hungry, Ted?' said Israel.

'No.'

'Not even a little bit?'

'No.'

'Not even a tiny, teensy-weensy little bit?'

'No. Why? Are you hungry? I thought you were feeling sick a minute ago.'

'Yes. I am. But I wonder if a little something

93

would . . . You know, settle my . . . But if you're OK. I was just wondering if you were . . .'

'No, I'm fine.'

'Good. We'll keep on going then, shall we? We wouldn't stop at the services yet, would we?'

'No,' agreed Ted.

'You don't need the toilet or anything?'

'No.'

'Don't want to buy anything?'

'No.'

'A paper, or a . . . souvenir, or anything?'

'No, Israel. We're here working. We're not on holiday.'

'Yes,' agreed Israel. 'Quite. Lunch though. We'll be stopping for lunch somewhere?'

Ted gave a huge eloquent sigh. Israel shut up.

Somewhere down the road, somewhere south, somewhere after the M62, on the M6, just after the Knutsford Service Area – the manifold facilities of which, much to Israel's disappointment, the pair did not avail themselves – Ted started to relax and decided to put on the audiobook of *The Da Vinci Code*. Again.

Israel had had to listen to *The Da Vinci Code* – all six and a half hours of it, repeatedly, narrated by a man who did comedy French accents – for much of the past six months in the van. It was Ted's favourite.

'No!' he groaned, as Ted extracted the first of the cassettes from its special box. 'No! Please! Not that bloody book again.'

'It's good,' said Ted.

'It's not good at all. It's total crap.'

'Have ye read it?'

'No. But—'

'Well then.'

'I may not actually have read it. But I have had to listen to it being read out loud by Dan fucking—'

'Language,' said Ted.

'Sorry. Flippin' Brown.'

'It's not Dan Brown who narrates it. He's the author.'

'I know he's the author.'

'It's another fella who narrates it. He's an actor.'

'Yes! Fine! And I've been listening to him read the bloody thing for what seems like most of my adult life, so I think I have pretty good grounds to be able to form a judgement on the book!'

'Maybe,' said Ted.

'And it's crap,' said Israel.

'It's not crap.'

'It's even worse than Harry bloody Potter, and that bloody accordion music. It's total nonsense.'

'What, the Field Marshal Montgomery Pipe Band?'

'No! *The Da Vinci Code*. It's rubbish.'

'It is not.'

'It is!'

'The Priory of Sion,' said Ted. 'Fact.'

'What?'

'The sacred femimime. Fact.'

'What?'

'*Holy Blood, Holy Grail.* That was a great book also,' said Ted.

'Oh, God.'

'Stop it,' said Ted.

'Sorry,' said Israel.

'And what are you reading at the moment, then, Einstein?'

'Paul Auster, actually.'

'Well, that's a lot of crap,' said Ted.

'Have you ever read any Paul Auster?'

'I don't need to: if youse are reading it then I know it's a lot of crap.'

Israel agreed to allow Ted to play *The Da Vinci Code* – again – if they could stop at the next service station. Which they did.

And which Israel instantly wished they hadn't. He hadn't been at a service station for a long time: they didn't seem to have any service stations in Northern Ireland; there weren't enough motorways, and people still believed in doing flasks and their own sandwiches, and taking rugs and fold-up chairs for the lay-by. He'd forgotten what service stations were like: they were like England, complete, but in miniature. Women in tight T-shirts giving out Peanut Butter KitKats; men in shiny suits trying to sell credit cards; young men in football shirts; older men in baseball caps; fat women dressed for the gym; celeb mags, sweeties, super-value meals. Machine coffee. Spoliation.

'This is great, isn't it?' said Ted, tucking into an

all-day five-piece fry. 'I've not had an English fry for years,' he said. 'You miss the potato bread, but.'

Israel had gone for the vegetarian option – a fried egg on toast. The egg had not been recently fried.

When they got back into the van, Israel got into the driver's seat.

'Look, Ted, you have a rest. I'll drive. You can navigate.'

'No,' said Ted. 'You navigate. I'll drive.'

'No!' said Israel. 'I insist. We need to share the responsibility.'

Ted sat with the burgundy *AA Illustrated Road Book of England & Wales* unopened on his lap.

'Concord De Le Elegant,' said Ted sleepily to himself as they motored down the M6, down, down towards the south of England.

'Concours D'Elégance,' corrected Israel.

'That'll give that wee nigger bitch Linda a—'

'What?' said Israel. 'You can't say that.'

'What?' said Ted.

'That! What you just said.'

'What? Wee nigger bitch?'

'Yes! That! That's racist! And sexist!'

'It is not.'

'Of course it is.'

'Are ye calling me a racist?'

'Yes, I am. You can't call someone a nigger bitch.'

'Why not?'

'Because it's offensive!'

'Aye. But Linda is a wee nigger bitch, so she is.'

'Ted! No. No. Also, Linda's not black, she's Chinese.'

'I don't mean she's black, ye fool.'

'"*Nigger*"?' said Israel.

'Aye. D'ye not say that in English?'

'No, we don't. Unless you're . . . you know.'

'Like, "niggerly" but?' said Ted.

'Niggerly?' said Israel.

'Aye.'

'Niggardly, do you mean? Nig-*gard*-ly?'

'Aye,' said Ted. 'Same thing.'

'It's not the same thing at all, Ted.'

'Well, it might not be to you, but it is to me.'

'Well, it's still outrageous. You better stop talking like that now we're here.'

'Oh!' said Ted, again putting on the strangulated, nasal voice that was supposed to be his approximation of an English accent. '*You want me to start speaking proper?*'

'You could try,' said Israel.

'Aye, and you can try the back of my hand,' said Ted.

Hours passed. They crawled along: the van shuddered at anything over fifty. Places. Muhammad slept. M6. M1. Newport Pagnell.

'It'll be stiff competition,' said Israel.

'What?' said Ted.

'The Mobile Meet. It's the UK's Premier—'

'Aye. But we've the luck of the Irish,' said Ted.

'Ted?' said Israel, sucking on a fruit pastille; he'd

stocked up on sweets at the service station: two Snickers, Maltesers, some M&Ms and a Daim bar; they were so good; the fruit pastilles now were just to clear his palate.

'Aye.'

'You know when you're in Northern Ireland you insist you're Northern Irish.'

'That I am. Ulsterman and proud.'

'Yes. Well. Did you know now we're in England you've started to refer to yourself as an Irishman? Just, Irish?'

'And?' said Ted.

'It's interesting though, isn't it, multiple identities? How we shift and redefine ourselves according to our environment.'

'Aye, right, d'ye read that in a book?'

'No. I—'

'Just give over, Israel, will ye? And get ready to pay out one thousand pounds.'

Coming into the Great North Way, off the M1. Mill Hill. Israel could feel his pulse rate increasing.

'What are you doing now?' said Ted.

Israel was humming 'London Calling' by the Clash. He could almost smell the tartan moquette on the old Routemaster buses.

'I'm home, Ted.'

Ted looked around.

'This is it?'

It was mostly light industrial units.

'Not like North Antrim, eh?' said Israel.

'You're right there,' said Ted.

England is a complete mess, of course – everybody knows that – and London is at the heart of the mess, the guts, the nub: vast, cosy, labyrinthine, stinking, fresh and alive; like a bucket of still beating offal. Israel loved it. It was hard to explain, but it felt to Israel as though he'd been in a place where the house lights were permanently dimmed, and now suddenly someone had turned on the lights, turned up the volume, and thrown open the windows.

'The ripeness!' he called out, as they came through Hendon.

'What?' said Ted.

'The ripeness,' repeated Israel. 'The full, rich, frothing . . . richness of it all,' said Israel.

'Jesus,' said Ted.

'Woof,' said Muhammad.

As they came closer and closer to Finchley, Israel was filled with excitement. He could almost feel a *Time Out* in his hand.

'*Time Out!*' he said out loud.

'What?'

'London's premier listings magazine.'

'Are ye having some sort of nervous breakdown?' said Ted.

Time Out: The almost pornographic thrill of it in his hand: the pictures, the absurdly boostering coverage of the Arts, the Books, the Films, the Theatre, everything! He could see himself once again at the Royal Opera House! At the Ritzy Cinema in Brixton! At the Serpentine Gallery!

The V&A! (Not that he'd ever been to the Royal Opera House. Or the Serpentine Gallery.) This was his city!

'This is my city!' he announced to Ted.

'Aye, right. Well, which road do we want here then?' said Ted.

'Erm.'

It was as though they were drawing close to the very cradle of humanity, the omphalos, the whirlpool, the centre of the universe. First every few miles, and then the half-mile, and quarter-mile, and finally by yards, feet and inches he was confronted by and consumed with memories: the DIY centre where he'd gone with his mother when his father had died, to buy a lighter lawn-mower; the place they'd bought his bed and his wardrobe; the shop he'd bought his first bike; the cinema; the bus stop; the school; the youth club; the post box; his street.

Home!

He parked outside the house – not bad. He didn't even clip the kerb. It was like he was driving on air, in a fantasy, or a dream.

'We're here,' he said, amazed.

'Well,' said Ted.

'*This* is home,' said Israel, gesturing at the long bare suburban street, no different to suburban streets anywhere else in England, Scotland, Wales, or Northern Ireland. Telegraph poles, flower-pots, a touch of mock-Tudor, front gardens paved over for cars. Not much different, in fact, to Tumdrum.

'What do you think?'

'Hmm,' said Ted. 'I thought it'd be—'

'What?' said Israel.

'The way you santer on . . .' said Ted.

'Yes?'

'I don't rightly know. I was expecting maybe knights and turrets, and streets paved with gold.'

'Right.'

'Mansions. Rolls-Royces.'

'OK. Yep. Anyway . . . Come on,' said Israel. 'Mum'll be delighted to see us.'

He jumped down out of the van and Ted followed.

He rang the doorbell of his parents' standard suburban semi.

'Mum!' he said, when his mother opened the door.

'You're late,' said his mother. 'Dinner's already on the table.'

'Sorry.'

She leaned forward and kissed him and then looked over his shoulder, past Ted, at the van.

'Is that your van?'

'Yes.'

'You can't leave the van there.'

'Why not?'

'You're blocking the drive.'

'Well, that's OK, isn't it?'

'It would be better if you parked it elsewhere.'

'Why?'

'Just park out of the way, somewhere round the corner.'

'But—'

'Do hurry up, Israel, and do what you're told.'

Home?

Definitely.

He felt like a child again already.

CHAPTER 7

Israel's mother was not a good cook. It was a myth about Jewish mothers, in Israel's experi-ence: he knew a lot of Jewish mothers who were good eaters, but good cooks? Gloria's mother, for example, had ambitions as a cook, but her meals were always somehow inappropriate, or undone by her own ambition: meals made with a random *coulis* of this and an inexplicable *jus* of that; and a Puerto Rican fruit and chicken dish she liked to make, soaked in sherry for two days, and garnished with candied fruit and raisins; and stuff she liked to do with braised celery; and weird shiny food; and breakfast soups; all of it just . . . not a good idea. Israel's mother specialised in half-raw roast chicken dinners – put in too late, or taken out too early – and also crispy plasticised ready-meals, burnt beyond recognition while she was talking on the phone, overcooked casualties of hasty multi-tasking. In Israel's experience, the only good food in the Armstrong household came direct from the deli counter at the Waitrose in Finchley.

As a welcome-home meal, Israel's mother had

prepared her signature dish, paprika chicken, which was basically chicken with a lot of paprika sprinkled over it – one part chicken to one part paprika – and cooked with tomatoes and rice until all the constituent parts had broken down to roughly the same size and consistency and were indistinguishable; you could almost drink Israel's mother's paprika chicken. Israel had eaten this meal probably at least once a week for fifteen years before becoming a vegetarian; if he had to identify a particular dish, a particular meal that had turned him vegetarian, then it was probably paprika chicken: the sickly smell of it, the oils, the colours. The paprika chicken sat now, liquid and fragrant and oily and orange, centre stage on the Armstrong family dinner table. For Israel, in respect of his status as honorary returning family vegetarian, there was a side dish of glistening fried mushrooms.

'Thank you for having us, Mrs Armstrong,' said Ted.

'Thank *you*, Mr Carson.'

'Please, call me Ted.'

'If you'll call me Eva,' said Israel's mother.

'Is that an Irish name?' said Ted.

'I don't think so,' said Israel's mother. 'Although my late husband was Irish.'

'Oh,' said Ted.

'So we certainly have something in common,' said Israel's mother, who was clearly in good spirits: she'd lit candles, and there was a tablecloth.

105

The meal felt like a special occasion; a family gathering. Israel was there; his mother; his sister, Deborah; and Ted. Deborah's fiancé would be arriving later.

'Well,' Israel's mother was saying, looking at her watch.

'Ari won't be here till later,' said Deborah.

'So we're just waiting for Gloria,' said Israel's mother.

'I'm sure she won't mind if we start,' said Israel.

'Are you sure?' said Israel's mother. 'I wouldn't want it to get cold.'

'Yes, absolutely.'

'I'll serve, at least,' said Israel's mother. 'She may be here by then.'

Israel had told Gloria what time he'd be arriving, and she said she'd be there. Probably she was busy.

Israel texted again.

She was not there by the time the food was served.

'So. Shall we?' said Israel's mother, looking at her watch again.

'Let's,' said Israel.

'No sign of Gloria then?'

'She's probably busy.'

'Well, good. First, a toast. To Israel! It's lovely to have you back! And to Mr Carson!'

'Please, call me Ted,' said Ted.

'Ted. Yes,' she said. 'And your lovely dog.' Israel's mother hated dogs. 'What was it he's called?'

'Muhammad,' said Ted.

'How unusual!'

'After the boxer,' said Israel.

'Woof!' said Muhammad.

'Quite!' said Israel's mother. 'Lovely to have you here. We missed you,' she said to Israel, placing a hand on his arm.

'I missed you too, Mum,' said Israel.

'I didn't,' said Israel's sister Deborah.

'You wouldn't,' said Israel.

'She's joking, Ted,' said Israel's mother. 'They like to tease each other. Of course she missed him.'

'Have you had your hair cut?' said Israel to his sister, sipping his wine.

'Yes, of course I've had my hair cut. You think I'd grow my hair for six months without having it cut?'

'Well, it looks . . . different,' said Israel.

'And you look like you've been sleeping in a ditch,' said Deborah.

'Thank you,' said Israel.

'Mmm,' said Ted, who was enjoying his first experience of Armstrong paprika chicken. 'Delicious.'

'And what about me?' said Israel's mother.

'Sorry?' said Ted.

'My hair, Israel?'

'Yes,' said Israel. 'Yours is—'

'It's shorter,' said his mother. 'More modern.'

'Is it . . .?' Israel thought perhaps his mother's hair colour had gone a shade too far towards burgundy.

'There's a touch of colour in it,' she said.

'Right,' said Israel. 'And there's something else . . .'

'My nails?' said Israel's mother. 'He's very observant. He gets that from my side of the family,' she explained to Ted. 'I've started getting my nails done.' She held up her hands and stretched out her fingers as though about to play a two-octave scale. Her hands were all wrinkly and slightly liver-spotted, but the nails were pure bright white and shiny; like old wine skins stoppered with brand-new plastic corks. 'French polish,' she said.

'I thought that was something to do with furniture,' said Israel.

'Tuh!' said Deborah.

'But they're nice,' said Israel. 'Really nice.'

'Thank you,' said his mother.

'And your eyebrows,' said Deborah.

'Ah, yes, my eyebrows.' Israel's mother raised an already arched eyebrow. 'I go to a woman now that Deborah knows in Swiss Cottage.'

'I thought she needed some updating,' said Deborah.

'Right,' said Israel.

'A woman needs to take more care of herself as she gets older. Isn't that right, Ted?' said Israel's mother.

'Mmm,' said Ted. 'Lovely chicken.'

'After all, I'm only sixty-two. There's plenty more, if you want some.'

Ted looked bemused.

'The chicken?' said Israel's mother.

Ted smiled and graciously accepted another ladleful of paprika chicken.

'Now,' said Israel's mother. 'Just for a quick catch up on all the news, Israel, seeing as you've missed so much while you've been away. Mrs Metzger?'

'Who?'

'Mrs Metzger, of the Metzgers?'

'Oh.'

'She's been in hospital. They cut out half her intestine.'

'Ouch,' said Israel.

'And Mrs Silverman?'

'Sorry?'

'Her husband taught the girls the violin.'

'Ah. Right.'

'He's dead.'

'Oh.'

'Cancer.'

'Oh dear.'

'Of the nose.'

'I didn't know you could get cancer of the nose.'

'You can get cancer of the anything,' said Deborah.

'Are you sure?'

'Of course I'm sure.'

'It can kill you,' said Israel's mother.

'Cancer of the *nose*?'

'For sure. He's dead. And Mrs West, her Israeli cousin, her son, he's dead. He was killed.'

'Oh dear. In Israel?'

'No, in Tunbridge Wells,' said Deborah. 'What do you think? Of course in Israel!'

'And we're doing *Guys and Dolls* again with the amateur dramatics. It's a shame you're going to miss it.'

'Yeah. That is a . . . shame.'

'Gerald—'

'An old Armstrong family friend,' noted Deborah.

'Calls it *Goys* and Dolls!'

'Ha!' said Israel. 'Very funny.'

Ted looked perplexed.

'Anyway, we know the news, Mother,' said Deborah.

'Israel doesn't know the news.'

'He knows it now. What we want to know is *his* news. So how is the world of *information services*, brother of mine?'

'Well. Erm. Good, thanks,' said Israel. 'It's . . . very interesting.'

'I'm sure Israel has made a lot of good friends over there, hasn't he, Ted?' said Israel's mother. The Irish are renowned for their warmth of welcome and hospitality, aren't they?'

Israel almost choked on a mushroom.

'Aye,' said Ted, who had paprika around his mouth. 'That we are.'

'We're in Northern Ireland, Mother,' said Israel.

'Ah, yes, of course,' said his mother. 'The IRA bit.'

'Yes. Well . . .' said Israel.

'How's all that going these days?' said Israel's mother.

'Fine,' said Israel. 'It's this whole peace process thing and the devolution, so—'

'Ah, yes, good, good. My late husband was an Irishman,' said Israel's mother. 'Did Israel tell you, Ted?'

'Aye,' said Ted.

'From Dublin.'

'County Dublin,' said Israel.

'So good they named it twice,' said Deborah.

'That's what he always used to say,' said Israel's mother. 'He'd kissed the blarney stone. Have you kissed the blarney stone, Ted?'

'Ach, no,' said Ted.

'He was great crack, my husband, Ted. You'd have got on. Do you have crack where you are?'

'Aye,' said Ted. 'Craic? We do.'

'Good,' said Israel's mother. 'I am glad. I do love the Irish – such a sense of fun and adventure.' Israel couldn't tell if she raised an eyebrow, or if it was permanently raised.

Israel's mobile phone vibrated. Text message from Gloria: she was going to be later than she thought. OK. That was fine. That was OK.

They were sitting in the back room – the best room, the room with the curtain tiebacks and the swags. Israel looked up at the photos on the walls: his father, his grandparents, the Irish, and the Jews, all tiny, all reduced and captured in neat shiny silver frames; his mother liked a nice silver frame. All ship-shape, present and correct. And there, there was the old wooden gazelle on the mahogany sideboard under the window, a wooden gazelle that Israel remembered as having belonged to one of his mother's aunts; and next to it a couple of elephants made of coloured glass, which he recognised as having once belonged to his granny. Things had slowly migrated to this room from other houses, or got washed up, like wreckage; it was a room completely stuffed to overflowing, teeming, bobbing with booty, and ornaments and furniture; barely enough space to edge round the dining table (which had for years been in situ in Colindale, at Israel's mother's brother's, before coming adrift and floating downstream to the Armstrongs). The whole thing was like a palimpsest of other rooms, a stratum, layer upon layer of other people's lives. The only thing that Israel could iden- tify as being absolutely native, something original, and aboriginal, and uniquely of their own, was a stainless-steel hostess trolley which had never been used for hostessing, as far as Israel was aware, and had only ever been used for storing newspapers and the *Radio Times*; though by the looks of it his mother seemed to have converted since his depart- ure to the *TV Times*. Standards were slipping.

Half an hour after the meal had begun, on the verge of the end both of the conversation and of the paprika chicken, Deborah's fiancé arrived. He was wearing the kind of shirt that had obviously recently seen a tie, and he had a thick, luscious head of hair, the hair of a lead character in an American made-for-TV courtroom drama.

112

'Hi!' said the thick-haired fiancé loudly, entering the room, to everyone and no one in particular. 'Sorry I'm late.'

'Long day?' said Israel's mother.

'You could say that!' He kissed Israel's sister – on the lips. And then – unbelievably – he went over to Israel's mother and kissed her also. On the cheek. Israel didn't like this at all; this was definitely a new development. Israel was pretty sure that his sister's fiancé hadn't previously been in the habit of kissing his mother; Israel would definitely have remembered that.

'Israel!' he said, reaching across and shaking his hand, in a man-of-the-household fashion. 'No, no, don't get up. Good to see you. You're looking well. And . . . Hello!' He shook Ted's hand. 'I'm Ari.'

'Say again?' said Ted.

'Ari. My name.'

'Hello,' said Ted. 'I'm Ted. Nice to meet you.'

'Ari and Deborah are engaged to be married,' said Israel's mother.

'Oh,' said Ted. 'Congratulations.'

'Ted works in information services over in Ireland with Israel,' explained Israel's mother.

Ari and Deborah exchanged amused glances.

'Really?' said Ari. 'Information services? I'd be very interested to know about that. I'm kind of in information services myself.'

'Ari works in financial PR,' said Israel's mother.

'Oh,' said Ted.

'He's very successful.'

'Oh,' said Ted.

'Paprika chicken, Ari? And Ted, perhaps can I tempt you?'

For someone who was very successful Ari ate as though he hadn't eaten in a long time – or maybe that's just how very successful people eat, like tramps, or emperors; determined, heedless. Ari paused from stuffing himself only to heap absurd, lavish praise upon Israel's mother's cooking, and to provoke and dominate conversation, and to share sly whispered asides with Israel's sister. Israel had fantasised for months about returning to his family. And this was it. This was his family. This was home.

Oh, God.

'So, Israel, you followed this business in Lebanon?' said Ari, mid-forkful. 'What do you think?'

'I don't know,' said Israel. 'What do you think?'

Ari knew full well what Israel would think. And Israel knew full well what Ari would think.

'You get the news OK over there then?' said Ari.

'We manage,' said Israel. He didn't want to admit that he was mostly listening to BBC Radio Ulster and reading the *Impartial Recorder*.

'I'm trying to wean your mother here off the *Daily Mail*.'

'I like Melanie Phillips,' said Israel's mother.

'My aunt knows Melanie Phillips,' said Ari.

'Yes, his aunt knows Melanie Phillips,' said Israel's mother.

'I like to read *The Times*, the *Telegraph* and the *FT* every day. To get a rounded view of things,' said Ari, who didn't talk so much as make statements and request information.

'I'm sure you do,' said Israel.

'I read the *Telegraph*,' said Ted.

'That's the *Belfast Telegraph*,' said Israel.

'Oh,' said Ari.

'So, Israel, you haven't answered the question, what should we do in Lebanon?' said Deborah.

'I think we should pull out, of course,' said Israel.

'Well, well,' said Deborah. 'There's a surprise.'

'And I think all Israelis should come out and protest.'

'Like that'd help,' said Deborah.

'It'd be a show of solidarity.'

'Now, I hope we're not getting into politics?' said Israel's mother.

'It's not politics, Mum,' said Israel.

'I do apologise, Eva,' said Ari.

'That's OK, Ari,' said Israel's mother. 'More chicken?'

'Yes, please. Delicious.'

'Are there any more mushrooms?' asked Israel.

'No, sorry,' said his mother.

'Ted,' said Ari. 'I'm sure you must have an interesting perspective on things, coming from Northern Ireland.'

'On mushrooms?' said Israel.

'On the situation in Lebanon. Obviously,' said Deborah.

'One man's terrorist is another man's freedom fighter,' said Israel's mother. 'That's what your father used to say.'

Ted picked at his chicken bones.

'Ted?' said Ari.

'I . . .' began Ted, blushing.

'How anyone could think it was OK to plant a bomb and kill people,' said Israel's mother.

'As they're drinking a cup of coffee, or on their way to work,' said Deborah.

'Exactly,' said Israel's mother. 'Disgraceful.'

Ted was flushed, and coughed, and adjusted himself awkwardly in his chair.

'Are you OK, Ted?' said Israel's mother.

'Fine, thank you.'

'I blame Tony Blair,' said Israel.

'Tony Blair?' said Ari. 'For Lebanon?'

'Evil man,' said Israel.

'Evil?' said Ari. 'He's not evil.'

'He is evil.'

'What, the same as Hitler or Stalin or Saddam Hussein were evil?' said Ari.

'No, of course not,' said Israel.

'So in what sense evil?' said Ari, stroking his luxuriant hair. 'Like who? Like Jeffrey Dahmer was evil?'

'Don't be silly,' said Israel.

'Israel, please, treat our guests with respect,' said his mother.

'I am treating him with respect,' said Israel. 'He's not—'

'It's OK, Eva,' said Ari. 'I hardly think Israel and I are ever going to agree over the Middle East.'

There was a suggestion here in what Ari said, and the way in which he said it – coolly and calmly – that this was in some way Israel's fault.

'It's just, I'm very' – Ari continued, spearing another chicken thigh – 'very suspicious of this whole anti-Israel lobby.'

'I'm not anti-Israel,' said Israel.

'Really?'

'And I'm not part of a lobby. I just think people should be allowed to criticise Israel when it's made a mistake. Like, for example, going into Lebanon and committing atrocities.'

'Israel, Israel,' said Ari, patriarchally. 'You know, it's funny, I do often find it's self-hating Jews who make these wild accusations about the—'

'They're not wild accusations,' said Israel. 'And maybe I am a self-hating Jew, because—'

'You're not a self-hating Jew,' said Deborah. 'You're a self-hating person.'

'Children!' said Israel's mother. 'Ted doesn't want to hear this, do you, Ted?'

Ted smiled, non-committally.

'Coffee everyone?'

Israel helped his mother take the dishes through to the kitchen, leaving Ted to battle it out alone over Lebanon with Ari and Deborah.

'So, where's Gloria?' she asked, when they were alone together in the kitchen.

'She's just texted,' said Israel. 'She's having to finish some work.'

'But she knew you were coming back tonight?'

'Yes, it's just something she couldn't get out of.'

'I see.'

'Mother, let's not get started on Gloria.'

Israel's mother didn't trust Gloria.

'I'm not getting started on anything. So, you've not met any nice girls over in Ireland?'

'Mother!'

'I'm only asking.'

'Well, anyway, no, I haven't. Not really.'

'Not really? Does that mean yes?'

'No!'

'Well. He's lovely, though, isn't he?' said Israel's mother.

'Who? Ari?'

'No! Ted.'

'Ted?' said Israel.

'Yes,' said Israel's mother. 'I think he's very charming.'

'Ted? Charming?' Israel thought back to when he'd arrived in Tumdrum and Ted had physically threatened him on a number of occasions. 'Ted is certainly a lot of things, Mother,' he said, 'but I hardly think charming is one of them.'

'I do like his accent.'

'His accent?'

'It's very cute, isn't it?'

'He's Northern Irish.'

'Yes, I know. Reminds me of your father.'

'Dad was from Dublin.'

'Well, it's the same sort of thing, isn't it? It's all an accent.'

'Mother! It's not the same thing at all.'

'He's a big hog of a man, though, isn't he?'

'What?' said Israel.

'Ted. How old is he, do you know?'

'No! I've got no idea how old he is. Seventy?'

'Don't be silly, Israel, he's not seventy. I'd place him early sixties. So he'd be about the same age as me, maybe a little older. He's really very well preserved, isn't he?'

'Mother!'

'He reminds me of Leo Fuld.'

'Who?'

'The singer. "*Wo Ahin Soll Ich Geh'n*".'

'I'm sorry, I have absolutely no idea what you're talking about.'

'I don't know,' said Israel's mother. 'Young people. Where did we go wrong?'

'Maybe you've just got old?'

'Thank you.'

'Don't mention it.'

'Anyway, come on, make yourself useful and take this tray.'

They returned with coffee – proper coffee! – and dessert. Israel's mother's desserts were much better than her main courses.

There was a good reason for this.

'This is delicious,' said Ted, once they'd started in on dessert. 'What is this?'

'Baklava,' said Israel.

'Ba-whatter?' said Ted.

'Baklava,' repeated Israel.

'Aye. Right. What is it?'

'It's pastry, with pistachios,' said Israel.

'No,' said Ari. 'It's not pistachios. It's almonds.'

'I always thought it was pistachios,' said Israel.

'You can have either almond or pistachio,' said Deborah.

'I've had walnut, actually,' said Ari.

'Sounds lovely,' said Israel's mother.

'Walnut?' said Israel.

'Uh-huh.'

'I've never had walnut,' said Israel. 'And I've had a lot of baklava.'

'It's filo pastry,' said Deborah, explaining to Ted.

'Aye. Nice.'

'It was on a business trip to New York I had the walnut baklava,' said Ari.

'And the sticky stuff is – what's the sticky stuff, Mother?' said Deborah.

'Orange-blossom water.'

'Ah, that's right.'

'Are you sure it was walnut?' said Israel.

'Of course I'm sure.'

'What?' said Ted.

'It's lovely baklava, Mum,' said Israel. 'Did you make it?'

'Israel!' said Deborah.

'What?'

'You never ask a lady if she's made a dish.'

'Do you not?'

'No.'

'Do I look like I have time to make baklava?' said Israel's mother.

'Erm.' Israel looked at his mother's French-polished nails. 'So where's it from?'

'Israel!' said Deborah.

'It's from Israel?' said Ted.

'It's from Jacobs, on the High Street, where we've been buying our baklava for thirty years,' said Israel's mother.

'Oh,' said Israel. 'Of course. I was only asking.'

Soon after the baklava Ari and Deborah had to go: Ari had a big presentation the next day.

'*Big* presentation,' he said, slipping into his suit jacket, Israel's mother holding it out for him, like a personal valet. 'You know what it's like, Eva.'

'Hardly!' said Israel's mother, twittering.

'Ted, it's been a pleasure,' said Ari.

'Aye,' said Ted.

Ted and Israel and his mother cleared the remaining dishes and then sat around drinking coffee. There was still no sign of Gloria. Israel texted her again.

No reply.

Israel's mother opened another bottle of wine.

'Are you from Dublin, Ted?' she asked.

'Mother!' said Israel. 'I told you. He's from Northern Ireland.'

'I'm from Antrim,' said Ted.

'My late husband was from Dublin,' said Israel's mother dreamily.

'In Ireland doth fair Dublin stand,' said Ted. 'The city chief therein; and it is said by many more, the city chief of sin.'

'Oh!' said Israel's mother. 'That's very good. Did you make that up?'

'Ach, no,' said Ted.

'I have a couple of Van Morrison albums somewhere,' said Israel's mother, getting up.

'Aye, he's a Belfast lad,' said Ted.

'It's like name the famous Belgian, isn't it?' said Israel's mother, who'd gone over to the cupboard where Israel's dad had kept his records. 'Van Morrison. George Best. He's from your neck of the woods, isn't he?'

'Aye,' said Ted.

'Terrible waste,' said Israel's mother.

'D'ye know the joke?' said Ted.

'Which joke?' said Israel's mother.

'So,' said Ted. 'George Best is in the Ritz Hotel in bed with Miss World.'

'Right,' said Israel's mother, facing Ted, hand on hip, wine glass in the other.

'And the bed is covered with money – fifty-pound notes. The waiter comes in with room service – another bottle of champagne.'

'Uh-huh,' said Israel's mother.

'And the waiter takes in the scene and shakes his head and he says, "Where did it all go wrong, George?"'

'Oh, that's very funny!' said Israel's mother, her face creasing up with laughter. 'That's very funny! Isn't it, Israel?'

Israel frowned. Ted had told him the joke several dozen times before.

'Yes,' said Israel.

'I don't think I know any other famous Northern Irishmen,' said Israel's mother.

'Wayne McCullough?' said Ted.

'Is he a singer?'

'He's a boxer,' said Ted.

'The Corrs?' said Israel's mother.

'They're from down south,' said Ted.

'Oh.'

'Liam Neeson,' said Ted.

'Really?' said Israel's mother. 'Oh, I like him. Did you ever see him in *Schindler's List*?'

'I don't think so,' said Ted.

'No? We've probably got it on video somewhere if you'd like to see it. Although you'd be better seeing it in a cinema really. We have wonderful cinemas here. I prefer the theatre myself.'

'Mother! You never go the theatre!'

'I went to see *Les Misérables* with my book group. And *Mary Poppins* – that wasn't awfully good actually; not nearly as good as the film. Do you remember the film, Israel? We used to watch it when you were children. We had that on video too. I don't know where all the videos are now. Anyway, how many have we got then, Ted, Northern Irishmen. Five?'

'Not far off,' said Ted.

'Israel?' said his mother.

'What?' said Israel, who was staring at his mobile phone, willing Gloria to ring.

'Famous Northern Irishmen?'

'Or women,' said Ted.

'Yes, of course,' said Israel's mother, who'd returned to rifling through the old LPs. 'We don't want to forget the women.'

'Certainly not,' said Ted. 'Mary Peters,' he added.

'Ah!' said Israel's mother, standing up triumphantly with a copy of *Moondance*. 'Who did you say, Ted?'

'Mary Peters.'

'Ah, yes. That dates us a little bit, though, doesn't it?'

'Who's Mary Peters?' said Israel.

'She was in the Olympics, wasn't she?' said Israel's mother.

'She was,' said Ted.

Israel's mother was fiddling around with the turntable.

'I can never get this right. Ted, would you mind?' she said.

Ted went over and stood beside her, taking the record from her hands.

'You just need to bring this over here, and put this here,' said Ted.

'Ah!' said Israel's mother. 'Yes, of course, I'd forgotten. My husband used to do all the . . .'

Israel's mother allowed Ted to reach right round her, and lift the stylus.

Israel coughed loudly. But no one seemed to hear him.

'Do you like folk music, Ted?' he heard his mother saying, rather breathily, he thought.

'No. I can't say I do, to be frank with ye, Mrs Armstrong.'

'Do call me Eva,' said Israel's mother.

'Sorry, Eva,' said Ted.

'Good,' said Israel's mother. 'My late husband liked folk music. But I feel there's enough misery in the world already.'

'Aye. I'm more of a Frankie Lane and Nat King Cole kind of a man meself.'

'Oh, how lovely. I went to see the Drifters a while back, with some friends; they were fantastic.'

'The original Drifters?'

'I'm not sure,' said Israel's mother. 'It was in Croydon.'

'Were they good?'

'Oh, they were fabulous! They did – oooh, what did they do? – "Under the Boardwalk" and "Saturday Night at the Movies". And "You're More Than a Number in my Little Red Book".'

At which point – to Israel's utter horror – his mother started actually singing, and – worse! – Ted joined in, and suddenly they were duetting. *'You're more than a number in my little red book, you're more than a one-night stand.'*

'Anyway,' said Israel, coughing much louder. 'Anyway!'

'Sorry?' said Israel's mother, turning away from Ted and towards him.

'Hello?' said Israel, as the opening bars of 'And It Stoned Me' came from the speakers. 'I could sit here all night listening to you talk about music and discussing famous Northern Irishmen—'

'And women,' said his mother, who'd sat back down at the table.

'—and women,' said Israel, 'all night long. But—'

'Are you a Catholic, Mr Carson?' asked Israel's mother, staring up at Ted.

'Mother!' said Israel.

'What?'

'Ted's a Protestant.'

'Oh, is he? Do they have those in Ireland as well?'

'In the north of Ireland, Mother. *Northern* Ireland.'

'Ah, yes, of course. My late husband was a Catholic. He didn't take it very seriously though.'

'No,' said Ted, sitting down. 'I'm only a Sunday worshipper myself.'

'Oh? Isn't that what you're supposed to be?'

'Not if you're a Presbyterian, no.'

'Really?' said Israel's mother. 'I've never met a Presbyterian. Is it like Jehovah's Witnesses?'

'Not exactly,' said Ted.

'It's a Christian religion though, is it?'

'Aye. Though according to most Presbyterians I would be a failed Christian.'

'Oh, I'm sure that's not the case.'

'Ach, well. It's my decision, ye know. I like a drink. I smoke.'

'Oh, I am glad,' said Israel's mother. 'I thought I was the only one.' She poured Ted another glass of wine. 'We need to stick together, Ted,' she said, winking. 'Have you noticed how everything that used to be good for you is supposed to be bad for you?'

'Aye,' said Ted. 'You mean smoking and drinking?'

'Yes, and eating, even, for goodness, sake.' Israel's mother patted her ample hips.

'Aye,' said Ted.

'More baklava, Ted?'

'Maybe just a small piece.'

Israel went to take a piece as his mother offered the plate to Ted.

'Guests first,' she said, slapping Israel's hand. 'I do like to see a man with a healthy appetite.'

'I have a healthy appetite, Eva,' said Ted, 'that I must admit.'

Israel thought he might be sick.

'Have you ever met Gloria, Ted?' said Israel's mother.

'Who?'

'Israel's girlfriend. She was meant to be here this evening. Still no sign, Israel?'

'No,' said Israel.

'They live – lived?'

'Live,' insisted Israel.

'Together.'

'No, I've not met her,' said Ted.

'Thin as a rake,' said Israel's mother. She held up her little finger. 'Like that. Thin. As. A. Rake. She's a high-flyer,' she said to Ted.

'I thought you'd given up smoking,' said Israel, changing the subject.

'I have,' said his mother. 'But I just have one or two occasionally, for the sake of my health.'

'For the sake of your health?'

'My mental health. Goodness, I'm sorry. He's a terrible nag, Ted, isn't he? I hope he's not like that with you?'

'We have a healthy working relationship,' said Ted.

'Well, anyway. If Mr Health Police here would excuse us, perhaps, Ted, you would like to join me for a cigarette on the terrace.'

'We don't have a terrace, Mum.'

'The patio, then,' said Israel's mother, getting up from her seat. 'You are so pernickety. And perhaps Gloria will have arrived before we're all through?'

Ted got up obediently and to the strains of 'Moondance' followed Israel's mother into the kitchen and out into the back garden.

Israel looked again at the photos on the walls. Checked his mobile again; nothing from Gloria.

He couldn't believe she'd missed the meal.

He was desperate to see her.

Gloria: she looked like Giulietta Masina as Gelsomina in Fellini's *La Strada* – a film they'd gone to see together at the National Film Theatre, years ago. They used to go to the cinema two, three times a week back then.

In fact, Gloria looked nothing like Giulietta Masina as Gelsomina in Fellini's *La Strada*. Sometimes he could barely remember what she looked like. She was definitely beautiful though. She was . . . What could he say? She was just . . . Gloria.

When Israel's mother and Ted returned, laughing and smelling of cigarettes, Israel was picking miserably at the remains of the baklava.

'He was a terribly greedy child,' said his mother.

'Mother!'

'You were though. Chocolate biscuits. He was a fiend for the chocolate biscuits, Ted. Honestly. I had to hide them. And then the girls would beat him up. He never learned to stick up for himself.' She walked over towards the hi-fi system. 'No sign of Gloria then?'

'No, she—'

'Has stood you up, I think.'

'No,' said Israel. 'She has not stood me up, she's just . . .'

'And not for the first time,' said Israel's mother. 'She—'

Israel's mother simply waved her hand at Israel dismissively, and knelt down to the record cabinet.

'A change of mood, I think,' she said. 'It turns out Ted and I have an interest in common, Israel.'

'What, winding me up?' said Israel.

'Now, how many times do I have to tell you? Don't be rude to our guest, please.'

'What then?' said Israel. 'What interest have you got in common?'

'Line-dancing,' said Israel's mother.

'Ha!' said Israel. 'Good one. You don't go line-dancing.'

'I do now.'

'Since when?'

'Since you've been gone. I do have a life, you know.'

'Yes, of course, but—'

'What?' said Israel's mother.

'*Line-dancing?*' said Israel, as though she'd confessed to participating in some kind of Satanic abuse rituals.

'What's wrong with line-dancing?' said Israel's mother, her back to him, searching for records.

'Well, there's nothing wrong with line-dancing. But couldn't you have done . . . I don't know, tango, or something?'

'In Finchley, dear? Don't be such a snob. You're like your father. He wouldn't go to discos or anything when we were young. And also it's very good exercise. Keeps me in shape.' She patted her hips.

'Ted?' said Israel. 'You don't dance, do you?'

'Aye,' said Ted. 'I do.'

'Really?'

'Best feet in the parish,' said Ted. 'First Friday of every month in the First and Last.'

'He never really joined in with anything, you know,' said Israel's mother.

'Mother! I am here, you know. I can hear you.'

'Yes. Ah! Just what I'm after.' She stood up, record in hand. 'We're fine here, you know, if you want to leave us.'

'Well, it has been a long day,' said Israel. 'But I'm sure Ted is tired as well. Shall I show you where you're sleeping, Ted?'

'Oh, leave Ted with me, Israel, he'll be fine,' said his mother.

'Are you sure, Ted?'

'Aye,' said Ted. 'We're grand.'

'That's it, you pop along and read your books there.'

'Mother, I'm not a child.'

'Of course not! Goodnight then!'

So Israel left them to it.

He went upstairs to his childhood bedroom, the room where he'd done all that groundwork on *verfremdung* and *ostranenie* in his teens. It had been decorated several times since then, and with the chintz it just wasn't the same; you couldn't really feel properly alienated under a nylon sunflower-print duvet cover.

His first night back in England and he was alone.

Except for the dog: his mother had put Muhammad in with him; he sat whimpering in his travel basket.

'Shut up!' said Israel. Muhammad continued to

whimper. 'No, really. I'm not joking.' Whimper. Whimper. 'Shut up!'

Sometimes in Tumdrum Israel had had dreams about this room, but in his dreams it was much larger, a palace, where he would weigh his conscience and enjoy his princely pleasures. But of course it wasn't a palace; it was a room furnished with cheap melamine furniture and miniature Monet prints in lilac-coloured pine frames. Israel could no longer even imagine his excitement at reading *Portnoy's Complaint* in here, let alone recreate in memory that wet afternoon when Gloria had first let him kiss her here. It was all gone. All his books were gone. Everything of his own was in the flat he shared with Gloria.

He rang her number again. Ten thirty: it wasn't late.

No reply.

He texted.

No reply.

Downstairs he could hear the sound of his mother's records. They'd never upgraded to a CD player. He remembered his father swivelling the records between his fingers, blowing gently on them, as if they were votive candles. And he could hear his mother singing, '*Don't tell my heart*' and Ted singing back, '*My achy breaky heart*' and both of them duetting on '*I just don't think it'd understand.*'

And he crawled, exhausted, alone, unhappily, into bed.

Muhammad was snoring in the corner.

CHAPTER 8

For a long time he couldn't get to sleep. First it was Ted and his mother downstairs: '*It's a marvellous night for a moondance.*' Oh, God. Then it was the dog. Then it was dreams. Bad dreams about Gloria.

He was awake at one, and then half past one, and two o'clock, half past two. Eventually, he sat up in bed, and tried to remember what his room had looked like before his mother's recent thoroughgoing chintz makeover. He tried to picture the whole pre-chintz thing, *his* thing, the posters – Nelson Mandela, and U2, the Pogues and Woody Allen – and the bookshelf, the wardrobe, the desk, right down to the position of the books on the shelves. He imagined himself as a hostage or a prisoner, held against his will in a one-piece nylon sunflower-print duvet cover, in a tiny chintz cell, with a small snoring Jack Russell, having to reconstruct his life from scraps and memories, and he found to his surprise that if he shut his eyes very tight he could do it, he *was* Brian Keenan, with John McCarthy, he could see every peeling scrap of wallpaper and every book:

The Alexandria Quartet in their horrid puke-murky covers, and a big fat swollen jumble-sale Norman Mailer, *The Naked and the Dead*, and *A Clockwork Orange* from the Oxfam shop in Mill Hill, and Jack Kerouac, and William Burroughs, and Allen Ginsberg. And seeing them, picturing them, he immediately regretted almost every one of them, regretted having spent any time on them at all: they seemed suddenly bogus, pointless, a pose.

There were of course some books he could see on his shelf, in his mind's eye, that he didn't regret – his Kurt Vonneguts, for example. How could he possibly – how could anyone possibly – regret Kurt Vonnegut? He could see the covers of his beloved old Vonneguts, pixel-perfect in his imagination, books bought from charity shops, tattered and worn, their pages crisp and yellow with age, with their tacky, instantly outdated covers. *Welcome to the Monkey House. Mother Night. Player Piano.* He loved those books, and yet none of them had really lasted; they weren't canonical books; they were cheaply produced, rubbishy-looking books; they had no place in the pantheon of great literature; he would never read them again, and probably wouldn't even enjoy them if he did. But he couldn't deny them; he couldn't deny any of them, actually, even the books he regretted; they had made him who he was; they had interpenetrated him; they were instantiated within him. He was his books; and his books were him.

These were his 3 a.m. thoughts. Israel Armstrong. Twenty-nine years old. Shambolic. Sixteen stone. Just short of six feet tall. Hair, brown. Eyes, brown. Glasses. No distinguishing features. Though he did know the word 'instantiated'. Did that count as a distinguishing feature?

Probably not.

He got up out of bed and sat on the chair by the window and drew back the curtains and looked out at the deserted street, lit by pale, sickly yellow lights. He tried to let his mind go blank, but whenever he thought about anything it seemed ugly, and sad, and pathetic – memories of Gloria, and his father. So he got back into bed.

And then when he finally drifted off to sleep at around half past three in the morning he had more strange, merging dreams, in which people and places came together in bizarre and horrible combinations: his father was with Linda Wei, and they were both naked, and dancing and singing karaoke; and then Ted was there with one of Israel's old school friends, and they were drinking beer and whispering about him, keeping secrets; Gloria was there too, riding a unicycle; and his mother in a giant terracotta pot, sprouting. The dreams made him feel dizzy, even in his sleep, as though he were awake; he could hear voices; he thought he could hear his mother saying, 'Careful! The children may be listening.'

When he woke he felt light-headed.

The first thing he did was check his phone. Nothing from Gloria.

He lay still, already defeated.

The house was quiet, except for a strange scratching sound that seemed to be coming through the walls, like mice or rats, nibbling at the very foundations of the building. He thought for a moment it was Muhammad the dog, but he was still asleep; and then Israel thought he was going mad, but then he got up and went into the bathroom and the scratching sounds went away. The bathroom was safe; the bathroom was quiet; the bathroom was fine; the bathroom was familiar; he could remake himself in the bathroom, as he had done in his adolescence. Except that when his father had died his mother had had a big clear-out and done a lot of things she'd been meaning to do for years, like changing the avocado suite for something more modern, and white, and redecorating with tiny off-white tiles and down-lighters so now the bathroom felt like a three-star hotel in an up-and-coming former Eastern bloc nation. He stood under the hot jet of the shower for almost fifteen minutes, trying to put himself back together again. He hadn't had a shower for eight months, not since arriving in Tumdrum. The Devines had a bath with a hand-held attachment, and sometimes he'd kneel there and try to remember what it felt like, the cleansing power of a good shower, but his imagination had always proved inadequate.

After the shower, he shaved. There was no shaving mirror any more; he wondered what his mother had done with his father's shaving mirror, the mirror he'd first shaved in when he was a boy. Instead, there was now a circular spotlit mirror with a frosted rim attached to the wall; with the mirror, and the flowers and the candles, also new additions, the bathroom was like an opera diva's dressing room. He followed the contours of his face, scraping at his stubble, trying to remember the name for that little trough that runs from under your nose to your mouth; he used to know it; he used to know the name. His face looked deathly white under the glare of the lights, and when he finished shaving he could see there were still little tufts adhering around the corners of his mouth, and under his chin, and he had to pull around at his face to get at them. He thought to himself, So this is how the fat shave. Finally, he put on his glasses to get a better look at himself. It was still him. He was here.

At home.

He went quietly downstairs into the kitchen and put the kettle on. Gloria still had his coffee maker in their flat – it was a little baby Gaggia. He loved that machine, and all the rituals associated with it: the tamp and the grind, and squeezing out the perfect crema right down to the last drop. Gloria had bought it for him for his birthday, and it sat on the worktop in the corner of their kitchen, a big silvery symbol of their good fortune and their lives together; it spoke of quality, and sturdiness and style. It had been way too big to take to

Ireland, and anyway would have looked out of place in the chicken coop. At least his mum had a good supply of ground coffee, and a filter cone, and some papers, and the old red enamel coffee pot they'd had as long as he could remember – the one with the lid tied on with wire. He could remember as a child watching his dad, during the summertime, from out of the back bedroom window, watching him sitting in the garden, doing his paperwork on the garden table, with the red enamel coffee pot at his elbow, a picture of perfect contentment. His dad always reused coffee grounds. He would grill them in a pan every morning. And that was the smell that Israel remembered from his childhood most clearly: the bitter smell of burning coffee grounds.

He stood looking at the little patch of garden, waiting for the kettle to boil. He'd been away less than a year. Everything was exactly the same, and everything had changed. He popped a couple of Nurofen. He texted Gloria.

It'd all be fine when he got to see Gloria.

Too early to ring? It wasn't too early to ring. He rang their flat.

'I'm not here at the moment,' said the answerphone. Where was she then? And how could that possibly be true: I'm not here at the moment? In the act of utterance? 'I'm not here at the moment'? She was there. She had to be somewhere. 'I'm not here at the moment'? How could she not be?

His mother came downstairs.

'Ah. Mum.'

'Here he is then, His Royal Highness.'

Ted came into the kitchen directly behind her.

'Hello, erm . . . Ted. Did you sleep well?'

'Like a log,' said Ted.

His mother was wearing a smart white towelling dressing gown, and had her hair wrapped in a towel. Ted was wearing his cap, Muhammad at his heels.

'How did you sleep?' she asked, absent-mindedly.

'Not very well,' said Israel.

'Oh dear. And what exactly are you doing?'

'I'm making coffee.'

'Using last night's grounds?'

'Yes.'

'Just like your father.'

'I suppose,' said Israel.

'You were overtired, I expect.'

'Maybe,' said Israel. 'And I thought I heard these weird noises upstairs.'

'Weird?'

'Sort of scratching noises.'

'Oh, that'd be the pigeons,' said Israel's mother.

'The pigeons?'

'Aye, there's a wee nest outside your room,' said Ted.

'I see. Really?' Suddenly Ted seemed to know more about his house than he did.

'Ted's going to sort that out for us today, aren't you, Ted?' said Israel's mother.

'Aye.'

'Is he?'

'Oh, he's been very good to me already,' said Israel's mother.

'Has he?' said Israel.

'Oh, yes. He was out first thing this morning to that little hardware shop, you know, which used to be owned by Mr Thompson. He got a drill bit, some bolts.'

Ted held up a little blue plastic bag and grinned.

'He's doing the back gate later.'

'I'll need a hand with the pigeons though,' said Ted.

'Right,' said Israel.

'And he's seeing the neighbours later,' said Israel's mother.

'So-called neighbours,' said Ted.

'What?' said Israel. 'Mr and Mrs Stevens?'

'No, Israel. Do keep up! They moved. I told you.'

'You never told me.'

'I did tell you.'

'I don't think so.'

'Anyway, it's this new couple. They keep blocking access to the drive.'

'That's terrible.'

'That's neighbours,' said Ted.

'Ted said he'd have a word with them later today.'

'Ted?' said Israel.

'D'ye want to come and have a look at the guttering?' said Ted.

'I'd love to,' said Israel. 'But not now. I've not had my breakfast or—'

'Only take a minute,' said Ted.

'Go on,' said Israel's mother. 'If Ted's ready . . .'

'Do I have to?' said Israel.

'Yes, go on. Ted has to know what he needs to get to sort it out, don't you, Ted?'

'Aye.'

'Mother!'

'Go on. I'll make the coffee.'

'But I'm not even dressed yet.'

'That's all right,' said his mother. 'Go on, no one's going to see you. He was always very shy,' she said to Ted.

'Mother, please!' said Israel.

'Go on!' she said. 'It'll take you two minutes.'

Ted had already borrowed an extending ladder from somewhere.

'He's very resourceful,' said Israel's mother.

'I've really not got a head for heights,' said Israel. They were outside, looking up at the guttering.

'It's not that high,' said his mother.

'Wouldn't Ted be better to climb up?'

'He might fall,' said Israel's mother.

'Well, I might fall!'

'Yes, but Ted's a guest,' said his mother. 'That'd be awful. Up you go! Go on!'

So Israel, too tired to do otherwise, climbed the ladder, Ted and his mother down below holding it steady.

'What d'you see?' shouted Ted, when Israel, coffeeless and still in his pyjamas, had made it to the top.

'Ah. The gutter's full of . . . ah, God! The smell is . . . It smells like . . .'

'What?'

'Pigeon shit.'

'Aye, well, that'd be right,' said Ted. 'How thick's it?'

'Ugh. Really thick,' said Israel.

'Inch?' said Ted.

'I don't know,' said Israel. 'I've not a tape measure with me.'

'Just stick your finger in,' shouted Ted.

'I am not sticking my finger in!' said Israel.

'Does it fill the gutter to the top?' said Ted.

'Pretty much,' said Israel.

Ted whistled.

'Well?' said Israel's mother.

'We'll need pigeon wire all the way along,' said Ted.

'Hello?' Israel called down. 'Can I come down? Hello?'

His mother and Ted were discussing where best to find pigeon wire in Finchley.

Israel looked around him. London had always seemed to him to be fully alive, but from up high it seemed to be a place in rigid repose. He surveyed the houses – row upon row, blocks of flats in the distance. The tiny suburban gardens, patio heaters and decking. It looked like a little model village.

'Quite a view!' he shouted down to Ted and his mother.

'Aye. But scenery doesn't get the job done,' said Ted.

It was a beautiful crisp morning. The sun was shining, birds were singing. Israel could see glass glittering on pavements, signalling the extent of last night's fun and the loss of yet more stereos, CD players, and old hot-hatches to the many local joy-riders and thieves.

'I can probably see the van from here, Ted,' he shouted down. 'If I twist round a bit.'

He carefully twisted round on the top of the ladder. Some neighbours had planted leylandii. But through the gaps he could clearly see where he'd parked the van.

Except the van wasn't there.

'Erm. Ted?' he called down.

'Can you not interrupt please, Israel,' said Israel's mother. 'It's very rude.'

'What?'

'Don't interrupt!'

'Did you move the van, Ted?'

'No. I'm just talking to your mother here,' said Ted.

'But, Ted!'

'What?'

'I can't see it.'

'Well, you're looking in the wrong place, sure.'

'No, it should definitely be over there.'

'Aye, right. Wind your neck in, will ye?'

Israel started climbing down the ladder.

'Everything all right?' said Israel's mother.

'Mum, you've not moved the van, have you?'

'What van?'

'The mobile library van?'

'No. Moved it? Of course I haven't moved it. What would I want to move it for?'

'It's just it's not there any more.'

'Where did you leave it?'

'It was round the corner, outside the Krimholzes.'

'The Krimholzes!'

'Yes.'

'No! You shouldn't have parked it there!'

'You made me park it round there!'

'I did not!'

'You did!'

'I said park it round the corner, not park it outside the Krimholzes!'

'It was the only space I could find.'

'Oh, Israel! We're all in trouble now.'

'What do you mean, we're all in trouble now?'

'The Krimholzes!'

'So? Can't you just ring them?'

'What for?'

'To see if they've moved it.'

'Mr and Mrs Krimholz?'

'Do they have keys?' asked Ted.

'Of course they don't have keys!' said Israel's mother. 'And I'm not ringing them to ask about your mobile library.'

'Why not?' said Israel.

'Because,' said his mother.

'Because you're ashamed of me working on a mobile library?'

'No! I am not!'

'Are you sure that's where you left the van?' asked Ted.

'Of course I'm sure!' said Israel.

'Well, there's only one way to find out,' said Israel's mother. 'Which is for you to go and check.'

'Fine. I'll go and check,' said Israel.

'You might want to get dressed first,' said Ted.

'Give the neighbours a shock, wouldn't it!' said Israel's mother.

'Thank you.'

'He's probably just forgotten where he parked it,' said Israel's mother, *sotto voce*, to Ted as Israel went upstairs. 'He's like that. Very dreamy.'

Once he was dressed, Israel went round the corner to check if the van was there.

The van had gone.

CHAPTER 9

Stolen cars in London are of course ten a penny, but a stolen *mobile library* is a little rarer: maybe ten a two-penny; or five to two farthings; or two to half a sixpence; none of your old tu'penny ha'penny or how's your father; cor blimey, guv'nor; would you Adam and Eve it; Jesus H. Christ; there's a funnyosity; you're having me on; I beg your Covent Garden; there's a turn-up for the books.

A stolen mobile library? It was certainly unusual.

But, still, nonetheless, the police weren't interested. When Israel's mother rang to report the missing vehicle, she was simply issued with a crime number, and that was it.

'That's it,' she said, putting the phone down, and explaining the procedure to Ted.

'That's it?' said Ted, who'd gone into shock when he realised the van really was missing. Israel's mother had been feeding him with hot sweet tea and soothing words, but Ted just kept saying, over and over, 'I don't believe this. I don't believe it.'

They were all sitting around the kitchen table.

'It's post-traumatic shock,' Israel's mother whispered to Israel. 'We need to be gentle with him.'

'I just don't believe it,' mumbled Ted.

'You'd better believe it, Ted,' said Israel. 'We have been well and truly TWOCed!'

'Israel!' said Israel's mother.

'TWOCed!' repeated Israel.

'What?' said Ted who, despite the shock, could still rise to irritability with Israel; it'd take more than a shock to stop him getting annoyed with Israel.

'That's what they call it. Taken without owner's consent,' said Israel.

'That's only on television,' said Israel's mother.

'I just don't believe it,' said Ted.

'You can report it online, apparently,' said Israel's mother.

'I don't believe this.'

'TWOCed,' repeated Israel. 'T. W. O. C.'

'D'ye not know a local policeman we could talk to?' said Ted.

'No,' said Israel's mother. 'We've never had anything to do with the police.'

'Ach,' said Ted, putting his head in his hands. 'I don't believe this.'

'There, there,' said Israel's mother. 'Don't worry.'

'Don't worry,' repeated Israel, trying to be helpful.

'Don't *you* be telling me not to worry!' said Ted. 'It's your flippin' fault in the first place!'

147

'How is it my fault?'

'I knew we should never have come over to the mainland!'

'It's not my fault!' said Israel.

'Well, whose fault is it then?' said Ted, who was definitely returning to his usual self; the hot sweet tea was taking effect. 'I never should hae listened to yer stupit slarrying nonsense.'

'My what?' said Israel.

'It's you that brought us over for this stupit Mobile Meet and now look at what's happened!'

'Don't be blaming me for someone else stealing—'

'All right, calm down now, boys, please,' said Israel's mother. 'I'm sure it'll turn up.'

'It's a van, Mother. It's not a pair of spectacles,' said Israel.

'I am aware of that, Israel, thank you.'

'What are we going to do?' said Ted, slumping down in his seat.

'Well, first of all, I'm going to put the kettle on, and then we can make a few calls,' said Israel's mother.

'Who're we going to call?' said Ted.

'Ghostbusters?' said Israel.

'Don't be facetious, Israel,' said his mother. 'Can't you see Ted's very upset about this?'

'Sorry.'

'Good. Now,' said Israel's mother, producing a Biro and small notebook from her handbag. 'Let's make a proper list, shall we?'

Israel's mother was a great one for lists; she'd have done well in the Army Service Corps, or as an estate agent, or as a primary school teacher, preparing for a new class at the beginning of September. If something had to be done, it first had to be listed: making a list, for Israel's mother, was almost more important than doing the thing itself. Indeed, often, if you put something on a list, Israel had learned from his mother from an early age, you didn't then actually have to do it; the list effectively substituted for the thing. Israel's father had been exactly the same, except with figures. As an accountant he'd understood numbers as a principle, and on behalf of other people, and yet had somehow failed to translate this successfully into the business of making actual money for himself. Which was maybe why Israel had ended up as a librarian – he was doing what his father did with numbers, and what his mother did with lists, except with books. Those who can, do; those who can't learn classification and cataloguing.

Israel's mother was jotting down notes.

'OK. Number one, first of all, while I'm making the tea someone's going to have to go and speak to the Krimholzes.'

'Oh, no. Not the Krimholzes. Why?' said Israel.

'Because you parked the van outside their house.'

'Well, I'm not going round there,' said Israel. 'I've just been round there.'

'Yes, but you didn't think to actually speak to them, did you?'

'No.'

'Well, they might have seen something, so you need to—'

'They won't have seen anything.'

'And you know that, do you? Go on now,' said Israel's mother. 'It'll only take you two minutes.'

'Why me?' said Israel.

'Well, I'm hardly going round there, am I?' said Israel's mother.

'So what about Ted?' said Israel.

'I don't mind,' said Ted.

'No!' said Israel's mother. 'Certainly not! That's hardly fair on Ted, is it?'

'Why not?' said Israel.

'They don't know Ted from Adam.'

'Fine. So you go,' said Israel. 'They know you best.'

'No, don't be silly. I've already said I'm not going,' said Israel's mother.

'Well, I've already said I'm not going.'

'What's wrong with these people?' asked Ted.

'It's just . . .' began Israel's mother, as the kettle started to boil.

'Well, Mother?'

'Because . . .'

'She's funny about it,' Israel said to Ted.

'I am not funny about it!' said Israel's mother. 'They're just not the sort of people you want to . . . know your misfortune, that's all.'

'Ah,' said Ted. 'Neighbours.'

'Precisely!' said Israel's mother triumphantly. 'See! Ted understands. He's a man of the world.'

Ted blushed, there was a lull in conversation, and the kettle came to boiling point.

'So, when you're gone, Israel, I'll start making some phone calls,' said Israel's mother.

'Oh, no. No. I'll tell you what, I'll make the calls instead and you can—'

'No. *I'll* make the calls. You're going round to the Krimholzes.'

'No, I'm not!' said Israel.

'Well,' said Israel's mother, brandishing a tea bag in one hand and a pint of milk in the other. 'Someone is going to have to go to the Krimholzes. And it can't be Ted, and it's not going to be me. Which leaves—'

'Mother!' said Israel.

'Don't be so babyish, Israel,' said his mother.

'I'm not being babyish.'

'Yes, you are.'

'No, I'm not.'

'You are now! Just go round and find out if they saw anything.'

'Oh, God!' said Israel.

'Language,' said Ted.

'Shut up!' said Israel.

'Don't be rude to our guest,' said Israel's mother.

'I'm not being rude, he's just . . . Agh!'

'Go on!' said his mother. 'Go!'

'Ugh!' said Israel. 'I don't want to go!'

'They'll be delighted to see you,' said Israel's mother.

'No, they won't.'

'Of course they will. Go on. We'll have some breakfast when you come back.'

'Agh!'

'Go on!'

'All right, I'm going,' said Israel. 'But only because you and Ted won't.'

'Good,' said his mother. 'Go then! We need to act quickly.'

'The van's not been kidnapped,' said Israel. 'It's only been stolen.'

'Time is of the essence though.'

'That it is,' said Ted.

'Right,' said Israel, getting up to leave. 'And while I'm hurrying round there what's Ted going to be doing exactly?'

'He's going to stay here and help me,' said Israel's mother.

Ted grinned sheepishly.

'Right,' said Israel.

'Go on then,' said his mother. 'Run along!'

This was what always happened to Israel: he always ended up in this predicament, doing the thing he didn't want to do; doing the favour; running the errand. It wasn't that he was solicitous or particularly eager to please. No. He knew why it was. He was just weak. He knew he was weak. He seemed to lack the necessary resistance to others to be a fully formed person; he lacked a sense of his own established boundaries; he wasn't so much a person as a gas, or an amoeba. He couldn't say no. It was a shame. Because he didn't know his limits he was restricted in what he could achieve; because he lacked design, he lacked purpose; or vice versa. He lacked certainty. Or at least, he thought he did. He was never sure which came first, his chicken, or his egg; he wasn't sure if his existence preceded his essence, if God was dead, if abortion or the European Union were good things, or what he would throw out of a balloon if the balloon was plummeting towards earth and he had to throw something out. He wished he could work any of this out, and understand himself better, and become himself. But he didn't know how.

Oh, God.

He walked to the Krimholzes like a man walking to the gallows.

Mr and Mrs Krimholz's house had no front garden. They'd had it gravelled years ago, to make way for his and hers Mercedes. Their house was detached: Israel's parents' house was semi-detached. The Armstrongs had PVC windows and guttering: the Krimholzes had replacement sashes and mock-Tudor gabling.

Israel rang on the door, and Mr Krimholz answered; he was wearing chinos and a polo shirt, his hair and moustache cut close and neat. The Krimholzes were in their seventies, but they looked as though they were in their fifties. They liked to holiday; when other people were still going to Wales, the Krimholzes were going to France; when other people started going to France they moved on to Spain; when other people started going to Spain, they moved across to Florida. They currently had a little time-share in Cape Verde. They were in the avantgarde of mass tourism.

'Israel!' said Mr Krimholz. 'Israel Armstrong!'

'Mr Krimholz,' said Israel, shaking him warmly by the hand, though not as warmly as Mr Krimholz shook his; Mr Krimholz's handshake was on the business side of firm.

'Israel! Israel Armstrong,' repeated Mr Krimholz, looking Israel up and down as though he were a slightly unpromising suitor, or a newly delivered chest freezer. 'How are you, young man? I thought you were working away in America?' Mr Krimholz had dyed his hair black. It made him look like the proprietor of a small Italian backstreet restaurant; he had in fact run a little electrical supplies whole-saler in Wembley.

'Ireland,' said Israel.

'Ah, yes. Computers, isn't it, your mother said?'

'Er.' Israel looked down at his shoes. 'Sort of.'

'Come in, come in. Don't stand there. Come on! Sarah!' Mr Krimholz called into the house. 'We have a special visitor! Come through. Into the lounge! Come, come, come! So you're back on business?'

'Yes. I suppose.'

'Good! Business is good?'

'Well . . .' Israel gazed around the lounge. It had changed since the last time he was here. They'd redecorated, with a Louis XIV theme: gilt mirrors, elaborate rugs and furniture with ornamental feet. Before that, it had been Scandinavian; and before that American Colonial. The Krimholzes changed their home furnishings as often as some people changed their cars. And they changed their cars almost as often as some people changed their sheets.

'The Internet, isn't it?' Mr Krimholz was asking. 'Was that it? We've got broadband now. Mostly' – he pretended to lower his voice – 'so she can go shopping without leaving the house!'

'Lionel!' said Mrs Krimholz, coming into the lounge, grinning. 'Don't listen to him! Israel!' She kissed Israel on both cheeks. Her skin was incredibly smooth. She seemed to be getting younger and slimmer.

'He's back on business,' said Mr Krimholz. 'Information superhighway.' He made a swooshing superhighway kind of movement with his hand.

'Kind of,' said Israel. 'It's a sort of conference.'

'Good!' said Mr Krimholz. 'Networking opportunity.'

'Yes.'

'Now, coffee?' said Mrs Krimholz, smiling a doll-like smile. 'And what are you doing standing? Sit down! Sit down!' She gestured towards a grand sofa with an excess of cushions.

'No,' said Israel. 'I can't . . . I just . . . It's . . . I'm looking for something.'

'Not money I hope!' said Mr Krimholz, chuckling. 'Israel! Investors? You're looking for investors?'

'No, no!'

'We've just reorganised all our investments, you see,' said Mrs Krimholz.

'That's fine,' said Israel. 'I'm not looking for investors.'

'Excellent financial adviser, if you're looking for one,' said Mr Krimholz, bending towards Israel and whispering, as though someone might overhear. 'Hungry, you know? He's got that –' and here, disconcertingly, Mr Krimholz barked loudly, as though a young puppy had got its teeth into a brand-new inflatable toy and was tearing it to pieces.

'Good,' said Israel, backing away slightly.

'You know Adam has his own business now?' said Mrs Krimholz.

'Really?' said Israel.

'NMR scanning.'

'Right,' said Israel, unsure whether this was the name of the company, or what the company did.

'*And* he's doing his interneeship at Harvard Medical School *at the same time*!' said Mrs Krimholz, as though announcing the ending of hostilities in the Middle East. 'I don't know how he does it.'

'No,' agreed Israel. 'No. I don't know how he does it either.'

'Hard work,' said Mr Krimholz sagely.

'And talent!' said Mrs Krimholz. 'Hard work and talent.'

Adam Krimholz was Israel's oldest friend. He was the kind of person who always got top marks in everything he did, and yet – and Israel had never been able to understand this – he wasn't actually that smart. Adam Krimholz was average. In fact, depending on the average, Adam Krimholz was very possibly *below* average. He was naturally a C grade sort of a student. And yet he had somehow succeeded at everything way *above* his ability, while Israel, on the other hand, Israel Armstrong, who was naturally an A grade sort of a student, seemed to have failed to succeed at a level commensurate with his talents. It was a mystery. Adam Krimholz just seemed to have the knack, whatever the knack was; Israel had no idea what the knack was. Israel's mother used to say, 'Krimholz! Knishes! K'nockers!' which roughly translated meant, 'The Krimholzes! They have the brains of dumplings, but they act like they're big shots!' You could go a long way, it seemed, with the brains of a dumpling, all the way to the top, in fact; dumpling brains were no bar to success; certainly the Krimholz children had become variously successful as surgeons, and lawyers, and parents, and marathon-runners and champion this-and-thatters, and the Krimholzes' front room was a museum to them and their extraordinary dumpling-brained achievements. There were certificates and photographs everywhere. There was Adam, at his bar mitzvah, on top of a console. And there he was again, with his brothers, at various graduation ceremonies, and on tables small, round and oblong with ornamental feet. And there they all were, the dumpling brains, receiving various trophies on top of the sarcophagus-style TV cabinet. The Krimholzes were the family Forrest Gump of Finchley, though much better looking. There was a definite suggestion of family private medical care, and cosmetic dentistry.

'Actually,' said Israel, utterly depressed, 'I wanted to ask you about a van. I'm looking for a—'

'A van?' said Mr Krimholz. 'For the business? You're not buying, no? Leasing, I hope. Leasing is much better, tax-wise. But you know that, of course! I'm not telling you anything you don't know, am I? You're your father's son, am I right?'

Israel nodded.

'Do we know anyone who does vehicle leasing? Sarah? What was it the Goldman boy is doing now?'

'That's a car showroom,' said Mrs Krimholz. 'Not vans.'

'Ah.'

'BMWs, I think,' said Mrs Krimholz. 'Or Bentleys.'

'Premium marque vehicles,' mused Mr Krimholz, nodding his head in approval.

'Yeah, sorry,' said Israel. 'It's not . . . I'm not looking to buy—'

'Or lease?' said Mr Krimholz. 'Lease, remember.'

'No, I'm not looking to buy or lease a van as such. It's more . . . We've . . . lost a van.'

'Lost a van? Oh dear.'

'Yes . . . You've not seen a van?'

'What sort of a van?'

'It was parked here yesterday. It's a . . .'

'Did your mother tell you Adam has another baby?' said Mrs Krimholz.

'Really?'

'Yes. With his wife? Rachel? And the two girls already. You remember them?'

'Yes.'

'Rachel's father is Mr Solomons. You know, from Hampstead—'

'Israel was at the wedding, Sarah,' said Mr Krimholz. 'He remembers.'

'Ah, yes, of course,' said Mrs Krimholz.

'He drank so much he passed out in the toilets!' said Mr Krimholz, slapping Israel on the back. 'Do you remember, Israel?'

'Er, yes, yes. I . . . Sorry about—'

'You're not married yet?' said Mrs Krimholz.

'No, not . . . yet. Not married. No.'

'Children?' said Mr Krimholz, laughing.

'No,' said Israel. 'No children either.'

'We have eight grandchildren now,' said Mrs Krimholz. 'How many does your mother have?'

'Er. I don't know, actually. I've never stopped to count—'

'Three,' said Mrs Krimholz.

'Right, yes,' said Israel.

'Your sister's.'

Israel noticed that when Mrs Krimholz spoke

her face didn't seem to move: it was like listening to a recording of someone speaking from inside the body of Mrs Krimholz, as though the mind-body split had *actually* split, flesh from self, and soul from court shoes, scoop-top, cardigan-round-the-shoulders and slacks.

'Yes,' he said. 'That's right. Anyway, it's about the van.'

'The van?' said Mrs Krimholz.

'Yes,' said Mr Krimholz. 'What is this van?'

'It's a . . . mobile library van.'

'A mobile library van? Really?'

'Yes.'

'I haven't seen one of those for years,' said Mr Krimholz. 'They're still going?'

'Yes,' said Israel. 'Actually, there are over five hundred mobile libraries still operational all around the—'

'Really?' said Mrs Krimholz.

'You sound like an expert!' said Mr Krimholz.

'Yes!' said Israel. 'It's just a . . .' He'd been reading the Mobile Meet brochure.

'You know,' said Mr Krimholz, 'now you mention it, I think there was a thing like a . . . an old ice-cream van there last night?'

'Yes,' said Israel. 'That'd be it. Did you notice what time it was there?'

'Well, it's funny. When I went to bed, I remember looking out and thinking, There's an ice-cream van.'

'Right,' said Israel. 'What time would that have been?'

160

'Well, these days, I go to bed the same time every night. Around nine o'clock I like to have a cup of tea—'

'Right,' said Israel.

'And then I maybe check my e-mail.'

'OK.'

'And then I watch the ten o'clock news. I always watch the ten o'clock news. I feel I've sort of tucked up the world for the night, you know?'

'Right,' said Israel. 'And so you saw the van at what time?'

'You know the trouble in Israel at the moment?'

'Terrible,' said Mrs Krimholz.

'Anyway?' said Israel.

'Yes. I remember thinking to myself, that's an unusual sort of ice-cream van. And then this morning, it was gone.'

'OK? Time?'

'I don't know. Half past ten?'

'Well, thanks, that's . . . And you didn't see any sort of suspicious . . . things, did you?'

'Suspicious?'

'Well, people, or . . .stuff?'

'No,' said Mr Krimholz. 'No more suspicious than usual!'

'Why are you looking for a mobile library van?' asked Mrs Krimholz.

'It's . . . I'm . . . Sorry,' said Israel, reaching into his pocket. 'That's my phone. I need to take this one.'

'Business?' said Mr Krimholz.

'Business,' said Israel. He shook the phone slightly, pretending that it was vibrating. 'I've got it on, er . . . vibrate.' He shook it slightly again and then pretended to answer it. 'Ah! Yes.' He put his hand over the phone and whispered to the Krimholzes, 'Sorry, have to take this one.'

'OK,' mouthed Mr Krimholz. 'Business is business.'

Israel backed out of the house, pretending to talk into the phone. 'Really?' he was saying. 'That's a lot. You know, we could maybe try to meet them halfway on that one, and . . .'

'Strange boy,' said Mrs Krimholz, shutting the door.

'Yes,' said Mr Krimholz. 'I don't think his phone was vibrating. I think he was sort of shaking it . . .'

And they went back inside to their Louis XIV-style furniture.

By the time Israel, disconsolate, had got back home, his mother had swung into action and set up the kitchen as a centre of operations. There were telephone address books piled on the table. There was paper everywhere. She was finishing a call.

Ted had an apron on and was standing by the counter.

'Bagel?' said Ted.

'What?' said Israel, already disorientated by his encounter with the Krimholzes, and now shocked to be offered a bagel by Ted; Ted might as well have been offering to help him tie on tefillin, or suggesting they share a crack pipe.

'You want a bagel?' said Ted. 'They're delicious. Why did you never tell me about bagels before?'

'I . . .'

'I've never had them before. Muhammad loves them.' Muhammad barked in agreement. 'They're from . . . what's that place called?'

'Jacobs?' said Israel.

'That's it,' said Ted. 'Great bagel bakery.'

'Yeah.'

'We've got poppy-seed, onion, plain?'

Israel's mother was finishing her conversation on the phone.

'Yeah,' she was saying. 'Sure. Bye. Bye. Ciao.' She turned to Israel. 'So?'

'Can I just say, Mother, that I am never, never going round there again, under any circumstances, for anybody, for *anything*.'

'Fine, fine,' said his mother. 'But the van?'

'They are the most appalling people I have ever—'

'They're not that bad,' said Israel's mother.

'Well, if you think they're not that bad, then why didn't you go round there?'

'Let's not get into that again, please, Israel. Did you think she'd had work done, Mrs Krimholz?'

'What?'

'Did you think she'd had work done? You know, around the eyes, or . . .'

'She did look a little strange.'

'That's not just Botox,' said Israel's mother, touching her face, 'let me tell you. Anyway, the van?'

163

'Mr Krimholz saw it last night. But it wasn't there this morning.'

'What time did he see it last night?'

'He thought about half past ten.'

'OK, good,' said his mother, who wrote something down in her notebook. 'And did he see anything suspicious?'

'No.'

'OK. Fine. Good. We're getting there.'

'We're getting where exactly?' said Israel, helping himself to a poppy-seed bagel.

'You've got to try the onion,' said Ted.

'I'm fine with poppy-seed, thanks,' said Israel.

'Well, I've made a lot of calls,' said Israel's mother. 'But so far no one seems to have seen anything.'

'So, who are you calling?' said Israel.

'Do you want it toasted?' said Ted. 'They're good toasted.'

'No, I'm fine as it is, thanks,' said Israel. 'Who are you phoning, Mum?'

'People.'

'Which people?'

'Friends.'

'Right. Who? People in your line-dancing class?'

'No. Not just them!' said Israel's mother. 'People in my book group as well.'

'Well, that's . . .' said Israel. 'Any coffee?'

'Sure,' said Ted.

'It's a start,' said Israel's mother.

'Yeah, but I hardly think we're going to get very far in tracking down the van with a bunch of middle-aged women from Finchley who happen to have read *Reading Lolita in Tehran*, are we? We need to get a proper plan together.'

'Fine. So what's your proper plan?' said Israel's mother.

'I haven't got a plan,' said Israel. 'I'm just saying, we need to get a plan. It can't be that difficult to find a stolen mobile library in north London, can it? You can't just make a mobile library disappear. Someone must have seen it.'

'We could put out an appeal on *Crimewatch*,' said Israel's mother.

'Mmm. Now *that* is a good idea, actually,' said Israel, swallowing a piece of bagel. 'God, yes. If you think about it, there's a great media angle on this. "The Book Stops Where? Have you seen this Mobile Library?" We could get national coverage. We should ring the papers. It's definitely a *Guardian* sort of a story.'

'Great!' said Israel's mother. 'We'll start a campaign. Ari's aunt knows Melanie Phillips.'

'No,' said Ted. 'I don't think that's a good idea.'

'Why not?' said Israel. 'You don't like the *Daily Mail*? I thought you liked the *Daily Mail*?'

'No,' said Ted.

'No?' said Israel's mother.

'No . . . I wouldn't want people to know we'd lost it.'

'You wouldn't want people to know?' said Israel's mother. 'But why? How else are we going to find it?'

'Linda would love it.'

'Ah,' said Israel. 'Good point.'

'Who's Linda?' asked Israel's mother.

'Don't ask,' said Israel.

'Our boss,' said Ted.

'Huh,' said Israel's mother. 'They're all the same.'

'She's a Northern Irish Chinese lesbian single parent,' said Israel.

'Well, they're all more or less the same,' said Israel's mother.

'We can't do any publicity,' said Ted.

'It'd be a shame not to,' said Israel's mother.

'I bet we'd find it that way,' said Israel.

'No,' said Ted.

'Any better ideas?' said Israel.

'I know!' said Israel's mother. 'Let's make a list.'

While Israel and his mother started another list Ted busied himself finishing off the rest of the bagels.

'Yes! Of course! I've got it!' Israel's mother began. 'Number one! Insider contacts! We have to start with any insider contacts we have.'

'What do you mean, insider contacts?' said Israel. 'Contacts in the mobile library-stealing fraternity?'

'Exactly,' said Israel's mother.

'I've a cousin who works in a pub,' said Ted, finishing off his second onion bagel. 'He might be able to help.'

'I doubt that very much,' said Israel.

'Perfect!' said Israel's mother. 'People in pubs, people on the street, that's just where we should start.'

'Mother!' said Israel.

'Where is it, Ted?' said Israel's mother. 'Your cousin's pub?'

'It's . . . Hold on,' said Ted. 'I've a wee scrap of paper here.' He took some crumpled papers from his pocket and sorted through them. 'Here we are,' he said. 'I wrote it down. It's called the Prince Albert, in Camden Town. I thought I might look him up while I was over here.'

'That's a lead!' said Israel's mother.

'That is not a lead,' said Israel. 'Ted's cousin who works in some grotty pub in Camden is not a lead. I might as well go and ask some of my friends if they've come across a stolen mobile library recently.'

'That's not a bad idea either,' said Israel's mother. 'We've got to cover every angle.'

It's a wild-goose chase, Mother.'

'It's not a wild-goose chase.'

'Yes, it is.'

'Well, have you got any other leads?'

'No.'

'And how do you know it'll be grotty?' said Israel's mother.

'What?'

'Ted's cousin's pub.'

'Of course it'll be grotty!'

'You don't know that. It could be like a gastropub,' said Israel's mother.

'Yeah, right,' said Israel. 'Maybe we should go there for lunch then?'

CHAPTER 10

I srael was glad that he'd managed to persuade his mother not to join him and Ted for lunch at the Prince Albert.

The Prince Albert was *not* a gastropub.

The Prince Albert sits on the corner of Georgiana Street and Royal College Street, in Camden, London, NW1, a big wedgy-shaped red-brick and terracotta building. It reminded Israel of the Flatiron Building in New York. Israel absolutely *loved* the Flatiron Building; to Israel, the Flatiron Building represented Manhattan itself, which in turn represented the good life, the cosmopolitan, the sophisticated, and everything that Israel aspired to – intelligence, wit, repartee, and profound, geeky men in suits and sneakers, and complicated, elegant women in sunglasses, and evenings out with high-end friends in hip new neighbourhood cafés discussing the latest intellectual fashions and comparing stock portfolios. To Israel, the Flatiron Building represented a way of life.

Unfortunately, it wasn't his way of life. (Israel had never ever been to the Flatiron Building: he'd seen it in *Spiderman* films. The Flatiron Building, like Grand Central Station, and the Empire State, and the Statue of Liberty, and the whole of the rest of New York, and Boston, and San Francisco, and all America, indeed, as well as most of continental Europe, and Asia, and Africa, and Australia, and Antarctica, existed only in Israel's mind, where they had all come to resemble each other: cities, plains and mountains fabulously, exotically and glamorously *there*, a world of un-discovered and unreachable El Dorados compared to Finchley and Tumdrum's unavoidable and everyday *here*. Israel had travelled widely in his imagination, and gone absolutely nowhere; he was imprisoned by limitless horizons. Just the thought of travel gave him a headache.)

And inside, of course, inside, the Prince Albert was nothing like the Flatiron Building. Inside, comparisons to Manhattans both real and im-agined quickly evaporated. Inside, the Prince Albert was a typical stinking London Irish boozer: dirty, depressing, dull, and completely empty, except for one lone drinker who wore a pork-pie hat, and dirty boots, and a ravaged-looking suit, and who didn't look up as Israel and Ted approached the bar.

'Gastropub!' said Israel. 'God!'

'Language,' said Ted.

'Sorry,' said Israel. 'But I mean . . . Couldn't they at least give the place an occasional sluicing out?'

There was music playing, a tinny radio-cassette

player behind the bar, its shiny silver plastic rubbed black and white with age, the sound of a female singer sighing and deep-breathing and claiming that she wanted to be a slave to your rhythm, over ululations and ecstatic drumming, and a bass-line that sounded like it was being played on very tight knicker elastic. In a too-small alcove off the bar there was an old, frayed and chipped pool table, with a big dark stain on the baize that looked as though someone might once have given birth on it. The table was wedged in with just a few feet to spare all round – London Irish pool players having notoriously short arms – and it was flanked and shadowed by big faded, framed posters on the walls all around it, showing the Mountains of Mourne sweeping down to the sea, and County Kerry, and Cork, and a framed jigsaw of the Giant's Causeway, which made it look as though the basalt rocks had been machine-cut and pieced together on a Sunday afternoon by bored children and their maiden aunts.

Above the bar a chain of pathetic, dirty nylon Irish tricolours hung down like leprechauns' washing, a set of rainbow flags hanging even more pathetically below them, and behind the optics, tacked to dirty mirrors, there were nicotine-stained, crumpled, damp cartoon pictures of the Great Irish Writers: James Joyce, and Samuel Beckett, and Seamus Heaney, and W.B. Yeats, and also, incongruously, ABBA, and Barbra Streisand, all crowded together and looking as though

171

someone had pissed all over them. Brown paper peeled from the walls, and yellow paper hung down from the ceiling. The floor's grey lino was cracked and turning black with age, and the paint-work on the doors and windows was worn almost through to the wood. You could hardly say that the Prince Albert was a bar in decline; the Prince Albert had already declined; it had long since stooped, and slipped, and was starting to go under.

'Tricolours!' murmured Ted. 'Bloody tricolours!' while he ordered drinks from the barman, who was not blessed with English as a first language, but who coped manfully, square-jawed with it as perhaps his fourth or fifth, and who could certainly manage any instructions that included the word 'Guinness', if spoken loudly. He fared less well with Ted's asking if his cousin Michael was in working that day, and if not, where they might possibly find him. After a few minutes of complex misunderstandings – involving the barman talking about *his* cousins, who were somewhere back home in Silesia, apparently – the barman dis-appeared behind a beaded curtain. He came back a few moments later.

'Name?' he said.

'My name?' said Ted.

'Yes.'

'Ted,' said Ted.

'Sorry. Again?'

'Ted,' said Ted. 'T. E. D. Carson. C. A. R. S. O. N.'

'OK. One minute please.'

'Foreigners!' said Ted, as the barman disappeared back behind the beaded curtain.

'*You*'re a foreigner here, remember,' said Israel.

'I don't think so,' said Ted.

'Yes, you are,' said Israel.

'Aye,' said Ted. 'The *United* Kingdom? *United* Kingdom of Great Britain and Northern Ireland? Ever heard of it?'

Israel harrumphed and tutted – did Ted never get tired of being a relic? – and as he tutted, almost as a kind of tut echo, there was a sound as of a large object, a man, or a side of beef, or a beer barrel perhaps, being rocked slowly down a stairway, and then suddenly the barman re-emerged from behind the beaded curtain, with an old man following him.

The old man walked stiffly, loudly, with a crutch – like a beer barrel or a side of beef being rocked slowly down a stairway – and he had worn, patchy white hair and an unshaven, furry sort of puce-coloured face, as though someone had just rolled a little baby pig's head around in pinhead oatmeal. He wore tight grey nylon slacks and a too-large tomato-red shirt with pure white cuffs and collar, a shirt of a kind that Israel had only ever heard rumours of; the kind of shirt that now existed only in retro TV dramas. He also wore a polka-dot black and white silk scarf. And then there was the jewellery, lots and *lots* of jewellery: rings, bracelets, a big chunky gold necklace, and a huge watch of the kind that looked like you could fly to the moon with it and still not have exhausted all its unique features. The old man may have had a head like a pig and may have struggled to walk further than a couple of hundred yards, but he was utterly, utterly blingtastic.

'Ladies and gentleman!' he boomed, the old pig-and-mealy-faced man, 'IN THE *RED* CORNER, TED CARSON!' He then dropped his shoulders slightly and bobbed unsteadily, like a boxer on a crutch, before reaching forward across the bar to shake Ted's hand, with his thick, beringed and trottery fingers.

'Michael?' said Ted. 'It's yerself?'

'I fecking hope so!' said Michael, patting his chest. 'Certainly the last time I checked it was! But for feck's sake! Ted Carson! Jesus!'

'Michael!' said Ted, shaking his head in wonderment. 'Ach, Michael! What about yerself?'

'Doin' bravely, Ted. Doin' bravely. Can't complain.'

'Good,' said Ted. 'That's good.'

'Because you know if ye did—' began Michael.

'No one would listen to ye anyway!' said Ted.

They thought this was hilarious, Ted and Michael. They both creased up at this, laughing like they were boys who'd let off a stink-bomb, or slipped a whoopee cushion onto the headmaster's seat. Israel had never seen Ted laugh like that before; it was uninhibited laughter. Israel hadn't laughed like that in a long time.

'Boys-a-boys,' said Michael, coming out from

round behind the bar on his crutch. 'Look at ye now. I haven't seen ye in, what, ten? Twenty?'

'Forty,' said Ted.

'Forty years?'

'Forty years,' agreed Ted.

'Forty years,' said Israel, joining in.

'Ach, Israel, quiet,' said Ted.

'Seems like yesterday we were wee lads,' said Michael. 'Out in the fields.'

'Aye,' agreed Ted.

'Y'member yer mother'd have the sandwiches set out ready for us when were in?'

'Aye. Thick as the duck-house door.'

'Happy days,' said Michael. 'Wonderful woman, yer mother, Ted.'

'Aye,' said Ted quietly.

'But now, come on, Ted, we're being awful rude here. Introduce me. Who's yer young friend then?'

'Who?'

'The wee pup here.' Michael gestured at Israel with his crutch.

'Him? He's Israel.'

'How ye doin', sir?' said Michael, bracelets jangling, shaking Israel's hand. 'Pleased to meet you.'

'Nice to meet you too,' said Israel.

'Israel?' said Michael, rubbing his wide, white-stubbled chin. 'Israel. Now, tell me the truth, young man, and I'll tell you no lie, would you be of the Hebrew persuasion?'

'Erm. Yes, I suppose, I—'

'Well, well,' said Michael. 'Isn't that a coincidence. Some of my best friends are Jewish.'

'Right,' said Israel.

'Did I ever tell you the story of the rabbi and the priest?'

'No,' said Israel hesitantly. He'd never met Michael before, so exactly how he might have told him the story before . . .

'All right,' said Michael, leaning across towards Israel. 'Come here.' Israel stepped reluctantly a little closer. He'd never really warmed to men who wore chunky gold jewellery. Michael grabbed hold of his elbow. 'So,' he said, breathing cigarette fumes over Israel. 'There's a rabbi and a priest, and the priest says to the rabbi, "Tell me, you're not allowed to eat bacon. Is that right?" And the rabbi says, "Yes, that's right."' Michael looked at Israel for confirmation of this fact of Jewish dietary law; Israel smiled weakly.

'Anyway, "Just between ourselves," says the priest, "just out of interest, have you ever tried it?" Well, "I must admit," says the rabbi, "many years ago, I did taste bacon." "It's pretty good, isn't it?" says the priest. And, "Yes," says the rabbi, "I have to agree, it's pretty good."'

Israel continued to smile uncertainly.

'"But tell me," says the rabbi – now listen,' said Michael to Israel, '"priests are not allowed to have *sex*, is that right?"'

Israel grimaced slightly.

'"Yes, that's right," agrees the priest. "We're not

allowed to have sex." They're celibate, right, Catholic priests?' said Michael.

'Yes,' said Israel.

'So, "Between ourselves," says the rabbi, "have you ever tried it?" Sex? Right? "No," says the priest, "I must admit, I have never tried it." Never had sex. "Not even once?" asks the rabbi. "No," says the priest, "I've not had sex even once." Now listen,' said Michael, drawing Israel closer, 'this is the punchline. "That's a shame," says the rabbi, "*because it's a hell of a lot better than bacon!*"'

'Right,' said Israel.

'Sex, you see!' said Michael, 'better than bacon!'

Ted was roaring with laughter.

'Ah, that's a good one,' he said, wiping his eyes.

'It's the way I tell 'em!' said Michael, which sent Ted into further paroxysms of laughter.

'That's it?' said Israel. 'That's the end of the joke?'

'It's the way he tells them!' said Ted.

'Clearly,' said Israel.

'Come on, fellas,' said Michael, 'enough joking around. Come and have a seat here. Come on, come on. Look. I've reserved the best table in the house.'

Michael ushered them over to a table, a table that hadn't had a wipe in some time – years, possibly. The surface was tacky and crusty, as though covered in a thick film of mucus.

'You're getting drinks now, are ye?' said Michael.

'Aye,' said Ted. 'Guinness.'

The barman looked up and across at the word 'Guinness' and nodded.

'So, you all right?' said Ted.

'Not so bad,' said Michael. 'Few troubles with the old leg, but.' And he slapped his leg.

'Aye,' said Ted. 'What's that all about then?'

'Bone cancer,' said Michael. 'It was me or the leg, they said, so that was it, away.'

'What?' said Ted.

'The leg,' repeated Michael. 'Got the chop.'

'Almighty God!' said Ted. 'That's awful, sure. You mean you've only got the one . . .'

'Aye,' said Michael.

'Well. I'm . . . Sorry for your loss,' said Ted.

'Ah!' said Michael. 'That's very good. "Sorry for your loss"! I like that. God, it's good to speak to someone from back home. The English, ye know . . .' He smiled a dirty-toothed smile at Israel. 'No sense of fucking humour. Present company excepted.'

'When did ye? Ye know? Lose the . . .' said Ted.

'That'd be, what? A year ago?' said Michael.

'And ye've the all-clear now, like, from the cancer?'

'Touch wood,' said Michael. 'Touch wood.' He slapped his leg. It gave a dull thud.

'It's a wooden leg?' said Ted.

'Ach, no!' said Michael. 'Wooden leg, Ted! Ye've got to get with it. This is the twenty-first century. I'm not a feckin' pirate, am I? Eh?'

'Ooh-aar, shipmates,' said Israel.

178

'Shut up, Israel,' said Ted.

'It's plastic,' said Michael. 'Ye can feel it if you want.'

'I'll not, thanks, Michael, no,' said Ted.

'Ye want to feel it?' said Michael, laughing, addressing Israel.

'No, thanks . . .'

'Me leg, I mean. She'll not bite,' said Michael.

'No, I'll skip on the . . . Thanks, anyway.'

At which point, thankfully, the barman came and set drinks down before them, three pints.

'Now *that*'s a pint of Guinness,' said Ted, admiring the pint, as though it were Athena in the Parthenon.

'Aye,' said Michael. 'Ye could trot a mouse across her.' Michael demonstrated this possibility by walking his fingers daintily across the top of his pint. 'It's the training. See yer man there now?' He gestured towards the barman while he licked the froth from his fingers. 'Months, it took me to get him to do what I wanted. Honest to God, Ted. Months.'

'Where's he from?' said Israel.

'Poland,' said Michael. 'Boleslaw.'

'Whatterslaw?'

'Like coleslaw,' said Michael.

'That his name, or where he's from?' said Ted.

'That's his name,' said Michael. 'Studying for a . . . what do you call it?'

'Don't know,' said Ted.

'One of those . . .'

'An exam?' said Israel. 'English as a foreign language? TEFL?'

'PhD,' said Michael. He shouted across to Boleslaw. 'Boles? Hey! What is it you're studying at?'

'Sublinear algorithms?' said Boleslaw, grinning behind the bar. 'King's College.'

'Right,' said Israel.

'Immigrants,' said Ted, stroking his pint glass as though it were a Jack Russell terrier. 'Pulls a good pint, mind. What, ye share the shifts, do ye?'

'What!?' said Michael. 'Share shifts!? Not at all. I'm not a barman any more, Ted.'

'Are ye not?'

'Not at all. Jesus! Did ye not know? I thought ye knew? I bought the place off the auld fella that owned it back in '73, when he was away over to America.'

'I didn't know that,' said Ted.

'Aye. I'm what they call an owner slash manager,' said Michael, prodding a finger at himself. 'Have been for years.'

'Well . . .' said Ted thoughtfully. 'Ye're the boss class now then?'

'Indeed!' said Michael, raising his glass. 'And who's not for us is a Guinness!' he said.

'Cheers,' said Ted.

'Sláinte,' said Michael.

'Sláinte!' said Ted, laughing. 'Sláinte! Ach, that's a good one, Michael.' He sipped his pint. 'Ye've done all right for yerself then?'

'Aye. True enough. Ye remember, I came over and I hadn't a fluke.'

'Aye.'

'But look at me now.' He gestured round the bar.

'Aye,' said Ted doubtfully.

Israel noted a group of small plastic model leprechauns posed with fiddles around a plastic crock of gold behind the bar, their green waistcoats rotting onto their chubby little plastic bodies.

'Retiring soon though,' said Michael.

'Never?' said Ted.

'Abso*fucking*lutely. You know what it's like. You get to this age, ye want to get in some golf.'

'Golf?' said Ted.

'Aye. So, I'm selling up.'

'Ye'll get a few pounds for this place then?' said Ted.

'Ha!' Michael laughed and slurped at his pint like a hungry dog. 'The price of the places these days, Ted, if I told you, you wouldn't believe me. Honestly. Godsamount of money.'

'Really?'

'I've been beating them off with a big stick, sure. London property prices, you could name a figure almost.'

'No?'

'Of course.' Michael set down his pint glass and leaned in close over the table to speak more quietly. 'I bought this place in 1973, with the money I'd saved from working on the roads, ye know, and a loan from the bank.' He took another sip of his pint. 'Four thousand pounds I bought the place for. Four thousand pound.' He shook his head in disbelief. 'Ye'll not believe me when I tell ye how much it's on the market for now.'

'How much?'

'Have a wee guess.'

'I don't know. I'm not good on the auld property prices.'

'Have a guess though,' said Michael. 'Bear in mind the London property prices.'

'London? Property prices? They've gone up rightly. I don't know. A hundred thousand?'

Michael smiled into his Guinness.

'Come on, Ted, ye couldn't even get yerself a wee one-bedroom flat in London now for a hundred thousand.'

'I don't know then. A couple of hundred thousand?'

'Ted! Come on!'

'No, you'll have to tell me.'

'Two and a half,' said Michael.

'Aye?' said Ted. 'Two and a half what?'

'What do ye think?' said Michael. 'Two and a half *million*!'

Both Ted and Israel spluttered – actually spluttered, spraying Guinness down and out and across the crusty tabletop.

'How much?' said Ted.

'Two and a half million of yer English pounds, Ted. That's how much she's worth.' Michael leaned far back in his seat. Israel gazed up at the yellowy ceiling with its architraves. The cracked, frosted, filthy windows. The peeling floor, the splitting vinyl banquettes.

'Holy God,' said Ted.

'Unbelievable, eh? Ye should have come over with me when you had the chance back then, Ted.'

There was a long silence then, during which Michael licked his lips and Ted looked mournfully down at his pint.

'The road not travelled?' said Israel.

'Shut up,' said Ted.

'Two and a half million,' repeated Michael.

'Are you sure?' said Ted.

'Of course I'm feckin' sure,' said Michael.

'Two and a half million,' said Israel. 'That's a lot of money. What are you going to do with two and a half million?'

'I'm buying a wee bit of land up in Antrim,' said Michael.

'A wee bit?' said Israel.

'Aye. Round Bushmills, Here.' Michael fished into his pocket and produced a wallet and a folded-up photograph showing what appeared to be a huge half-constructed hacienda in Spain, or Mexico, the sort of tasteless rural-bourgeois palace inhabited by some land-owning enemy of Zorro.

'That's a quare lump of house,' said Ted.

'Aye. Well, I want to keep myself in the manner to which I've become accustomed,' said Michael.

'Fair play to ye, Michael,' said Ted, raising his pint glass. 'Ye must have missed it sorely but, all these years away? The auld home country, like?'

'Ach, not really, Ted, to be honest with ye. A nice sliced pan maybe.'

'A what?' said Israel.

'A nice loaf,' said Michael, 'or a nice soda farl.'

'Aye,' said Ted.

'That's it?' said Israel. 'That's all you missed? The bread?'

'You're always going on about the bagels and croissants,' said Ted.

'Well, that's different,' said Israel. 'It's—'

'Apart from that, Ted,' said Michael, 'no, I haven't missed it. First couple of years mebbe. But hardly given the place a second thought since. Not till I thought of retiring, like. Nothing much changed, I'll bet, has it?'

'Well, ye know,' said Ted.

'First and Last still there?'

'Aye,' said Ted.

'What was yer man's name? The owner?'

'Elder? Elder Agnew.'

'That's him. He still there?'

'Ach, no, not any more. He passed on. The son's the business now.'

'And how's the Guinness?'

'Ach. You'd read a paper through it to be honest, Michael.'

As Ted and Michael solemnly finished their pints the barman, with an uncanny sense of timing,

184

appeared with three more pints. Israel had barely started on his first.

'There's you,' said Michael.

'Cheers,' said Ted. 'I'll tell you what, Michael, I'd take a sandwich and all, if it's not too much trouble, just to chase down the Guinness, like.'

'Me too,' agreed Israel.

'You'll start a run on the sandwiches,' said Michael, winking. 'The missis won't be pleased.'

'You married then, Michael?' said Ted.

'Ach, Ted!' said Michael. 'Confirmed bachelor. Yerself?'

'Aye, the same,' said Ted.

'Well,' said Michael. 'That's what I thought! Boles! We'll take some sandwiches here please?'

The barman nodded, and disappeared behind the beaded curtain.

'Anyway,' said Michael. 'That's enough about me, Ted. What about yerself?'

Ted was silent. It can be difficult following up someone's good news with no news of your own.

'Ye keepin' all right though?'

'Aye,' said Ted.

'Ye're not still boxing?' said Michael.

'Ach, no,' said Ted. 'Look at me.' He patted his considerable stomach. 'I gave that all up years ago.'

'Shame. Shame,' said Michael. 'I'll tell ye what though, Ted, look at ye here then.' He pointed above their heads with his crutch. 'These'll take you back.'

Ted and Israel swivelled round in their greasy,

worn, tub-bottomed seats. The wall above them was filled with photos of boxers, black and white photos, mostly, of thick-set, flat-nosed men in long shorts, and bare-chested, all standing slightly sideways, shyly almost, up on the balls of their feet, in lace-up boots, gloved fists held aloft, elbows in, as though protecting themselves from the camera. Ted stood gazing up at them all, cradling his pint.

'Ach, Michael.'

'Rogue's gallery, eh?' said Michael.

'Who's that now?' said Ted, pointing up at a photo. 'Is that wee Jim McCann?'

'That it is,' said Michael.

'Ach, wee Jimmy. Whatever happened to him?'

'God only knows, Ted,' said Michael. 'Long time ago.'

'Ach, seems like yesterday,' said Ted. 'God bless him.'

'Aye. Paddy Maguire,' said Michael, pointing at another photo. 'The great Belfast bantamweights. Hughie Russell. Davy Larmour.'

At that point, Israel successfully zoned out of the conversation – all he could hear were names that meant nothing to him, like the declension of foreign nouns, or the lists in Leviticus, or the place names in an Irish poem: Fra McCullagh; and Bunty Doran; and Kelly; and Rooney; and Cowan – and he stared down at his pint, as though he might be able to divine the secrets of the universe therein; as though the deep dark depths of Guinness might be able to reveal to him the meaning of existence, and the exact reason how and why he had washed up here with Ted on yet another wild-goose chase, and where was the bloody mobile library anyway, and why Gloria wasn't answering his calls, and why anyone was interested in boxing, when it's just men trying to knock each other down, because, really, what did that have to do with real life?

'Hey, you!' said Michael, jogging Israel's elbow, and almost knocking him out on the table.

'Who? Me?' said Israel.

'Yes, you, young man. Now who do you think this wee fella is?' Michael pointed to a photo showing a bulky young boxer with a crew-cut.

'I have no idea,' said Israel wearily. 'Not a clue.'

'Do you want to guess?' said Michael.

'Not really,' said Israel. 'No.'

'Go on,' said Michael. 'Who do you think that is?'

'I don't know,' said Israel. 'I'm not good on boxers.'

'Go on,' said Michael.

'Muhammad Ali?' said Israel.

'Muhammad Ali!' said Michael. 'You've a quare one here, Ted!'

Ted shook his head, as though contemplating the meaning of utter stupidity.

'Muhammad Ali was a black man, son!' said Michael.

'Oh, yes,' said Israel, attempting to communicate disinterest.

'Think of another one.'

'Erm . . .'

'That!' said Michael, without waiting for Israel to answer. 'Is! Yer man here!'

'Ted?'said Israel. 'It's you? Really?'

'Aye. He could have been a contender,' said Michael.

'Ach, Michael.'

'He could. He was one hell of a specimen when he was young, let me tell ye. Adonis, so he was.'

'Michael!' said Ted.

'He was a wee bunty one when he was a wean, but.'

'I was that,' said Ted.

'But that was before he got into the sports, like. You were on the same bill as Paddy Graham once, were ye not?'

'I was,' said Ted. 'Fiesta Ballroom. Fighting Sam Kelly.'

'That was a close fight,' said Michael.

'He cut me open like a butcher, so he did,' corrected Ted. 'Referee stopped it in the seventh.'

'You weren't far off,' said Michael.

'Aye, half a yard and a million miles away,' said Ted.

Israel was looking at the photograph showing Ted in regulation boxer's stance. He looked younger, of course, and about half his current body-weight, but there was a look in his eyes that Israel recognised, a look that could have been defiance. Or it could have been fear.

The sandwiches – white bread, margarine and

188

ham – and three more pints arrived. Ted and Michael seemed to be engaged in some kind of unspoken but deeply acknowledged drinking competition.

'Sláinte,' said Michael, as was his custom, tucking into the Guinness. Israel saw Ted wince again.

'Now, just . . .' said Ted, putting up his hand. 'Hold on there now, Michael. You are having me on, are ye?'

'With what?' said Michael. 'Having ye on with what, Ted?'

'With this auld "Sláinte" nonsense.'

'Sláinte?'

'Aye. We don't say "Sláinte", do we?'

'What do ye mean, "we", Ted?'

'In the north, I mean. It's . . . ye know.'

'Ach, Ted. It's just habit,' said Michael, picking up his pint again. 'I've been here that long.'

'Habit?' said Ted. 'Holy God, man.'

'Keeps the customers happy, you know,' said Michael. 'A touch of the blarney.'

'Aye, right, and the tricolours and all?'

'And leprechauns,' added Israel for good measure, pointing to the rotting plastic figurines gathered behind the bar. 'They're a nice touch.'

'Shut up, Israel,' said Ted. 'Yer father was staunch, but,' he said to Michael.

'I know, Ted, I know, I know.'

Ted shook his head. 'You might have expected to have gone, ye know, a wee bit Englishified over

189

here,' he said. 'That'd be understandable, like. But to have gone . . . Irish on us . . .'

'Ach, Ted!'

'I'm just finding it hard to understand, Michael, that's all.'

'Look, Ted, come on. It's a big wide world out there. You know as well as meself, you come over here, ye're just a Mick to people. It doesn't matter whether you're from the north or the south or orange or green or whatever. Ye play along with it a wee bit, ye're fine.'

'Aye, but the tricolours, Michael. The tricolours! The Republican flag, but.'

'Ach, for feck's sake, Ted, people wouldn't know we were an Irish pub otherwise, would they?'

'What about a red hand?' suggested Ted.

'Ach, Ted, wise up. A red hand!'

'Symbol of Ulster,' said Ted.

'You're having me on now, are ye? We're a business here, Ted, we're not into making sectarian—'

'The red hand is not a sectarian symbol!' said Ted. 'Was it not O'Neill who cut off his hand to claim the kingdom of Ulster?'

'I don't know, Ted. I'm not into the history, like. But I tell you what I do know: that you might as well put a swastika on the front of the pub if you're going to put the red hand up.'

'A swastika?' said Israel. 'Erm. Ahem. I'm not sure the red hand of Ulster is quite the same as a swastika—'

190

'Shut up, Israel,' said Ted.

'You've got to give people what they want, Ted. And a wee touch of the Irish doesn't do any harm. I tell you, we have the auld diddly-aye music in here once a week, and it's a coupla wee fellas from East Belfast. One of them was in a feckin' flute band, for goodness sake!'

'Ach.'

'It's a wee bit of craic, just.'

'Postmodern identities,' said Israel.

'Shut up, Israel,' said Ted.

'Anyway,' said Michael. 'Are ye's here on holiday, or what?'

'Well,' said Israel. 'Actually we were wondering if you could help us?'

'Really?' said Michael. 'And there was me thinking it was a social call!'

'Ach, it is, Michael, I've been meaning to look you up for years, like. It's just, with work, and—'

'Aye, all right, Ted, I'm only keepin' ye going. Now what sort of help was it ye were looking for?'

'We're in a wee spot of bother, Michael,' said Ted.

'Taxman is it?' said Michael, leaning back in his seat. 'Bloody bastards.'

'Ach, no. It's not the taxman. I pay my taxes, and glad to pay them.'

'That's your prerogative, Ted, your prerogative. So what sort of help would it be that you're looking for?'

'We've had our van stolen.'

'Van?'

'Mobile library van,' said Israel.

'Your what?' said Michael.

'We're librarians,' said Israel.

'Is that the word for it then?' said Michael, laughing. '*Librarian!* I've not heard that one before.'

'What?' said Ted.

'Librarians!' said Michael. 'Ah, you're an auld old queen, Ted.'

'What?' said Ted.

'You and your young man here. Librarians! Very cute!'

A few of the things Michael had said now suddenly started to make sense in Israel's mind.

'Hold on,' he said. 'You don't think . . . You're not implying that we're—'

'Young man?' said Michael.

'We're what?' said Ted.

'Shaved head,' said Michael. 'Leather jacket. And your friend the bear here.'

Ted looked to Israel, who looked to Michael.

'Ye do know what sort of bar this is, don't you?' said Michael.

'Aye, an Irish bar,' said Ted.

'Ha!' said Michael. 'We, Ted, are London's premier Irish *gay* bar.'

'As in?' began Israel.

'Homosexual?' said Michael.

'Homo . . . Homo?' said Ted.

Michael raised his eyebrows – which, it suddenly

occurred to Israel, were plucked eyebrows – and fingered the ends of his black and white polka-dot silk scarf.

Ted's eyes looked as though they might pop out of his head. Israel glanced around again: the rainbow flags with the tricolours. The poster of ABBA. Barbra Streisand.

'Some of my best friends are homosexual,' he said, trying to think of something to say. 'And I really like Alan Hollinghurst. *Queer As Folk*? Do you remember that? *Tales of the City*?'

'Ted?' said Michael. 'Are you all right?'

Ted looked as though someone had just punched him hard in the stomach. He shook his head. He'd flushed a deep red.

'Ted?'

'I . . . Michael? . . . Ye're not . . . I mean . . .'

'I thought everybody knew!' said Michael. 'That was the reason I left back in '69.'

'But . . . I thought it was because of the Troubles,' said Ted.

'Well, there was that too, of course.'

'I . . . But . . .'

'You could have come with me, Ted. You could have made a new life for yerself.'

'I . . . You're not . . .'

'I think he maybe needs a drink,' said Michael to Israel.

'Right,' said Israel, pushing one of his three as yet undrunk Guinnesses towards Ted. 'He could have one of my—'

'Actually, I think a wee drop of the craythur,' said Michael. 'That'd see you right, Ted, wouldn't it? A wee drop of the craythur?'

'I . . .' said Ted, who was struggling.

'Let's have a wee look here.'

Michael got up and hobbled over to the bar.

'Ted!' whispered Israel.

'What?'

'Snap out of it. Don't be so rude.'

'Ach. I . . .'

'Get a grip, Ted.'

'I just can't . . . He's a . . .'

'It's fine. He's still your cousin.'

'Yes, but a . . .'

'There are no buts.'

'I wouldn't have come if I'd have known he was . . .'

'Sshh!'

Michael came back over to the table with a bottle of clear liquid gripped under his armpit, and three glasses.

'Fella from Dagenham gets it over from Cork, so he does.'

'What is that?' asked Israel.

'Poteen,' said Michael.

'Isn't that illegal?' said Israel.

'Ha!' said Michael, uncorking the bottle, and offering the bottle forward for Ted and Israel to smell. 'Where'd ye get him, Ted, eh?'

'I . . .' said Ted.

'Smell all right?' said Michael.

'Aye,' said Ted.

'It is illegal, isn't it?' said Israel.

Michael called over to the man in the suit and hat drinking by himself.

'He says the poteen, Hugh, is it illegal?'

'As far as I know.'

'Hughie says it's definitely illegal.'

'He's your poteen expert then, is he?' said Israel jokingly.

'Aye,' said Michael. 'You could say that. He's . . . Hold on, what's your official title, Hugh?'

'DCI.'

'The police?' said Israel.

'There you are now,' said Michael. 'You're not going to take us in for the poteen are ye, Hugh?'

'What day of the week is it?' said Hugh.

'It's a Wednesday,' said Michael.

'You're all right, then, Michael. I'll turn a blind eye. But mind you've it drunk by tomorrow.'

'There we are now,' said Michael. 'So, a wee drop of the craythur?'

'No, I don't think so,' said Israel. 'Not for me, thanks.'

'Ye big drink a water. Come on now and have a wee try.'

Michael poured three generous measures of colourless liquid into the glasses.

'Cheers!' he said to Ted.

Ted remained silent and motionless until Israel jogged his arm.

'Ted, *cheers*!'

'Cheers,' said Ted mournfully, looking down at the table.

Israel's taste buds had become accustomed to strong alcoholic beverages since living in Tumdrum. He knocked it back.

'Good, isn't she?' said Michael.

'Not bad,' said Israel, gasping. It tasted like fermented beaver piss. 'You know the policeman there,' he said to Michael. 'Do you think he might be able to pull a few strings and find out who's stolen our van?'

'Hugh?' said Michael, calling over. 'Could you do me a wee favour?'

'Any time,' said Hugh.

'Tracing a stolen van?'

'No problem at all,' said Hugh.

'Thank you, darling,' said Michael. 'There,' he said to Israel and Ted. 'That's you all sorted now, Ted, isn't it?'

'Ach, Michael,' said Ted.

'That went well,' said Israel, when they left.

'We'll never hear any more of it,' said Ted. 'A bunch of homo . . .' He struggled to say the word.

They got the call the next morning.

CHAPTER 11

The address they'd been given was just by Wandsworth Bridge. They drove there in Israel's mother's new car; she'd traded up since Israel had gone to Tumdrum, to a shiny black Mini with a cream leather interior, the middle-aged woman's Harley Davidson: the perfect post-menopause vehicle.

'Now we're just like *The Italian Job*,' enthused Israel behind the wheel.

Ted, in the passenger seat, looked at him pitilessly.

Muhammad, in Ted's lap, remained silent.

It was a small industrial estate surrounded by high fences and barbed-wire decorated with several generations of wind-blown rubbish, and criss-crossed by a warren of potholed roads lined with dilapidated warehouse units and fenced-in areas in which Alsatian dogs barked and loud music played, and firms specialised in the manufacture of PVC products.

Israel and Ted drove around for fifteen minutes up and down the pavement-less streets, white vans everywhere going about their honest-to-God business, and not a soul around, and eventually, down past Worldwide Refrigeration Services, and KGB Engineering – what was that? – and edging right up to the side of the Thames itself, there it was: Britton's Second Hand Van Sales, Lease and Hire.

'Ted?' said Israel. 'We're here.'

Ted had been entirely silent on the journey.

'Ted?'

'What?' said Ted.

'I said we're here.'

When they'd arrived back at Israel's mother's the night before, after their long afternoon in the Prince Albert, Ted had excused himself, and spent the evening alone in the spare room.

'Is he all right?' Israel's mother kept asking Israel. 'Do you think he's OK? Is it something I said?'

'He's fine,' said Israel. 'It's just been a shock, I think, with the van, you know, and seeing his cousin after all these years.'

'Oy!' said Israel's mother. 'People change. You remember your Aunt Sarah? She was a brunette growing up in Finchley; now, twenty-five years later, she's a blonde-in South Africa.'

'Right,' said Israel.

'*And* she's had a boob job.'

'Yeah, but—'

'*And* a nose job.'

'It's not quite the same, Mum. It's—'

Her mobile rang.

'I've got to take this call,' said his mother. 'It could be a lead.'

Israel's mother was taking the hunt for the van seriously. She'd always been ambitious and organised, but her ambition and organisation had been focused largely on making packed lunches and arranging school concerts for the PTA. Now that she was faced with a bona fide challenge, she'd turned into Hillary Clinton. It had given her a new lease of life.

Israel's mobile hadn't rung.

He still hadn't heard from Gloria.

She was busy. Maybe she was away. Business.

Yes. That was it. She was definitely away.

'You can talk to me about it, if you want,' said Israel.

Ted remained silent.

'Or not. "Whereof one cannot speak, thereof one must remain silent."'

'All right, Buddha,' said Ted.

'Actually, that's Wittgenstein.'

'Who?'

'Wittgenstein, Ludwig, famous Austrian philosopher.'

'Aye,' said Ted, 'we had one of them, but the wheels fell off.'

'Are you all right though, seriously?' said Israel, as he parked the car.

'What?' said Ted, stroking the dog.

'Well, it's just, you've not said anything all morning,' said Israel. 'I was just wondering, you know, if you're all right?'

'Am I all right?' said Ted irritably. 'Am *I* all right?'

'It's a straightforward question,' said Israel.

Ted shook his head, either in rage or despair, it was difficult to tell which. Muhammad barked in sympathy.

'There's nothing wrong with *me*,' said Ted, with implication.

'Are you thinking about your cousin?' said Israel.

Ted huffed.

'I know it was a shock, but . . . You can't know everything about people, Ted, not even your own family. Everybody has to lead their life the way they see fit. And it's just . . . something we all have to face, one day or another. Sometimes you just have to embrace difference and change and try to move forward.'

'Israel?' said Ted.

'What?'

'I'll tell you what would make me feel better.'

'What?'

'If you shut up.'

'Right.'

'Completely.'

'All right. OK.'

'Which means not speaking.'

'OK, sorry.'

'Ever.'

'I—'

'At all.'

They got out of the car and walked in through the gates of Britton's Second Hand Van Sales into a forecourt filled with white vans, a vast drift of vehicles looking as though they were floating upon the brimming Thames behind them and beyond: Citroên, Fiat, Mazda, Mercedes, Toyota, Vauxhall, like big wheeled swans ready to fly up and away and soar over the capital.

'Wow,' said Israel. 'Looks like they've got them all here.'

'Except ours,' said Ted.

'Come on, let's think positive,' said Israel.

'I thought you were staying silent?' said Ted.

A man came down a flight of steps from a Portakabin office raised on stilts and approached them.

'Right,' said Israel.

'Do not speak,' said Ted. 'Leave the ba-flum to me.'

'The what?' said Israel.

'Leave it to me,' repeated Ted. 'The ba-flum.'

'All right, I will,' whispered Israel, as the man approached. 'Even though I have no idea what bum-flum—'

'*Ba-flum,*' said Ted.

'—ba-flum might be,' said Israel.

'Hello, gents!' said the man. He had thinning, slicked-back hair. He wore a cheap-looking suit with an expensive-looking purple lining and he was finishing off a bacon sandwich, licking his fingers clean of grease and crumbs. He'd had acne. He couldn't have been much older than Israel but he looked like a bloated, out-of-condition Bill Clinton. He was, definitively, a second-hand car salesman.

'Gentlemen, gentlemen. Lovely to see you.'

They all shook hands. Israel wiped his hands on his trousers.

'Barry Britton,' said the man. 'How can I help you?'

'Great view,' said Israel, nodding towards the River Thames, out past the high wire fencing.

'Yeah, well. It's OK,' said Barry. 'You get used to it. It's like looking up a bit of skirt I always think. D'you know what I mean?' He had a long, lop-sided smile – a smile so big and so false, so gaping, that it looked as though if he smiled a little longer the top of his head would fall off.

'Erm . . .' said Israel.

'We're looking for a van,' said Ted.

'You're looking for a van?' said Barry, pointing finger and thumb at Ted, as though cocking a gun.

'That's right,' said Ted.

'You are *look*in' for a *van*?' repeated Barry, amused, almost singing the words, cocking both hands at Ted.

'Yes,' said Ted mirthlessly.

'Well, my friend,' said Barry, slapping Ted on the back. 'You have come to the right place! *This* is where you're going to find your van. What did you say your name was?'

'I didn't,' said Ted.

'Ha!' said Barry. 'You're good! You're not giving anything away, right?'

Ted looked at him silently.

'Yeah. Good! Now, my friend, what sort of a van

are you looking for? We specialise in light commercial and fittings, as you know. And you are looking for . . . No. Don't tell me . . .' He stood back and eyed up Ted and Israel. 'You're plumbers? Am I right, or am I right?'

'No,' said Ted.

'No? We get a lot of plumbers,' said Barry. 'Roof racks for the pipes, you know, and racking and what have you. Super racking. We've got a deal on that at the moment, if you're interested.'

'We don't want a plumber's van,' said Ted.

'That's fine,' said Barry. 'Not a problem. What is it then? Erm. You are . . . No, don't tell me . . . Chippies, are you?'

'No,' said Israel.

'We're not chippies,' said Ted.

'That's all right,' said Barry. 'Just guessing. You can't always judge a book by its cover, eh! Doesn't matter what you are, or what you do. Whatever it is, I can guarantee you, Britton's has the van for you.' When he spoke Barry sounded like he was rapping; Israel suspected a fondness for Eminem.

'It's a very particular sort of van we're looking for,' said Ted.

'Good!' said Barry. 'Excellent! You know what you want. That's good. I like a man who knows his own mind. I'm the same myself. A man's got to know what he wants in this life, and go get it, if you know what I mean. Eh?'

'The van,' said Ted, 'we're looking for—'

'Yeah. OK. Let me tell you this. You just name

203

your vehicle and spec, and if by some fluke we haven't got it – you're not going to believe this, but it's true – we'll get it; week, two weeks max, no problem. But first look. Look. Look at that. Little Citroën C15 over there. Lovely vehicle.' He gestured towards a small white van. 'And then we go all the way right up to the big Mercedes.' He gestured towards a big white van. 'I'm guessing there's going to be something here that's gonna suit you but if not, like I say, if we haven't got what you're looking for today, right here, right now on the forecourt, we'll source it. At Britton's we're all about customer service.'

'We're looking for a Bedford,' said Ted.

'Ha! Right, now,' said Barry. 'A Bedford? Well. Now . . . Phew! Don't take this the wrong way, all right, but I'm afraid you might be showing your age a little bit there. Yeah.' He patted Ted on the arm.

Ted looked for a moment as though he might knock him out.

'Only joking!' said Barry, sensing danger, stepping back. 'But the Bedford – OK? – that's more of a collector's item these days. We've not had a Bedford in for . . . Phew! I don't know how long. More of my dad's generation of vehicle, d'you know what I mean? No offence, like.' He pointed at him again with two fingers. 'If you're thinking Bedford, I don't know, let me think . . . You'd probably be better off these days with a Fiat. Depending on what you're after.'

Ted did not look amused.

'I *say* Fiat. Toyota might do you just as well. Nice little Ducato maybe?' He pointed over to another white van.

'It's got to be a Bedford,' said Ted.

'Right. You sure?'

'I'm sure,' said Ted.

'Well, now. I'm not saying here that we couldn't get you a Bedford. But just at the moment . . . You collectors or what?' said Barry.

'We're librarians actually,' said Israel.

'Come again?'

'Librarians.'

Israel thought that Barry's face coloured slightly at the mention of the word 'librarian' and that perhaps he twitched nervously inside his cheap suit with its expensive-looking lining. But then twitching nervously in the presence of a librarian wasn't an uncommon response – librarians, like ministers of religion, and poets, and people with serious mental health disorders, can make people nervous. Librarians possess a kind of occult power, an aura. They could silence people with just a glance. At least, they did in Israel's fantasies. In Israel's fantasies, librarians were mild-mannered super-heroes, with extrasensory perceptions and shape-shifting capacities and a highly developed sense of responsibility who demanded respect from all they met. In reality, Israel couldn't silence even Mrs Onions on her mobile phone when she was disturbing other readers on the van.

'Librarians?' Barry was saying. 'Librarians. Well. I've got to hand it to you, on that one you might just have caught me out. That may be a Britton no-can-do, boys. Library vans. No. I don't think we've had a library van at all. We do commercial, that's it.'

'We didn't say we were looking for a library van,' said Ted.

'No?' said Barry. 'I thought your mate here said—'

'I said we were librarians,' said Israel.

'Right,' said Barry, whose face was beginning to resemble the colour of his expensive lining. 'Yeah. Well, you know, I just put two and two together?'

'Aye,' said Ted. 'Right. And what d'ye come up with?'

'Four,' said Barry, hesitating for a moment.

'Correct,' said Ted. 'So the thing is, we heard you did have a library van.'

Barry shook his head. 'No. I don't know who you heard that from.'

'A mutual acquaintance,' said Ted.

'Oh, right! I see,' said Barry, seizing back the opportunity to be smart. 'Mutual acquaintance, is it?' He gestured with his thumb at Ted and spoke to Israel. 'He's hilarious, isn't he, your mate?'

'Is he?' said Israel.

'Now, not being funny, right, but I doubt very much we have any mutual acquaintances: I am very choosy, acquaintance-wise.'

'Me too,' said Ted.

'Ha!' Barry laughed, patting Ted on the back. 'So, anyways, gents, there's plenty of other vans for you to look at it, if you're interested, otherwise you'll understand I've got a—'

'We want the library van,' said Ted.

'Ah! He's a joker, isn't he?' Barry said to Israel. 'Sorry. I explained. We haven't got a library van.'

'We want the library van,' repeated Ted.

'Right. Hello? Sorry,' said Barry, gesturing to Israel and tapping his finger against his forehead. 'I don't mean to be rude here, Grandad, I don't know if your hearing's right. Is his hearing right?'

Israel nodded in confirmation.

'Is it?' continued Barry. 'Because what I just said was, we *don't have* a library van, all right?' Barry wasn't smiling now. Barry was frowning. 'I don't know how you've ended up here, boys, but I think someone's been winding you up.' He turned to Israel. 'I think you need to take your old man home here, before he—'

'Come on, Ted,' said Israel, turning to leave.

Barry Britton was already walking away.

'Hughie Jones sent us,' said Ted.

Barry turned back.

'DCI Hughie Jones?'

'Aye.'

'Really? How do I know Hughie sent you?'

'He said to remind your father not to miss the Masonic meeting next week.'

'Right,' said Barry, eyeing Ted and Israel up and

down. 'You do know Hughie then? Are you police?'

'We're friends,' said Ted.

Barry hesitated. 'All right,' he said. 'So what's your interest in the van?'

'It's our library van. And we want it back.'

'Ah!' said Barry. 'We'd better go and speak in private.'

They went up some steps to Barry's Portakabin on stilts. Inside, Barry settled himself down behind a large wood-laminate desk. The window behind him showed blue sky.

'So how do you know Hugh?' said Barry, rocking back on his chair.

'He's a friend of a friend,' said Ted.

'All right,' said Barry. 'Friend of a friend. So what do you know?'

'You and Hugh have an understanding.'

'That's right. We have an understanding. I scratch his, and he—'

'Scratches yours?' said Israel.

'Correct,' said Barry nervously. 'And I know Hugh wouldn't send me any time-wasters.'

'Good,' said Ted. 'We won't waste your time then. Where's our van?'

'Hold on,' said Barry, leaning forward.

'We know you've got the van,' said Ted.

'I don't actually,' said Barry.

'Oh, really?' said Ted.

'Yes. Really.'

'Where d'you get it from?'

'Ha!' Barry spoke again to Israel. 'He's hilarious, your mate, isn't he? I'm running a business here. I don't go around telling everyone where we source our vehicles.'

'Who stole our van? Did you steal it?'

'Steal it? Stole it? No, no. I don't know what Hugh told you. I wouldn't be dealing with stolen vehicles. That'd be illegal. We *source* vehicles for people. Like special acquisitions.'

'I want to know who stole our van,' said Ted.

'I can't tell you, mate, sorry. I don't have that sort of information.'

'So what can you tell us?' said Israel.

'About the library van?'

'Yes.'

'Well, look, because you're friends of Hugh's, I can confirm that we were recently in possession of an exlibrary van.'

'Great!' said Israel.

'But,' said Barry, 'it's been sold.'

'Sold? It couldn't have been sold,' said Israel.

'Why not?' said Barry. 'They're very popular, PSVs. Paki wagons, we call 'em.'

'Right,' said Israel.

'All these immigrants, they love 'em. Get the whole family in there, you know, or the mosque, whatever.'

Israel tutted.

'I speak as I find, mate,' said Barry.

'Who'd ye sell it to?' said Ted.

'To whom did I sell it?' said Barry.

'Yes,' said Ted.

'Look, I'm sorry, Grandad, I can't tell you that.'

'Why not?' said Israel.

'Well. Put it this way – that is what you might call commercially sensitive information.'

At which point Ted calmly reached a hand into his pocket – Israel winced, foreseeing violence – and took out his wallet. Israel had never seen his wallet before. Ted took a wad of notes from the wallet and placed them carefully on the desk in front of Barry Britton.

'We'd like to buy some of your commercially sensitive information,' said Ted.

'Well, well,' said Barry. 'Let's have a little look here, shall we?'

Barry began counting the money: five hundred pounds in twenty-pound notes.

'You know this is more than the van's worth, do you? I mean, it's scrap, basically.'

'It has sentimental value,' said Ted.

'There's very little room for sentiment in this life, my friend,' said Barry, wagging his finger at Ted, and patting the pile of notes with the other hand. 'That's one of the lessons you learn in business.'

'Who bought the van?' said Ted.

'All right, I'm just getting to that. Let me think . . . Er . . . Ah, yes!' he said. 'The library van! Now I remember. It was some travellers what bought it.'

'Travellers?' said Ted.

'Yeah. I've done a few bits of business with 'em. They're all right actually. Once you get over the smell and that: women more disgusting than the blokes really. They're not bad-lookin', some of 'em. But the state of 'em, you know. They'd have to pay you, if you know what I mean.'

'Where are they?' said Ted.

'The old dreadlocks and that. Dogs on string.'

'Where are they?'

'The travellers? They're based out in Essex somewhere. Out round Harlow, I think. Epping. I don't know.'

'Where's that?' said Ted.

'I know where that is,' said Israel.

'Good, well. There you are then, boys, that's you sorted. Thank you very much.' Barry got up to usher them out.

'Essex is quite a big county,' said Israel. 'Could you be a bit more specific?'

Barry sighed. 'Look, boys, I can understand you're keen to get a hold of your van, but these characters are not the sort of people who leave behind their business card, if you know what I mean.'

'So you can't be any more specific?' said Israel.

'Well, I dunno. I probably could . . . Under the right circumstances.'

'Can't you just tell us where they are?' said Israel.

'That sort of information might cost extra, mightn't it?' said Barry, sitting back down expectantly at his desk.

'Extra?' said Israel.

'Knowledge is power, gents, as I'm sure, you know, you librarians can appreciate. Power, you see. Knowledge. Two things. And you don't get the one . . . without the other. So it's got to be worth it to me.'

Ted had made his way slowly round Barry's desk to where he was sitting.

'Is it information worth me not breaking your fucking neck for, you piece of shit?'

'Yeah, ha! All right, Paddy, calm down,' said Barry.

If he'd had the good sense to ask, Israel would have been able to tell Barry not to use the 'P' word, but it was too late.

Ted had grabbed Barry Britton by the lapels of his cheap suit and had jerked him up violently out of his seat.

'What did you call me?' he said.

'Get off! You fucking—'

'I said, what did you call me?'

'Oi!'

Barry was struggling to break free from Ted's enormous grip.

'Nothing!' said Barry. 'I didn't call you—'

'You said something.'

'Fuck off!' said Barry, spitting his words into Ted's face.

Before Israel could intervene Ted had leaned forward and head-butted Barry, and there was a crunch like the sound of a hammer cracking a sheet of nutty slack.

Israel leaped round the desk.

'Ted! What the hell are you doing!' he said, grabbing hold of Ted's arms and pulling him back.

'Ah! Fuck!' yelled Barry, cupping his hands under his nose, as blood poured down his face. 'Fuck! You've broken my fuckin' nose!'

'Good,' said Ted, straining to release himself from Israel's grasp. 'And I'm going to break yer fuckin' arm next, ye gobshite. So what did ye call me?'

'Nothing!'

Ted freed an arm from Israel's grip and gave Barry an open-handed slap around the head, with force so strong it might have made him deaf.

'Ted!' yelled Israel. 'Stop it! Leave him alone, for God's sake. Come on.'

But Ted was in no mood to be pacified. He had his other arm free now and both hands round Barry's throat.

Israel was attempting to prise the two men apart.

'Stop it!' screamed Israel.

'What did you call me?' said Ted.

'Paddy!' whispered Barry, his eyes bulging.

'Ted!' said Israel. 'Leave him!'

'Sorry?' said Ted, speaking to Barry, relaxing his grip slightly. 'I can't hear ye?'

'Paddy!' said Barry again weakly.

'That's right,' said Ted. 'You called me Paddy.'

'Ted!'

'This doesn't concern you,' said Ted to Israel. 'So what do you say?'

'What?' said Barry.

213

'What do you say?'

'Sorry?' said Barry, starting to cry.

'Was that a sorry?' said Ted.

'Yes,' said Barry.

'Good, thank you,' said Ted, releasing his grip on Barry Britton, and picking up his own money from the table. 'Next time, I'll punch your fucking teeth down the back of your fucking throat, you fucking English racist bastard.'

Barry Britton was sobbing now.

'You're crazy,' he said to Israel. 'You bastards. You're both . . .'

'Look,' said Israel, 'I'm really, really sorry.' He put an arm round Barry's shoulder. 'Do you want me to get you some tissue or—'

'Fuck off!' said Barry.

'Where are they?' said Ted.

'Who?' said Barry.

'The people who've stolen my van!'

'I don't know,' said Barry.

Ted went to kick him.

'Ted!' yelled Israel.

'Ongar!' said Barry. 'Somewhere near Ongar!'

'Whatter?'

'Ongar! Near Harlow!'

'You ever heard of it?' said Ted.

'No,' said Israel.

'Are you lying to me, you wee shite?'

'No!' said Barry.

'You'd better not be,' said Ted. 'Because I'll be back.'

'Ted! Leave him!' said Israel. 'Come on.'

It was then, on the way back to Israel's mum's car, that the real argument began.

'What the hell was that about?' said Israel. 'Are you completely out of your fucking mind?'

'Don't you dare use that sort of language with me!' said Ted.

'Don't you dare correct my *fucking* language! You nearly killed a bloke back there!'

'I did not nearly kill him.'

'Yes, you bloody did! You broke his fucking nose, and if I hadn't pulled you off God knows what would have happened.'

'I just don't like people calling me Paddy,' said Ted.

'Paddy! He just called you a name, that was all.'

'Yeah, but not Paddy.'

'Why not?'

'I don't like it, that's all.'

'You're a fucking grown man, Ted! You're not a kid.'

'I just don't like it.'

'Oh, grow up!' said Israel.

'No, you grow up,' said Ted.

'I'm not going to be doing this with you if you're going to be throwing your weight around,' said Israel.

'So how else are you going to do it?'

'I don't know. By our . . . Powers of . . . We just . . . Not by punching people!'

'I didn't hurt him,' said Ted.

'You broke his bloody nose!'

'That'll mend.'

'I'm serious, Ted. You're going to end up putting someone in hospital, or ending up in hospital yourself if you carry on like this. *And* I'll report you to the police.'

'Aye,' said Ted.

'And then how would we get the van back. Huh?'

'I don't know,' said Ted. 'But I do know we're out in the big bad world now, and I want my van back, and I will do whatever I need to do to get it back.'

'Well, all right, Arnold Schwarzenegger, I want the van back as well, but next time don't be getting carried away like that. Jesus! You're a fucking embarrassment. I've never seen anything like it . . .'

'Yeah? Well, mebbe ye need to get out more in the real world, and mebbe next time, ye'll keep yer mouth shut and don't be entermeddling.'

'Entermeddling?'

'Aye.'

'God! Believe me, Ted, I have no intention of entermeddling with you.'

'Good.'

'Right then.'

'Aye.'

'Oh, yes, actually, and while we're at it, you can stop entermeddling with my mother, all right?'

'What?' said Ted.

'Keep your hands off my mother,' said Israel.

216

'I wouldn't lay a finger on yer mother.'

'I'm serious, Ted. You mess around with my mother, and you will . . . have me to answer to.'

'Is that a threat?' said Ted, as Israel unlocked the car and they opened the doors to climb in.

'Yes,' said Israel hesitantly.

'Now I'm scared,' said Ted.

'Well, so you should be,' said Israel, and then, 'Aaggh!' he said. 'What's that smell? Ugh. That bloody dog!'

Muhammad sat innocently on the white leather interior.

CHAPTER 12

Gloria still hadn't phoned. Or texted. Or indeed turned up, wearing perfume and a smile, bearing gifts and profuse apologies.

But then why should she?

She was probably away. She was busy.

And if she wasn't away? Maybe it was his fault? Maybe she was annoyed with him, staying at his mother's. But he'd not had time to go to their flat since he'd arrived, since the van had been stolen; it'd been absolute chaos; mayhem; utterly bonkers. He thought she might have understood that. But maybe she didn't.

He was confused.

He had a headache.

He rang again.

No answer.

He was depressed.

Oh, God.

Food. That was the answer. Food is always a great consolation in such circumstances, Israel had always found. He'd often turned to food in such circumstances in the past. When he and Gloria had argued in the past, for example, he'd usually find a way to slip out for a Chinese takeaway, or at least something from the corner shop; a packet of Pringles, at least: it was his version of therapy. It was always there for you, food. Everywhere, and always the same. A meal was a meal was a meal. And you couldn't say that about a therapist. Or a girlfriend.

They'd driven back to his mother's in silence, Israel and Ted, both shocked, and depressed, and irritated and annoyed by their encounter with Barry Britton. Ted said he needed time to prepare for their trip to Essex to find the van.

'What do you mean prepare?' said Israel.

'Prepare,' said Ted.

Israel imagined hunting gear and weaponry.

'We're not taking any weapons though, right?'

'Of course we're not taking any weapons, ye eejit; we're not the feckin' SAS.'

To prepare himself for going to Essex, Israel knew that he should probably have been doing yoga, napping and eating a freshly prepared salad, some steamed fish, and drinking some extract of wheatgrass, but he decided instead he'd be better off going to Grodzinski's for some cheesecake and an espresso. He rang round trying to rustle up a few old friends, managed to rustle up a couple, and arranged to meet up with them to kibitz and to help him try to get his head together. Maybe they could brainstorm on what to do about the van. And Gloria. He needed help. He needed to reconnect.

He left his mum and Ted scheming in the kitchen, as usual, drinking coffee, petting the dog. He wondered what his father would have thought: his mother and Ted, sitting there. He decided not to wonder.

His mother had put up posters everywhere on lamp-posts in the surrounding streets, stuck them up with Sellotape and drawing pins. She'd got a clip art image of a mobile library; it looked more like an American school bus. 'Have you seen this vehicle?' the posters said. 'Reward £100.' Her mobile number. The posters were so weird – and so useless – they could have been an art installation.

The High Street looked different. Not just the street. Everything looked different. The people. Especially the people: a woman wearing a mini-skirt and thigh-length suede boots; the man with his hair cut like something out of a Picasso; another man with – was that? – eye make-up. You didn't see that every day in Tumdrum. Israel walked from home in his worn-out old brogues, and his duffle coat – which was too hot for the summer, clearly, but he had no other jacket, because all his clothes were with Gloria, in the flat – and his eyes popped, and his mind boggled: the sight of men in T-shirts with huge, pointless muscles, men who had obviously recently and consistently been to the gym, and to a hairdressing salon, and to shops that sold *new* clothes; and women too, who had obviously invested heavily in shoes, and bags and accessories; and people who had had their teeth capped, or *something*, something shiny to do with their teeth; and people who had been sleeping rough; people who looked like they had been sleeping around; people indeed of every proverbial creed and colour and race and nation. Israel felt like he was in a novel by Zadie Smith.

To steady himself he stepped for a moment inside Verdi's Stores, the Asian newsagent-cum-greengrocer's and he was faced not only with shiny red apples, but also with watermelons, and ethnic vegetables, and sacks of peas and beans, and harissa paste, and big tubs of feta cheese, and cans of olive oil, and the newspapers! Piles of newspapers in a dozen different languages. And the magazines! Every taste and impulse catered for. And cigarettes. *And* high-energy drinks. He stood staring around, in a daze, like an idiot. Mr Singh behind the counter, wearing his turban: the bright orange of the turban. And a man who came in, who was wearing a beret – an actual beret. And a woman, who looked Mexican, or Spanish. And '*Shalom!*' someone was saying. And '*Arrivederci!*' And '*Adios!*' and other stuff in languages he could not understand and did not even recognise – Hindi? Czech? Geordie? It was too much. He had to get some fresh air. He had to walk out.

And out on the street, at a bus stop, a group of black teenage girls were talking together, the sheer uninhibited noise of them, rising up out of them, bold as brass and twice as shiny, the sound of the city. One of the women was doubling back, laughing a laugh that seemed to come from deep down inside her, almost from underground, and which made its way up through vast echoing chambers, a booming laugh, like organ pipes with all the stops pulled out; this was a laugh of a kind that simply did not exist in Tumdrum; it was a laugh that could not arise there; it would have to have stayed underground; it would have remained a distant rumble, or a polite tune on a backroom harmonium. And then a car going past with its radio on, playing some kind of music – bhangra? Bhangra! The sheer noise of the traffic. Impossible to distinguish between all the noises, or make sense of the sights. Past the hairdresser's – all that grooming! – and the nail bar next door, with false nails like miniature pelts, or butterfly wings, displayed in the window. And the bookshop – the bookshop where he had first gone to buy *Just William* books as a boy, and then the Bellows, and the Malamuds, and the Philip Roths, and he could see his reflection in the window of this shop, a shop packed full of shiny, new, good-looking books, books that you might actually want to spend money on; *non-library* books; and he could see his face in the window, *his* shop window, his wide, long nose, and somewhere behind his glasses, that was him.

And he realised – or rather, half-realised; or he felt; he *intuited* – that it was as if he were observing all this for the first time, that he was enjoying it as someone who was not *of* it. He realised – half-realised – that he had exchanged his life in London for a life somewhere else, somewhere he did not belong, and so without meaning to, without even noticing it was happening, he had become doubly foreign: he had lost his place, and failed to find another. He was a stranger even unto himself; the streets were no longer his home; they were for him now merely a tableau, something for him to observe, and to consume, and all these people, all these people with marvellous teeth, and extraordinary hairstyles, and the men in their berets and turbans, and the women in their fastidiously short dresses and skirts, they weren't real to him any more. They were a show.

And he felt insulted, as though the place had tricked him, or let him down, had turned its back on him. And so he hurried on to meet his friends at the café.

Which was no longer there.

Grodzinski's, which had been a fixture on the street for goodness only knows how long, had disappeared completely and in its place was the inevitable brand spanking new Starbucks. The jumbly, intricate interior of the old Grodzinski's had been completely gutted and stripped, and made over into the soft-edged comfy veneers of corporate creams and browns. There were none of the old posters, no nooks and no crannies, no mirrors; Grodzinski's had been full of mirrors. You could sit over your coffee in Grodzinski's and watch your-self sit over your coffee in Grodzinski's, watching yourself sit over your coffee in Grodzinski's, ad infinitum. It was a flâneurs' paradise. Israel had grown up there.

But now – what was it now? What was it supposed to be? What did it mean? In Grodzinski's you could have imagined Carson McCullers, and Karl Kraus and Frank O'Hara sitting down and enjoying some strudel together, and espresso in pure white espresso cups, but here, now, in Starbucks, the best you could imagine was Elton John getting together with the man with ginger hair out of Simply Red for a sunrise muffin and a skimmed milk latte in a stupid fat mug with a logo.

The smell of Grodzinski's – the smell of long-seated men and women of all ages, people with strong opinions and good humour – had been replaced by the smell of young people, of deodorant, and frothed milk. When you entered Grodzinski's, Mr Grodzinski would catch your eye – Mr Grodzinski, the son of the original Mr Grodzinski – and indicate to you with a nod of his brilliantined head where he expected you to sit, which table, or which booth, and then someone in a white shirt and black trousers, male or female – and often it was difficult to tell the difference, because Mr Jacobs employed a lot of little, hunched, elderly, wrinkled Lithuanians: 'So many little Litvaks!' Israel's mother would complain – would bustle over to take your order.

Now you could sit anywhere, and serve yourself, but why would you bother? The place was absolutely sickening; the place was a joke. He was never going to taste Grodzinski's coffee again, coffee so strong and so sweet and so thick it was like Turkish coffee, only better, because it was Grodzinski's.

The boys were already there, drinking coffee from the big heavy mugs with the logos on them, foam clinging to their lips, Scylla and Charybdis.

'Israel Armstrong!' said Ben.

'The wanderer returns!' said Danny.

'Hi!' said Israel. 'Danny. Ben. How are things?' Danny attempted to engage Israel in an embarrassing high-five, fist-knocking kind of a thing, and Ben shook his hand.

'Good.'

'You're looking well, gentlemen,' said Israel.

'You too,' said Ben.

'So, that's the pleasantries over,' said Danny. 'Now, are you buying me a coffee or what?'

Israel bought a grande – *grande!?* – cappuccino for Danny and a double espresso for himself and by the time he returned to the table the boys were deep in typical conversation.

'You can't rank writers like that, it's ridiculous,' Ben was saying. 'Tell him, it's ridiculous.'

'What?'

'Of course you can,' said Danny. 'Who says you can't? Firsts to the Renaissance; 2:1s to the nineteenth century; and then that leaves the eighteenth with the 2:2s and the Thirds to everything pre-Shakespeare.'

'Beowulf and Chaucer?' said Ben.

'They're exceptions.'

'Post-1945?' said Ben.

'Borderline Thirds.'

'What do you think, Israel?' asked Ben. 'He's got this idea you can mark authors like he marks his students.'

'Ha. Right. Very good,' said Israel. 'Very funny.'

'Did you read the new Pynchon?' asked Danny, his face deep in muggy cappuccino.

'No, I must get round to that,' said Israel.

'A 2:2,' said Danny, face full of froth.

'Oh.'

'So, what have you been reading lately?' asked Ben.

'Erm.' Israel had mostly been reading large-print true-crime books. 'This and that.'

'You should really check out the Pynchon though,' said Danny. 'I mean, a 2:2's respectable these days.'

Israel pondered for a moment the chances of the new 2:2 Thomas Pynchon making it into the acquisitions list for the mobile library in Tumdrum.

'Or that new Cormac McCarthy,' said Ben. 'Devastating.'

'Devastating,' agreed Danny. '2:1.'

'Right.'

'I've just been rereading *Cien Anos de Soledad*.' Danny never read books; he only ever reread them.

'*One Hundred Years of Solitude*', glossed Ben.

'Really?' said Israel. Danny did not read Spanish, as far as Israel was aware, but with Danny it was absolutely *de rigueur* to refer to titles in their original, so it was always *A la Recherche du temps perdu*, please, and *Der Zauberberg*.

'It's for a course I'm teaching.'

'Oh, yeah? How's that going then?' He knew Danny through Gloria: they were old friends; their families were friends. Danny taught English at University College London, which was like teaching at Oxford or Cambridge, except much hipper. According to Danny.

'It's OK,' said Danny. 'What can I say? It's teaching. Every day's kind of the same, you know.'

'Groundhog Day!' said Ben.

'Yeah.'

'That is a great film,' said Israel.

'Punxsutawney Phil,'said Ben.

'Bill Murray,' said Israel. 'I love Bill Murray in that film.'

'Yeah.'

'And in *Lost in Translation*.'

'Yeah.'

'Basically, I love Bill Murray!' said Israel.

'Excuse me, ladies,' said Danny. 'Did your mother not teach you it was rude to interrupt when you'd asked someone a question?'

'Sorry,' said Israel.

'So, as I was saying, when you *asked* me. The teaching is fine, thank you very much.'

'Good.'

'It's kind of like working in a factory, only in a factory you get longer lunch-breaks and get to knock off at five, and the stuff on the production-line doesn't talk back.'

Danny talked like he was in a successful HBO returning series; he talked like he was on all the time; and as he heard him spiel Israel realised that in Tumdrum he had effectively switched himself off, possibly for ever. Danny was transmitting on a channel that Israel no longer received.

'Huh,' said Israel. 'You're enjoying it then?'

'It's fine.'

'How about you, Ben?' asked Israel. 'How's work?'

Ben was smart, really smart – smarter than Danny. He was just quieter, and like Israel he'd drifted, had never quite found his niche; he was nicheless. Which was maybe why Israel got on with him so well; they were similar; they were on the same wavelength. Ben did something in the Civil Service which did not require a suit. And he was on flexi-time.

'Work's the usual,' he said. 'You know what it's like. Sometimes you feel like you can't go on—'

'But you go on,' said Danny. 'Samuel Beckett.'

'He went to school at Portora,' said Israel. 'Did you know that?'

'What?'

'Portora? It's a school in Enniskillen.'

'Weird!' said Danny.

Israel was about to ask them what they thought he should do about the mobile library.

'So, anyway, I was going to ask –' he began.

'How is life in bonny Scotland?' said Danny.

'Ireland,' said Israel.

'Oh, right, sorry. I thought it was Scotland.'

'Me too,' said Ben.

'They're all the same, though, eh? Celtic fringe.'

'Where are you based, then, Dublin?' said Ben.

'No, it's in Northern Ireland.'

'So what's it like with all the bogtrotters then?' said Danny.

'They're not bogtrotters,' said Israel.

'Top of the morning to ye!' said Danny. 'Begorrah, begorrah, begorrah.'

'It's *Northern* Ireland,' said Israel.

'Hoots, man!'

'That's Scotland,' said Israel.

'Ulster Says No!'

'Well, you got there in the end.'

'They're all sorted over there now, aren't they?' said Danny.

'You could call it sorted,' said Israel.

'Why's it called Ulster?' said Ben. 'I always thought that was a funny name.'

'Ulster is actually one of the four ancient provinces of the whole of Ireland,' said Israel. 'Three of the counties of the historic Ulster are a part of the Republic and—'

'Oooh,' said Danny. 'Who's been boning up on his Irish history then?'

'It's actually part of British history.'

'He's gone over,' said Danny. 'He's one of them now.'

'I have not gone over. I'm just—'

'He has. Are you voting for Sinn Féin?'

'No, I am not voting for Sinn Féin.'

'Well, you bloody well should be,' said Danny. 'They're much better than the other lot, aren't they?'

'The Scottish National Party?' said Ben.

'It's Northern Ireland,' said Israel.

'Plenty of crack then?' said Danny. 'The old ceilidhs and—'

'Oh yes, plenty of crack', said Israel irritably. 'Loads of it. The whole place is coming down with crack.'

'All right,' said Danny. 'I was only asking. It was a joke.'

'Right.'

'When are you moving back then?' asked Danny.

'I don't know at the moment,' said Israel. 'Soon. But I just wanted to ask—'

Israel couldn't understand why they weren't exactly following what he was saying, and why they were talking to him like he wasn't actually there, but then he noticed: Danny had his right hand under the table; he was texting. And Ben was texting too. They weren't listening. And they weren't talking. They were neither here nor there. They were double-tasking.

'Sorry,' said Ben, looking up.

'When are you going to tell him your news then?' said Danny.

'My news?' said Ben.

'The news.'

'Oh, the news. Yeah. I'm getting married.'

'No!'

'Yes.'

'Congratulations. Let me shake your hand.' They shook hands. 'To Louise?'

'No,' said Danny. 'He dumped her, and he's marrying a call girl he met in a bar.'

'Yes,' said Ben wearily, 'to Lou. That was her on the—'

'That's great, mate; when's the big day?'

'October. You and Gloria will be invited, of course.'

'Super. Great.'

'And how is the fragrant Gloria?' asked Danny.

'She's fine,' said Israel.

'You're still . . .'

'Oh, yeah. Yeah.'

'You sure?' said Danny with a smirk.

'Difficult being apart?' said Ben.

'It's fucking impossible if you're apart!' said Danny.

'Ignore him,' said Ben.

'Yeah, it's—' began Israel.

'When the cat's away the mice will play, eh?' said Danny.

'Erm . . .'

'Only to be expected,' said Danny.

'He's just jealous,' said Ben.

'Ooh!' said Danny, checking his phone again. 'You'll perhaps excuse me if I leave you ladies to discuss your scintillating love lives while I get more coffee.'

'He's published his book you know,' said Ben, when Danny was out of earshot. Danny had talking about his book for years. Talking about it had in fact been all he'd done until now.

'Oh.' Danny was insufferable before – but now! Oh, God. 'What's it like?' said Israel.

'*Postmodern Allegories?*' said Ben.

'Is that what's it's called?'

'Yeah. With a question mark.'

'Oh, God.'

'He gave me a copy,' said Ben.

'He didn't send me a copy,' said Israel.

'You're lucky.'

'Why? What's it like?'

'It got great reviews,' said Ben. 'In the *TLS* someone called him a genius.'

'Oh, no,' said Israel, finishing off his espresso.

'I wouldn't say it was a book for the general reader.'

'Really?' Israel felt himself to be no longer the general but rather the common reader.

'Suffice it to say that the acknowledgements run to two pages, the first chapter is called the "H – brackets – Owl of Minerva" and it's all about Facebook and MySpace, and virtual worlds, and Philip K. Dick, and contemporary American fiction, and he constructs this sort of argument based on Lacan, and Slavoj Žižek, and he uses the word "meta-epistemic".'

'Wow.'

'In his first paragraph.'

'Wow.'

'Twice.'

'Shit,' said Israel.

'Precisely,' said Ben. 'But don't tell him I said so.'

And then, as quickly as he had emerged into conversation, Ben disappeared back into the privacy of texting. And Israel twiddled his thumbs. He had no one to text: Gloria was not replying.

Danny's book. Ben getting married . . .

'Anyway,' said Danny, returning. 'Here we all are again. We're like the fucking Inklings, aren't we, eh?'

Israel couldn't quite remember who the Inklings were: were they *a cappella*, or was that the Ink Spots?

'So what are you planning while you're over?'

'Well,' began Israel, 'I was . . .' He hesitated, fatally, for a moment, trying to decide how to explain his predicament, and Danny stepped straight into the breach, cappuccino pint aloft.

'You want to know what I'm planning? I'll tell you. I'm planning to get *laid*.'

'Well,' said Israel, 'that is a very noble ambition.'

'Thank you,' said Danny.

'Actually, boys,' said Ben, 'I've got to go here. I'm meeting Louise in John Lewis – we've got to sort out the wedding list.'

'Right,' said Israel. 'Actually, I just wanted to—'

Ben was already up out of his seat. 'The planning, honestly, it would drive you—'

'You've got to leave it to the ladies,' said Danny.

'I'll maybe catch up with you again before you go?' said Ben, more as a question than a promise.

'Sure, yeah,' said Israel. 'And congratulations again, on the wedding. Send my love to Louise.'

'Yeah.'

And then Ben turned his back and was gone, still texting.

Which left Israel with Danny. Maybe Danny could help him to work out what to do about the van. And about Gloria. Maybe Danny would understand.

'Are you putting on weight, or is it my imagination?' said Danny.

'Actually,' said Israel, feeling a headache coming on, 'I've got to get back too.'

'But I haven't told you about my book yet.'

'Yeah, sorry. Maybe next time.'

'OK,' said Danny, 'suit yourself.' It didn't seem to bother him in the slightest. He'd already switched from under-table phone to on-the-table BlackBerry.

'Bye then,' said Israel.

Danny was already deep into scanning his e-mails. 'Yeah,' he said, without looking up. 'Sure.'

Walking back home, Israel no longer observed the dramas unfolding around him. His head was down, and his heart, and he felt like shit, and indeed when he reached his street he noticed that the pavement outside his mother's house seemed to have been smothered in what he thought at first was green and white paint, Jackson Pollock-style, but which on closer inspection he realised was in fact pigeon shit, in a kind of Off-White and Heritage Green, the Heritage Green the green of drawing rooms in gentlemen's clubs and of old libraries and leather armchairs, and the Off-White a white somewhere between the white of fine china and the ash-blonde hair of beautiful women; and stepping around these colours and associations, and into the gutter, onto the sleeping policeman, inches from the oncoming traffic, and yards from his childhood home, only reminded Israel once again of the many lives he did not lead, and the friends he no longer had.

Frankly, he might as well have been rubbing his nose in it.

He texted Gloria.

No reply.

CHAPTER 13

'This is madness,' said Ted.

'This,' said Israel, fingers thrumming on the steering wheel, 'is "The Road to Hell".'

'What?'

'"The Road to Hell", Chris Rea? It's a song, isn't it, about the M25?'

'I've never heard of it,' said Ted.

'Of course you have! "*This ain't no . . . something something something*,"' sang Israel, uncertainly, in his best unfiltered-cigarettes-and-alcohol kind of voice, '"*This is the road to hell.*"'

'No, never heard of it,' said Ted, gazing out of the window. 'Doesn't sound like much of a song to me.'

'Well, it is.'

'Aye. Right. What do you call this road? The M5?'

'The *M25*,' said Israel. 'It's famous. Like Route 66.'

'Aye. Well, it might be famous where you come from, but I tell ye, word of it's not reached us boys in County Antrim.'

'I'll bet it was built by Irish navvies,' said Israel.

'Aye, and you'd know, would ye?'

'No, I'm just saying. A lot of roads in England were built by Irishmen, weren't they? They all lived in Kilburn?'

'Aye. And they all wore shamrocks in their hair and carried shillelaghs and played harps and rode in donkey carts.'

'No! Don't be silly, I didn't say that.'

'Ach, you and your blinkin' stereotypes.'

'Me?'

'Yes, you.'

'Me and *my* stereotypes? What about you and your homophobic—'

'I'm not getting into the whole homophonic thing again!' said Ted.

'Homo*phobic*,' corrected Israel.

'Aye. I've got nothing against 'em. And anyway you're the one always going on about poster modern identity—'

'*Post*modern, Ted. *Post*modern! God!'

'Aye, right. Well, He's of the same opinion as me.'

'Who?'

'The Good Lord.' Ted shook his head. 'Homophonic! And you think all the Irish do is sit around playing bodhráns and building your English roads?'

'No.'

'You racist English b—'

'Ted! I'm just saying, it's a fact. A lot of English roads *were* built by Irishmen.'

'Aye, well,' said Ted, looking out of the window

of the Mini at the solid traffic; the M25 was full; as far as Ted could tell, *England* was full. 'Fat lot of good it's done ye. Look at it. I don't know how you cope with all this.'

'Coffee, actually, mostly,' said Israel, taking a sip from his insulated vacuum cup, which he'd had the foresight to bring when they'd set off from his mum's in the Mini early that morning. 'Speaking of which, if it's all right with you, I thought, seeing as we're, you know, down this way, I might just pop in and see some of my old friends at work.'

Israel was determined to find someone left in England who might want to talk to him.

'Oh, no, no, no,' said Ted. 'We're not mucking around here, boy. We're going to get the van and go. Where is it, anyway, Ongger?'

'On*gar*,' said Israel. 'It's in Essex. I looked it up.'

'Sounds African to me,' said Ted. 'Anyway, it's the van we're after here, not a trip down memory lane. You can do that on your own time.'

'It's not a trip down . . . Lakeside is sort of on the way.'

'What is Lakeside?'

'It's the shopping mall place where I used to work in the bookshop. I've told you about it loads of times.'

'I don't think so,' said Ted.

'Yes, I have. The Bargain Bookstore? Where I used to work? I thought I might just pop in and say hello to people.'

'Waste of time,' said Ted.

'It's not a waste of time,' said Israel. 'It's . . . Something I'd like to do. You know, reconnect with people.'

'Ach,' said Ted. '*Reconnect!*'

'Yes. Meet up with some of my old colleagues. We had some great times there. Honestly.' Israel sighed, remembering when he had a life in England. 'There was once, right, when it was a Harry Potter night – I think it was *The Goblet of Fire* – and we were doing a late opening, and we'd all gone to the pub, and we did this prank call to our manager, Simon, pretending we were from the police? Saying that there'd been a riot in the shop! And someone had stolen our whole consignment of Potters! Oh, God, that was fun.'

Ted did not deign to comment.

'Just ten minutes'll do it,' pleaded Israel. 'Pop in, say hello, we'll be back on the road again before you know it.'

'It's a bad idea,' said Ted.

'Well, I'm driving,' said Israel.

'In a manner of speaking,' said Ted.

'So I'm taking an executive decision,' said Israel.

'Ha!' said Ted.

Israel indicated left.

The road off the M25 and into Lakeside was like a merry-go-round, traffic being sucked in and down into a vast, empty, busy place that wasn't really a place at all.

'Now *this* is like hell,' said Ted, as Israel parked the car in a car park that stretched for miles.

'*This* is Lakeside,' said Israel.

Hundreds of people were flooding towards the main building.

'Where are they all going?'

'They're going shopping,' said Israel.

'On a nice day like today?'

'Of course. Come on.'

'It's like they're hypnotised,' said Ted, as people trailed past them towards the main mall.

'I suppose it is, yes,' said Israel. 'Hypnotised by consumerism.'

'Aye. All right, Siglund Freud. Let's just get you down memory lane and then get out of here. Muhammad, guard the car!'

'It's *Sig*mund,' said Israel. 'And you,' he said to the dog, 'don't shit all over the seats.'

Inside the shopping mall there were all the usual shops, spread out as far as the eye could see.

'An Argos!' said Ted. 'Look. There's not much you can't get out of Argos, I tell you.'

'What?'

'Argos. Great wee shop. We have one in Rathkeltair. There's one here as well. I didn't realise it was all over.'

'Ted, Argos is like a huge national chain of shops.'

'Is it?' said Ted. 'I thought it was just a local.'

'No. No. It's—'

'Look! And a Clinton Cards,' said Ted. 'There's one of these in Ballymena. They're bringing all our shops over here.'

'Yeah, and in England we have Starbucks as well. And Hoovers. And Ford motor cars?' said Israel.

'Woolworths,' said Ted. 'This place has got everything.'

'Anyway . . .' said Israel. 'Moving on.'

They went up an escalator, passed something that was meant to be a sculpture, and then they were outside the Bargain Bookstore.

'Oh,' said Israel.

The Bargain Bookstore was now called the Book Worm, the shiny new plastic shop fascia showing a huge fat yellow cartoon worm wearing a bib, with a knife and fork in its hands, tucking into a plateful of books, and winking suggestively. The name might have changed but the window display looked pretty much the same as it had when Israel had worked there, showing discounted autobiographies and biographies by footballers, and models and sportsmen, and huge, useless cookbooks.

'This is it?' said Ted.

'Yes,' said Israel. 'They've changed the name.'

'The Book Worm?' said Ted. 'Appealin'.'

'Well. Anyway. This is it. The old firm.'

'You made it sound like the British blinkin' Library,' said Ted. 'There's a shop like this in Coleraine.'

'No, no. Similar maybe,' said Israel. 'But not the same. This was a special place to work. Honestly. A lot of very interesting people work here.'

'Aye,' said Ted. 'I'm sure.'

'No, really. Great camaraderie. Each year we used to go on a day trip to Alton Towers.'

'Sounds amazing,' said Ted. 'Whatever Alton Towers is.'

'It's a theme park,' said Israel. 'Where they have this great water—'

'Let's hurry up then, shall we?' said Ted, striding into the shop. 'I'd like to get the van back this year, if possible.'

Inside the shop, Israel approached a woman who was wearing a shapeless red T-shirt with the words, 'The Book Worm!' emblazoned across her chest, the hungry worm on her back. She was unpacking a box of books.

'Hi!' said Israel. 'You're new here.'

'No,' said the woman.

'Newish?' said Israel.

'Can I help you?'

'Yeah. It's just, I used to work here myself, and I wondered if Simon was around.'

'Who?'

'Simon. The manager?'

'No. It's Justin who's the manager.'

'Right. Erm. Is Justin around then?'

'Yeah. Justin!' the woman shouted over a shelf. 'Justin!'

'What?' came a call back.

'Bloke here looking for a job.'

A Book Worm-T-shirted fat man with designer glasses emerged from behind some shelves.

'Yeah?' he said.

'Hi!' said Israel. 'I'm—'

'We're not taking anybody on at the moment,' said Justin. 'You need to write to head office for an application form. They'll keep it on file.'

'Erm. Sorry. I wasn't looking for a job. I *used* to work here. I was just looking for Simon.'

'Simon left six months ago,' said Justin, in a monotone.

'Oh, right. Did he?'

'Yeah. Sold his children's book for half a million pounds.'

'Did he?'

'Yeah.'

'Wow. Right. Gosh. The one about the forgotten world of dinosaurs underneath Lakeside, which is discovered by children who then embark on a magical journey of self-discovery?'

'Yeah, that one.'

'Wow. I never thought he'd . . . I mean, I knew, of course, he was . . . What about Amy?'

'Don't know any Amys.'

'Charlie?'

'Nope.'

'I see. What about Dwayne?'

'Bloke from Tottenham?'

'Yeah, that's right.'

'No, he's gone as well.'

'Oh, well, I'll—'

'Sorry. I've got a customer.'

'Right. Sure. Well. Say hello to Simon if you . . .'

Justin was already at the tills, ringing through a full-colour giant-size Diet Pasta cookbook.

Ted and Israel left the shop.

'Well,' said Ted. 'They certainly welcomed you back with open arms.'

Israel was silent.

'What was it you said to me the other day?' said Ted. 'Something about having to "embrace change" and try to move forward? Hoist by your petard and left danglin' by your—'

'Ted?'

'What?'

'Shut up.'

They drove for a long time in silence round the M25, and then onto the M11, deep into Essex.

'So,' said Ted, unable to restrain himself. 'Still planning to resign and move back here and pick up your old job at the shop again? Hook up with all your auld mates?'

'I'm not talking about it,' said Israel.

'Embrace change and try to move forward!' said Ted, chuckling. 'Isn't it? That's your advice.'

'I said I'm not talking about it.'

'All right,' said Ted. 'I'm only keepin' you goin'. Where are we now?'

'Harlow,' said Israel.

'Harlow!' said Ted, laughing.

'Yes, Harlow,' said Israel, unamused. 'What's funny about Harlow?'

'Harlow!' said Ted again. 'What sort of a name for a place is that?'

'Harlow? What's wrong with Harlow?'

'Harlow!' said Ted. 'Oh, hello, *Har*-low,' he said, in a Leslie Phillips kind of a voice. '*Hell-o, Harlow!* Named after the platinum blonde?'

'Sorry?'

'Jean Harlow? The actress.'

'I don't think so. Although my knowledge of the origin of Essex place names is not exactly—'

And then they picked up the first signs for Ongar.

'Look! Look!' said Ted. 'There we are! Ongaa! Ooga-booga-Ongaa.'

'*Ong*ar,' said Israel. 'It's just called *Ong*ar.'

'*On* guard!' said Ted. 'On guard!'

'All right, Ted, knock it off, will you.'

'Stupit English names.'

'I have trouble with Irish place names,' said Israel.

'Northern Irish,' said Ted.

'Yeah, whatever,' said Israel. 'Ballythis and Ballythat.'

'At least we don't have places called – what's that?' He pointed to another sign.

'Chelmsford.'

'*Chelms*-ford,' said Ted, sounding like Noêl Coward. '*Charmed* to meet you, *Chelms* Ford.'

When eventually they arrived in Ongar, which seemed to be several places under one name – '*Chipping* Ongar!' roared Ted, '*High* Ongar! Oh, Holy God! You English!' – Israel got out and asked at a petrol station if they knew where the travellers might be.

'Crusties?' said the man behind the counter.

'Erm, possibly,' said Israel.

'Bloody everywhere. There's some of them out by Willingale, up past Fyfield there,' said the man.

'Willingale?' said Israel.

'That's it,' said the man. 'Little village, just.'

They drove on, past huge old houses with high brick walls built up all around them, and fields, and barns, and honeysuckle-covered cottages.

'Quite bucolic round here, isn't it?' said Israel. 'Not like I thought it would be.'

'Bit like North Antrim,' said Ted.

'A *bit*,' said Israel.

'Except not as nice,' said Ted. 'We nearly there?'

'Yeah,' said Israel. 'We've just got to look out for some sort of, I don't know, encampment sort of thing, I suppose.'

'Gypsy wagons and that,' said Ted.

'I don't think it'll be gypsy wagons *as such*,' said Israel.

'The big old wooden wheels and the wee stove, and the jangling horse brass.'

'What d'you know about travellers exactly, Ted?'

'Gypsies?'

'I don't think they're the same as gypsies, no. These are more like . . . travellers, according to the second-hand-car bloke.'

'Well, he was a . . . Gypsies, I'm looking for.'

'I don't know if you're actually *allowed* to say gypsies these days, Ted.'

'Why not?'

246

'Because, it's not . . . you know. They're all called travellers now, I think.'

'I call them gypsies.'

'Well, a gypsy is . . .'

'I know what a gypsy is,' said Ted. 'Sean's a gypsy.'

'Who?'

'In Tumdrum. Drinks in the First and Last.'

'Oh, him, right, yes. You wouldn't call him a gypsy, though, would you?'

'No. I'd call him a tinker.'

'I don't think we call them tinkers these days either, Ted.'

'Lot of nonsense,' said Ted.

Willingale came and went, and they searched the horizon, looking out for signs of an encampment.

Then, 'Smoke!' called Ted suddenly, as they passed a little wooded area. 'Pull over! Pull over!'

Israel pulled the car drastically over to the verge.

'Where?' said Israel.

'Two o'clock!' said Ted, jumping out of the car.

'Hold on! Where?' said Israel, following him.

'There!' Ted pointed out a thin wisp of smoke.

'I can't see anything.'

'There! Up yonder, past them big oak trees.'

'Is that smoke?'

'Of course it's smoke.'

'Do you think that's them?' said Israel, who was starting to feel a little nervous.

'Gypsies love a fire.'

'They're not gypsies, Ted.'

'I reckon that's them all right.'

'Really? D'you think?'

'Only one way to find out,' said Ted, who was already bounding up the lane towards the smoke. 'Bloody thieving gypsies!'

The encampment was shaded by oak trees. There were about a dozen vehicles – buses, coaches, caravans – parked in a sort of horseshoe arrangement around a large fire. Everywhere on the ground there were tarpaulins, and paint pots, and scraps of wood, and engine parts, and despite the mess it all felt curiously prosperous and festive. There was washing strung up between trees, children running around.

'And lots of dogs,' Israel whispered, mostly to himself.

'Can I help you?'

'Aaaghh!' Israel gave a little yelp and twisted round in shock. There was a man standing directly behind him. He had a long plaited beard, multiple face-piercings, and was dressed in a black vest, black combat trousers, and wore no shoes.

'Ah! God, you gave me a fright.'

'Are you OK?' said the man.

'Yes, thanks, I'm . . . fine. Thank you. Just a bit of a . . .'

'You're lost?' The man had a warm, welcoming voice, curiously at odds with his fierce bepierced appearance.

'Yes, no, thanks. Erm. We're just looking for . . . are you the travellers?'

'Who are you?'

'Well, sorry, yes, very impolite of me. I'm Israel,' said Israel, putting out his hand to shake.

The man touched his forehead and bowed towards Israel.

'Peace, Israel.'

'Yes. Right. Peace, absolutely. And you're . . ?'

'You can call me Rabbit.'

'Rabbit?' said Israel. 'OK. Right, Rabbit; what, as in the John Updike novels?'

'No,' said Rabbit.

'Right. Yes. I read, erm, *Watership Down*, actually, long time ago now, but . . .'

Israel always talked nonsense when he was nervous.

And not only when he was nervous.

Other men and women had now appeared from the encampment and come to stand alongside Rabbit.

'This is Israel,' said Rabbit. 'And Israel, this is Bingo, and Bev, and Boris, and Scarlet.'

'Hi,' said Israel.

'Peace,' they said. 'Peace.' 'Peace.' 'Peace.'

'Right. Yes. Same to you.'

'Hello?' Another woman came walking towards them; she was taller than the others, distinguished-looking, with a Pre-Raphaelite, flute-playing sort of look about her. She had long, jet-black hair swept back from her face, with a flash of grey at her temples. She wore tiny gold earrings, and no make-up, and a long bright red skirt and an emerald green shift; she looked as though she might recently have been modelling for John Everett Millais, or a Scandinavian shampoo advertisement.

'This is Bree,' said Rabbit.

'Named after the cheese?' said Israel nervously.

'No,' said Bree. 'Named after the Fire Goddess, Bridgit.'

'Oh. Yes. Of course.'

'Also known as Brizo of Delos, the Manx Breeshey and Britomartis.'

'Gosh. Yes. That's . . .'

'And that's Spirit,' said Rabbit, referring to the large white dog that accompanied Bree and which was now licking Israel's left hand.

'Ah! Right. Hello, Spirit.' Israel lifted his hand away. Spirit leaped up towards him. Israel put his hand back down. 'Good dog! Good dog! Good dog!'

'Are you here to see us?' asked Bree.

'Actually, to be honest, I'm not – ahem – entirely sure,' said Israel. 'You see, we're two librarians. And our . . .'

He looked round, and realised that Ted had wandered off.

'Ted!'

He looked towards the encampment. There, by the little old camper vans, and the big old converted public service disability vehicles, Ted was standing in front of a brightly painted van.

'Ted?'

Ted did not reply.

'Sorry,' said Israel, addressing his new friends. 'That's my friend Ted.' He walked over towards him, followed by the travellers. 'Ted, are you all right?'

'The van,' said Ted, mesmerised, nodding at the vehicle before him.

'What?'

'The van.'

'What about the van?'

'It's our van.'

Israel glanced at the vehicle. 'It's not our van, Ted. Come on, these people, we need to—'

'It's the van.'

'Ted, it's not the van. It's doesn't look anything like the van.'

'I know my van, and *that* is my van.' He pointed at it.

Israel went up and peered through the windscreen.

The shelves inside were still intact. The skylight. The little issues desk.

It was the mobile library.

Fitted out with a sofa, and some rugs, and knick-knacks on the shelves.

'Oh, my, God!' said Israel. He walked slowly around the whole van, following Ted. 'Oh, my, God.'

Over the cab, where it used it read 'The Mobile Library' there was now a brightly painted eye, which made the vehicle look like it had just woken up. Above the eye, were painted the words 'The Odyssey'. Down the side of the van were painted the words 'The Warehouse of Divine Jewels'. Along the side, the lovely red and cream livery had been replaced with images of children playing. On the back, where it used to say 'The Book Stops Here' were painted the words 'Follow Us Towards Enlightenment', with a rainbow painted above it.

They wandered around again, astonished, to the front.

'My van,' said Ted. 'Look what they've done to my van!'

'Well, it's . . . It's certainly quite colourful, isn't it? I quite like it actually,' said Israel. 'It's rather well done. Is that a Cyclops eye on the front there?'

'It's the Eye of Horus.'

'Is it?'

'Yes. Horus was the Egyptian sky god.'

'Uh-huh.'

Israel turned to face the speaker, who had joined the crowd that had gathered around them. The man wore a bright red sarong and was bare-footed, and bare-chested, and tattooed up across his muscular arms, and he had his hair in dreadlocks, like fat hanks of wool, and silver bangles around his wrists.

'And you are?' said Israel, clearing his throat, just about managing not to say, 'Have you ever seen that Mel Gibson film, *Apocalypto*?'

'I'm Stones,' said the man.

'Sorry?' said Israel.

'Stones.'

'Right. Named after the Rolling Stones, eh?' ventured Israel.

'Named *at* Stonehenge. And you are?'

'Israel.'

'Named after the fascist state oppressing the Palestinian people?' said Stones.

'Erm . . .' said Israel.

'And you're the feckin' arse responsible for this . . . abomberation?' said Ted, coming over and squaring up to Stones.

'Abomination?' said Stones. 'I cannot claim responsibility for that, no. It's been a joint project.'

Ted and Stones eyed each other up and down, the small crowd watching them intently: the children with long hair, the men with shaven heads, the women wearing headscarves. And the dogs.

Stones was not quite as tall as Ted, but he was definitely younger, and fitter, and he had the clear advantage of popular support; Israel wouldn't have liked to have bet on Ted coming out on top in a fight under those particular circumstances. This, however, didn't seem to have occurred to Ted.

'Well, you tell me which one of yous dirty scroungers painted my van and I'll feckin—'

'Did you hear him, children?' said Stones, appealing to the crowd. 'Who painted the van?'

A dozen long-haired children put up their hands.

'I'll—' continued Ted.

'The children did it?' said Israel.

'Under supervision,' said Stones.

'D'you like it?' said Bree. 'We only finished it yesterday.'

'It's . . . Well, it's very colourful. It's just. It's our van, actually,' said Israel.

'*Your* van?' said Stones, chuckling to himself. 'It's our van, *actually*. We bought it only recently, and perfectly legally.'

'You bought it?'

'That's right.'

'From Barry Britton at Britton's Second Hand Van Sales, Lease and Hire, by Wandsworth Bridge?' said Israel.

Stones did not reply.

'Well, we'll take that as yes then, shall we?' said Ted.

'Mr Britton has helped us source many of our vehicles.'

'Source?' said Ted. 'Source? Stolen, more like. You bloody—'

'That is something you'll have to take up with Mr Britton, I'm afraid.'

Ted was still staring at Stones. And Stones was staring back. Stalemate.

'Erm, look,' said Israel, appealing to Stones. 'We need the van,' he said soothingly. 'You see, we're going to the Mobile Meet, which is a big mobile library convention sort of thing, and—'

'No,' said Stones. 'Sorry. I don't wish to appear cynical, obviously, but your arriving here unannounced and claiming that this vehicle once belonged to you is hardly proof of either current or past ownership, is it? And you expect us to just hand it over? You could be anybody.'

'We're librarians,' explained Israel. 'We're over from Ireland.'

'You don't sound Irish.'

'No. No. No, God, I'm not Irish. I'm from London. He's from Ireland.'

'Northern Ireland,' said Ted.

'Ah!' said Bree, as if this explained something.

'Well, clearly there has been some sort of a misunderstanding,' said Stones. 'But I'm sure we can resolve it.'

'I'll show you how we're going to resolve it!' said Ted, squaring up to Stones.

'Yes,' said Israel, tugging urgently at Ted's sleeve. 'I'm sure we can resolve this. Amicably.' 'Leave it to me,' he whispered to Ted.

'What?'

'The old ba-flum. I can handle this one.' He smiled at Bree and Stones. 'Perhaps we could, er, discuss the misunderstanding somewhere privately?'

Bree looked at Stones, who nodded.

'That's a good idea,' said Bree. 'Come,' she said, ushering Israel and Ted through the crowd and towards another brightly painted vehicle – 'Phun! Phun! Phun!' it announced in splashy lettering across the front – that might once have been a horsebox.

Inside the horsebox there was a little miniature wood-burning stove, and a wooden bed, rugs, cushions and wooden shelves fixed to the wall. Wind chimes and pieces of glass on string hung down from the ceiling.

Israel, Ted, Stones and Bree sat down cosily on the floor.

'Can we offer you some tea perhaps?' said Bree.

'I'm not drinking your tea,' said Ted.

'Coffee?' said Israel.

'We don't drink coffee,' said Bree.

'Right. Well. Tea would be lovely, thank you.'

'Nettle?' said Bree.

'Tea?' said Israel.

'Yes,' said Bree.

'Mmm,' said Israel, wishing he'd said no. 'Lovely. Yes.'

'I thought that was for women's problems,' said Ted.

'Sshh,' said Israel. 'So,' he said, trying to think of a friendly way into the discussion. 'Are you actual New Age travellers then?'

'Ha! Some people would call us that, I suppose,' said Stones.

'We call ourselves the Folk Devils,' said Bree, busying herself with a pot on the stove.

'Oh, really? Do you, you know, play music?'

'Yes,' said Bree.

'But we call ourselves the Folk Devils because that's how people regard us,' said Stones. 'As outcasts, or scapegoats.'

'Right,' said Israel. 'I've always wondered, actually, what you lot believe in?'

'Us lot?' said Stones. 'What do you mean, us lot?'

'You . . . sort of . . . people.'

'We're not a cult,' said Stones.

'We're more like an alliance,' said Bree.

'Yeah. That's right. There is no 'us lot'. Just among us here we've got pagans, and druids, and Crowleyites, witches,' said Stones. 'Personally, I believe in Jesus, and Buddha, and Karl Marx, and the Earth Goddess.'

'Aye, right, and what about Mother Teresa, and Bono then?' muttered Ted.

'You believe in all of them?' asked Israel.

'Yes.'

'At once?'

'Yeah. If God, as the Christians would have us believe, is great, then surely She is too big to be contained by any Church?'

'She?' said Ted. 'Hold on!'

'We don't really believe in God in the way you think,' explained Bree. 'Cosmic-energy is what we believe in.'

'Uh-huh,' said Israel.

'We are all daughters and sons of the Sun, and offspring of Mother Earth.'

'Speaking personally, like, I'm the son of a Ted Carson, of Cullybackey, and offspring of Margaret McAuley, from the Shankhill Road.'

'I'm talking about spiritual offspring,' said Bree. 'Obviously. Tea?'

Bree offered Israel a jam jar of what seemed to be warm, murky-looking water.

'Mmm. Great. Thanks.'

He took a sip. It tasted like the brewed floor-scrapings of a health food shop.

'And what do you believe in, Israel?' asked Stones.

'Erm. Good question,' said Israel. He coughed. 'A . . . Higher Being?' Hoping this was the right answer. It wasn't.

'Your Hebrew God is a lie,' said Stones.

'Right. Yes. Uh-huh. Well, I say I believe in a Higher Being—'

'And a lie, when repeated and repeated eventually comes to appear as the truth.'

'Yes, well. Anyway. I would love to talk theology all day with you, but—'

'Money, then?' asked Stones.

'Sorry?' said Israel.

'You believe in money, presumably?'

'Well, no, not exactly,' said Israel.

'Money's not a religion,' said Ted.

'Money,' continued Stones, '*is* a religion. People worship money. And yet in reality there is no such thing as money: money is a fiction; it's a symbol.'

'Ach!' said Ted. He fished into his pocket and produced a pound coin. 'What do you call this then?'

'I call it a curse,' said Stones.

'Aye, right. Well, I call it a blessing,' said Ted.

'That's perhaps where we differ,' said Stones.

'Anyway,' said Israel, desperate to avoid a confrontation. 'How did you sort of . . . end up, doing . . . this sort of thing?'

'Bree was with the Dongas,' explained Stones.

'The whatters?' said Ted.

258

'The Dongas. Road protests? Reclaim the Streets?'

'Oh, right.'

'We met in Seattle, 1999,' said Bree.

'Oh? I've got a friend from school who went to work for Microsoft actually,' said Israel. 'In Seattle.'

'We were at the G8 protest,' said Bree.

'Ah, yes, of course.'

'Bunch of Luddites,' said Ted.

'The modern world is a psychological and spiritual wasteland, Ted,' said Stones.

'Is it now?' said Ted.

'And you've never even lived in Northern Ireland!' said Israel.

'People want to reconnect with the Earth Mother,' said Bree. 'Israel, I sense that you are terrified of the Great Mother.'

'Am I?' said Israel, trying not to sip his tea. 'I mean, my own mother certainly, I—'

'I sense that you've closed yourself off to the creative goddess.'

'Right. Well, possibly, yes, I—'

'Shekinah.'

'Sorry?'

'Gaia, Mother Earth. Whatever you want to call her, that's her. You're denying her force in your life. You've closed yourself off to the cosmic part of the human psyche.'

'Have I?'

'Yes, you have.'

'Ach, Jesus,' said Ted.

'Sshh,' said Israel.

'Ach, come on,' said Ted. 'I have never heard such a lot of crap. I don't know how you can believe any of that stuff at all. It's like astrology. It's a lot of—'

'You believe in the sun and the moon, don't you, Ted?' asked Bree, with an ironic smile.

'Yes, of course.'

'Well, astrology is simply the study of the vibrations sent forth by the sun and the moon and their effect on our psychological make-up.'

'I don't believe in astrology.'

'You're Scorpio, right?'

Ted blinked. 'How did you know that? Did someone tell you that? Did he just tell you that?'

Israel shrugged.

'No!' Bree laughed. She had a phlegmy sort of laugh, which was quite sexy, actually, Israel found, but also suggested that she could have done with sleeping somewhere with cavity-wall insulation and central heating. She reminded him of Gloria. 'It's just,' she continued. 'You're temperamental. You have a tendency to the . . .' She was teasing him now. 'Tyrannous. Tell me, do you suffer from ulcers, Ted?'

Ted had been taking medication for ulcers on and off for years.

'How did you . . .?' said Ted.

Bree smiled serenely. 'I can do you a birth chart, if you'd like,' she said.

'I don't think so,' said Ted.

'Ha, Ted!' said Israel. 'She got you!'

'And what about you, Israel?' said Bree.

'Me? Sorry?' said Israel.

'I'd say you were probably . . .' Bree eyed him up and down. 'Sagittarius.'

'How did you . . .?'

'Long nose. Full lips.'

'He's Jewish, you know,' said Ted.

'Oh,' said Bree. 'Well, you of all people should understand our predicament here.'

'Well,' said Israel. 'I don't know if . . .'

'The travellers are the Jews of England,' said Stones.

'Erm. Well. Aren't the *Jews* the Jews of England?' said Israel.

'Stones often speaks metaphorically,' said Bree.

'Stones often speaks bullshit,' muttered Ted.

'When one of the trilithons went missing back in the eighteenth century, they blamed the gypsies,' continued Bree.

'We've been hunted down like dogs for centuries,' said Stones. 'My own parents were involved in the Windsor Great Park festivals, you know?'

'Erm. No, sorry.'

'My father was one of the Global Village Trucking Company. I was taken away from my family when I was only three years old, in 1984, after the Battle of the Beanfield. Taken to a children's home. It took them a year to get me back.'

'Really?' said Israel. 'God, that's—'

'All very interesting, I'm sure,' said Ted. 'But all I want is our van back.'

'Ah, yes, of course,' said Stones. 'You're very focused on the present, Ted.'

'Aye, that'd be about right.'

'We try to cultivate an eternal perspective.'

'Fine,' said Ted. 'You go ahead and crultivate your pspectre, and give me the van back. It's ours.'

'So you can. But as you can perhaps tell, we're not that interested in material possessions. My real interest is in English antiquarianism.'

'Antiques?' said Ted.

'The sacred sites of England. Avebury,' said Stones.

'Stonehenge?' said Israel.

'Yes,' said Stones. 'And we follow the ritual year and the festivals – Imbolc, Beltane, Lughnasa, Samhain.'

'The van?' said Ted.

'I sense you want to talk about the van,' said Bree.

They talked about the van for the best part of an hour, and in the end it was agreed that Ted and Israel would return the following day with any documents and evidence of their legal possession of the van and that Stones and Bree would then accompany them to Barry Britton's in the van to resolve the problem.

'Well,' said Israel, as they drove back to London. 'They seemed very nice.'

'Bunch of flippin' hairy fairies.'

'You can't say that.'

'I can say what I like,' said Ted. 'Bunch of work-shy, drug-using poke-shakings.'

'What?'

'I said—'

'I didn't see any drugs, as such,' said Israel.

'Aye, you could tell, but, the look of them.'

'And it looked quite hard work to me, actually,' said Israel. 'Collecting the firewood, and the cooking, looking after all those children.'

'They'd all a wee tinker tan.'

'A what?'

'A tinker tan. Dirty, like animals, so they were, the weans.'

'I didn't think they were that bad.'

'Like little Arabs, the lot of them.'

'Ted!'

'I'm only saying!'

'Well, don't! You make yourself sound bad.'

'And they were all dressed funny,' said Ted. 'The big fella there had a wee kiltie sort of thing on.'

'That's all right,' said Israel.

'Aye, it would be all right with you. He was full of the smell o' himself. And I didn't trust the big woman.'

'Bree?'

'Aye.'

'I rather liked her. She was very accurate in her astrological readings.'

'Ach, not at all! She was away with the fairies. I wouldn't trust her with one half of a bad potato. And the whole place stinks a' addle,' said Ted.

'Addle?'

'Aye.'

'Is?'

'U-rine, ye eejit.'

'No, I think it was patchouli oil or something.'

'Disgusting,' said Ted.

'I quite liked the smell,' said Israel.

'Aye, ye would.'

'I thought it was an idyllic sort of set-up actually. I wouldn't mind doing something like that myself. Get away from it all, life on the road . . .'

'Aye. Bunch a ill-set good-for-nothings, so they are. They're on the pig's back, the lot of them.'

'The—'

'Pig's back, that's right. And they've stolen our van, remember. Bunch o' bandits . . .'

'Well, they haven't actually stolen it, have they, it was more, you know . . .'

'What?'

'They were sold it under false pretences.'

'Aye. From the fella selling stolen vehicles. Caveat emperor,' said Ted.

'*Caveat emptor*, I think you mean,' said Israel. 'Anyway, this time tomorrow we should have it all sorted.'

'Never trust a hippy,' said Ted.

'They're fine, Ted.'

'Not as long as they've got my van they're not.'

'Well,' said Israel. 'They're clearly not going anywhere with the van at the moment, are they? Let's not panic, eh.'

CHAPTER 14

When Israel and Ted arrived back at the site the following day the travellers had gone – disappeared, vamooshed, packed up, beat a retreat and headed for the hills. The only evidence that they'd ever been there were a few black patches of bare earth where their fires had been, and some big rug-flattened patches of grass. Everything else was gone: no litter, no mess, no trace.

'Bloody gypsies!' roared Ted, as he stomped around the clearing, like a bear without his honey. 'Bloody lying gypsies! I told you! I said we should never have trusted those bloody gypsies. Ach!'

'Is this the right place?' said Israel, looking around. 'It looks different, without the—'

'Of course this is the right place!' said Ted. 'They've scarpered, the blinkin' gypsy—'

'Travellers,' said Israel. 'They're travellers, Ted. And at least they've left the place nice and—'

'When I get hold of them they'll feel—'

'Take only photographs, leave only—'

'My boot up the arse,' said Ted.

'Yeah. Fine,' said Israel. 'So now what?'

'I don't know,' said Ted. 'I just don't know. Ach! I can't believe this. We should never have come to England in the first place. The whole country's a f—'

'Yes, all right. I've heard it before, Ted. You're getting as bad as me on Northern Ireland. We just need to think logically and work this out. Maybe we should hunt for clues, should we?'

'Aye, Tonto,' said Ted, with a wave of his hand. 'That's right. You hunt away there.'

'Well. I just thought. You know. When we were in the Scouts we used to do this thing where we had to follow people's tracks.' Israel knelt down and began sniffing the ground. 'It had something to do with animal spoors, and and . . . bent twigs, and . . .'

'Holy God,' said Ted.

'What?'

'I tell you what. I've got a much better idea, Kemo Sabe.'

'Really?'

'Aye, you get off of your knees, and ring your mother.'

'Why?'

'Because she'll have a better idea of what to do than you, you eejit. Sniffing the ground, for goodness sake! God give me strength! I'm away here for a smoke.'

'I thought you were giving up?' said Israel, getting up off his knees.

'Until I came to England I was giving up. You,

and the . . . gypsies . . . and the homolosexuals . . . This whole flippin' country's gonna have me away to Purdysburn, d'ye know that?'

While Ted paced up and down and smoked in a furious, you'll-have-me-away-to-Purdysburn sort of a manner, Israel rang his mother on his mobile. She was preparing for a mobile library fundraising coffee morning back at the house.

'It's the Ladies' Guild,' she said, 'they'll be here in five minutes! What is it now?'

Israel explained that the trail had gone cold, and that they were standing in a field in the middle of Essex, and they had no idea what to do next.

'Ah, dear, that's not good,' said Israel's mother.

'Any ideas?' said Israel.

'Can you get back for lunchtime?'

'I don't know. Why?'

'You might find it easier to think if you've had something to eat. And you could maybe brief the ladies on the latest developments in the case.'

'No, Mother! We can get a sandwich or something. We just need to—'

'Get other people involved, no?' said Israel's mother. Israel could hear her gesticulating. 'That's what we need to do at this stage. It's completely ridiculous! We should ring the police.'

'Ted doesn't want the police involved,' said Israel, lowering his voice. Ted was glowering with his cigarette.

'Well, he's not going to have much of a choice now, is he? Israel, put him onto me. I'll talk to him.'

'No. I'll deal with him,' said Israel.

'I like talking to him,' said Israel's mother.

'Yes. I know. That's why I'm going to deal with him.'

'And what is that supposed to mean?'

'Nothing.'

'Well, anyway, look, I'll ring Deborah, and see what she and Ari are doing tonight; we can meet with them. He's very clever.'

'I'm clever,' protested Israel.

'I didn't say you weren't!' said Israel's mother. 'Don't be so sensitive. I just mean Ari's professionally clever.'

'What, and I'm an amateur?'

'He'll have lots of ideas.'

'No, Mother! Don't get him involved!'

'Hold on. Just let me check the calendar here, let me see how we're fixed for tonight.'

'Mother, no!'

'Here we are.' Israel could hear her peering at the calendar. 'Oh, look. It's your Uncle Bernard's birthday tomorrow.'

'Who?'

'In Montreal? He was married to the woman who was divorced, from Hendon? I must give him a ring. I always forget, but it's same every year. Summer solstice. And National Aboriginal Day in Canada.'

'Mother! Mother! Hold on! That's it!' said Israel.

'What's it?'

'They follow the ritual year.'

'Who do? Your Uncle Bernard and the divorcee from Hendon? No. They're Reform, I think.'

'No, not them,' said Israel.

'The Aboriginals?'

'No!' said Israel. 'They must have gone to Stonehenge.'

'Who? Stonehenge? What are you talking about? Hold on, there's someone at the door, Israel.'

'Fine. OK, Mum. Look. Got to go. Bye.'

'She have any ideas?' said Ted, finishing his cigarette and grinding out the stub.

'Don't leave any litter,' said Israel.

'It's not litter!' said Ted. 'It's a cigarette butt, but.'

'That's litter,' said Israel.

'Anyway?' said Ted.

'They're at Stonehenge.'

'And where's that when it's at home?'

'It's down in Wiltshire,' said Israel.

'And ye're sure they're there?' said Ted.

'No,' said Israel. 'But it was in Mother's calendar.'

'Stonehenge?'

'Yes. It's the summer solstice, and you remember the travellers saying they followed the ritual year?'

'No.'

'Well, they did. So, I'm guessing they're going to be at Stonehenge for the solstice.'

'What, like druids?'

'Exactly.'

'Ye think they've taken the van down to be with the druids at Stonehenge?'

'Yes.'

'Ach. That's it? That's the best ye can come up with?'

'Yes.'

'What does your mother think?'

'She agrees,' lied Israel.

Ted sighed. 'When I get a hold of those blinkin' hippies . . .' he said. 'Does she want to come with us?'

'Who?'

'Yer mother?'

'No, she does not!' said Israel. 'My mother come with us! Honestly, Ted. And you can just stop your sniffing around her, please.'

'What do ye mean, sniffing around her?' said Ted, drawing himself up to his full shaven-headed height. 'What are ye blerting about now, boy?'

'Come on. You know exactly what I mean. I've told you once to leave her alone, and I mean it. Stop it. Just stop . . . chatting her up, or whatever it is you're doing.'

'Chatting her up?'

They were walking back towards the Mini.

'Well, that's what it bloody looks like,' said Israel. 'Staying up late every night, listening to music together. I can hear you, you know, from upstairs.'

'Ye think I'm a sort o' belly-bachelor after yer mother?'

'I have no idea what a belly-bachelor might be, Ted. I'm just saying I want you to keep away from her.'

'Aye, well, and I'm telling you to mind yer own blinkin' business, or I'll—'

'Don't be threatening me, Ted!'

'I'm not threatening ye, ye eejit!'

They arrived back at the Mini.

'Well, that's what it sounds like to me. Now, anyway' – they got into the car, ready to go – 'So. To be clear. We're going to find the van – without doing any harm to anyone!'

Ted huffed.

'And we'll get this whole thing over and done with. And without my mother! Do you understand?'

'Ach.'

'Do you understand?'

'Aye, and who made you the head bombardier all of a sudden?'

'Head bombardier?'

'Aye, ye're all the same.'

'Who?'

'People.'

'Right.'

Muhammad barked at them approvingly.

'Stonehenge?' said Ted, as they set off, unable to let it go. 'Jesus!'

'Have *you* got a better idea, Ted?'

'I have not,' said Ted, as if the mere suggestion he might have an idea was an offence.

'So,' said Israel. 'As far as I'm concerned that's the end of the discussion. That's what we're doing. It's a long shot, but it might just work.'

'It's a stupit idea,' said Ted.

It was 6 p.m. by the time Ted and Israel eventually arrived at Stonehenge; they'd stopped off in a pub on the way for lunch, which was definitely not a good idea. ('I tell you what I'm going to have,' Ted had announced, hungrily, as they pulled off the motorway, and onto an A-road, and then onto a B-road, and into the pub fore-court. 'What?' 'A ploughman's. Nice fresh bread and cheddar cheese. A real traditional English pub lunch. You can't get that back home.' He was right. 'Your ploughman's, sir,' the barman had said. 'A ploughman's? That's not a ploughman's,' Ted said. 'It's . . .' 'It's sourdough bread, sir, with melted goat's cheese, and a cranberry and sweet chilli coleslaw, and baby gem lettuce.' 'Has this whole country gone completely mad?' said Ted. 'No,' said Israel, 'it's just gone gastro.') And then on round the M25, and on and on, on the M3, and the A303, and onto the A344, in the hot, steaming summer's night, and the approach to Stonehenge, which was like the approach to Lakeside, except this time instead of people being there for their actual shopping, they were there for the *spiritual* shopping, which is cheaper, admittedly, although some actual shopping was also available; as they approached the car park, there were young men and women wearing eccentric floppy rainbow-coloured hats going from car to car, offering juggling balls, and tarot cards, and giant Rizla papers, and novelty lighters. There were also stewards in fluorescent bibs, and policemen with dogs, and barriers, and fences, and burger and hot dog stalls, and vegetarian burger and hot dog stalls, and everywhere you looked, cars, and vans, and more cars and vans. It felt more like a motor show than anything else – a second-hand motor show, at which hippies jeered at the drivers of SUVs.

Israel had never seen Stonehenge before, and he could barely see it now; you just caught a glimpse of it from the car park. From a distance, in the shimmering heat, it looked like big heaps of old moulded Plasticine.

'Nice job,' said Ted, as they got out of the car.

'What is?' said Israel.

'The stones. Probably some sort of mortice and tenon at the top.'

'What?'

'Some sort of wee joggle joint. Must be.' Ted peered at the stones in the distance, as if surveying the quality of a roof on a new-build bungalow. 'Carpentry, basically, isn't it, applied to stones?'

'Right.'

'They're like lintels, if you look,' said Ted. 'Not bad. Must have been a job to do.'

'Right. OK,' said Israel. 'I think it's more the spiritual significance that most people are interested in, rather than the ancient building techniques.'

'Ah'm sure,' said Ted.

'So, anyway,' said Israel. 'I guess now we just look for the van.'

'Aye, it'll take some doing, mind,' said Ted. 'Look around ye. It's like Coleraine on market day.'

They agreed to split up, and went walking up and down the rows of parked cars and vans, which spread out as far as the eye could see, with crowds of people milling around, flying kites, playing Frisbee, playing the bongos; people hugging each other; people cheering and shouting; people crying; stumbling drunks. Occasionally, Israel would stop a sober-looking person and ask them if they'd seen the van.

'I'm looking for a van,' he'd say. 'An old Bedford?'

'Yeah. Nice vans. Good conversion.'

Or, 'Have you seen an old Bedford?'

'D'you want to buy a kite?'

And 'Excuse me, have you seen an old—'

'Could you give me fifty pounds?'

And, 'Have you seen—'

'Dope? Skunk? Crack?'

And, 'Have you—'

'Make Homebrew, Not War.'

And, 'Hello, I—'

'*Waaalllly!*'

Ted had fared no better.

'Any luck?' asked Israel, when they met up again, half an hour later.

'Ach,' said Ted. 'No. Not at all. Look at the place. Disgusting.' There was rubbish everywhere. 'It's like an outdoor bloody loony bin. All these sorts, all scunging about.'

'Scunging?'

'That's right. Load a thugs and auld hippies stocious with drink, playing the drums.'

'Bongos,' said Israel.

'Exactly,' said Ted. 'Completely blinkin' bongos, the lot of 'em.'

'I saw a nice-looking falafel stall, though, if you fancy something to eat,' said Israel.

Ted stared at him and tutted.

'Well, maybe you're right,' said Israel. 'Maybe later?'

A man came striding past them, wearing a yellow fluorescent vest with the word 'STEWARD' printed on it, front and back. He carried a satchel, and had a walkietalkie, and a long, greying goatee beard, down almost to his chest, and his hair was in a ponytail, and he was wearing frayed denim shorts, and walking boots, and a stained leather cowboy hat; he looked like a municipal Gandalf.

'Excuse me?' said Israel.

'Yes, brother?' said the man, halting abruptly, officially, and more than a little ironically, in his stride.

'Brother!' exclaimed Ted.

'Erm. I wonder if you might be able to help?' said Israel.

'That's what I'm here to do,' said the man. 'I Am Here to Help.'

'Good,' said Israel.

'You may call me Lancelot,' said the man.

'Right,' said Israel.

'I'll call ye something,' muttered Ted.

'And this might perhaps answer your questions,

gentlemen.' He handed them a leaflet from his satchel, announcing 'SUMMER SOLSTICE: CONDITIONS OF ENTRY AND INFORMATION'. 'No dogs!' the man announced, pointing to Muhammad. 'Sunrise at 4.58 a.m.,' he said, '*pre-cisely,*' and went to stride off again.

'Erm. Thanks. That's . . . lovely, Lancelot,' said Israel. 'But, actually, we're looking for a van.'

'OK,' said Lancelot, turning back. 'A van? Uh-huh.'

'Which has been . . . we have lost.'

'I see.'

'It's been painted. It has . . . What's it got painted on it, Ted?'

'Black,' said Ted.

'Yeah,' said Israel, 'and over the front there's a sort of big eye, and it says—'

'The Odyssey,' stated Ted, with distaste.

'Yeah, that's it,' said Israel. 'The Odyssey. And down the side it says—'

'The Warehouse of Divine Jewels,' said Ted, with disgust.

'Yeah.'

'OK,' said Lancelot.

'And on the back it says—'

'Follow Us Towards Enlightenment,' said Ted, his voice beyond emotion.

'Yeah,' said Israel. '"Follow Us Towards Enlightenment", with a rainbow painted above it.'

'Sounds like quite a van,' said Lancelot.

'Yeah. It belongs to . . . some friends of ours.'

'I see.'

'We were going to meet them here. You've not seen it?'

'No. No. I don't think so,' said Lancelot. 'But I could check with the other stewards, if you'd like?'

'Right, well, that'd be great actually,' said Israel. 'And this is where all the travellers meet, is it?'

'No, young man,' said Lancelot, 'oh, no, no, no, no, no. *These*' – he emphasised the word 'these' as though indicating his own wayward offspring – '*these* are mostly tourists.' He lowered his voice. 'To be honest with you, they're only here for Fatboy Slim.'

'Oh? Really? Is Fatboy Slim playing?' said Israel.

'No!' Lancelot laughed, as if this were the funniest thing he'd heard in a long time. 'He was on a few years ago – and very good, actually, I should say, though I'm more of a Steely Dan man myself – but now of course everybody expects a rave when they come. This is your first time, I presume?'

'Yes,' said Israel.

'And last,' said Ted.

'Henge virgins,' mused Lancelot, stroking his beard. 'I remember when I was a Henge virgin myself. Seventy-four,' he mused. 'Nineteen seventy-four.'

'Anyway, I'm sorry I missed Fatboy Slim,' said Israel.

'There were rumours this year that Snoop Dogg was going to play,' said the steward. 'I ask you!'

'Snoop Dogg!' Israel laughed. 'As if!'

Ted looked perplexed.

'A lot of your old-style New Agers,' continued the steward, 'they go up past Amesbury there, into the hills.'

'Ah, that'd be where our friends are then, I would have thought,' said Israel. 'Do you think, Ted?'

Ted shrugged.

'Do you still want me to check with the stewards for you?' asked the man.

'No, it's all right, thanks, erm, Lancelot,' said Israel. 'I think our friends'll probably be with the other . . . people. But thanks anyway.'

'Peace,' said the man.

'Off,' said Ted, as they got into the car. 'Lancelot! What sort of a name is that supposed to be? Lancelot? And Fat Boy Jim?'

'Slim. *You've Come a Long Way, Baby*?'

'Aye. And the Soup Dog?'

'Snoop Dogg,' said Israel. 'He's a rapper. *Doggystyle*? D'you not know it?'

'Israel. Let's just find the van and get home, can we?' said Ted. 'Because, I'm telling ye, everyone in this country's on the loonie soup, as far as I can tell. The whole blinkin' lot of ye . . .'

It took them even longer driving away from Stonehenge than driving towards it – diversions, single-lane traffic – but eventually they made it back onto the open roads and into the country.

'So?' said Israel. 'We are looking for—'

'Hippies,' said Ted. 'Gypsies. Troublemakers. Thugs. And ruffians.'

'Right. All of the above?'

'And rappers,' added Ted. 'Find one, we'll find 'em all. All together like Brown's cows.'

Which indeed they were, whatever it meant. Over on the other side of Amesbury, as dusk was turning to dark and they'd almost finished listening to *The Da Vinci Code* audiobook all the way through for the umpteenth time ('This bit, in the film, with Tom Hanks, is brilliant,' said Ted again; and again), they saw lights in the distance; not house or street lights, but what appeared to be fiery streaks and haloes shooting down the hillsides.

'What the hell's going on over there?' said Ted.

Israel peered through the windscreen. 'Well, from a distance it looks to me like it's people burning tyre wheels and rolling them down the hill.'

'That's what I thought,' said Ted. 'But why in God's name would anyone do that?'

'No idea. Some sort of pagan ritual?'

'Burning car tyres?'

'Well, maybe a sort of . . . reinterpretation of some . . . pagan ritual.'

'Aye. That'll be our lot then.'

Israel parked the Mini carefully in a lay-by and they clambered over a stile and began walking down across a field towards the tyre-burners.

It was dark now, but still warm, and there was

the sound of birdsong, and suddenly, here, just for a moment – a tiny moment; just a half even, maybe, or a quarter – in a field somewhere in England, for the first time since being back, Israel felt, for a piece of a moment, at home.

He felt overcome by the intensity of his own existence, and yet at the same time completely disembodied from it, as though he were observing his own experience. He thought for a moment of Robert Browning, and of Robert Bridges, and Thomas Hardy, and Ray Davies, and T.E. Lawrence, and Tim Henman, and of hedgerows, and cricket, and is there honey still for tea? He did not think, for a moment, of Gloria. He felt idyllic.

He decided not to mention this to Ted.

'Get down!' said Ted suddenly, as they approached a hedge. 'Down on yer hunkers.'

'Mywhatters?'

'Hunkers. Quick! Down. Get down! Quick!'

Israel did not get down on his hunkers quick enough, so Ted pushed him down flat into the damp mud.

'Ted!'

'Sshh!'

'What? Why?' whispered Israel. 'Have they seen us?'

'Look. There,' whispered Ted.

'Where?'

'A hint the hedge there.'

'A hint?'

'Aye.'

Israel looked ahint the hedge there.

It wasn't the travellers.

It was a long line of policemen, wearing dark blue boiler suits. And protective helmets. And carrying shields. Shoulder-to-shoulder. In total silence. And behind them, just over the hedge, piled up, were shovels and picks and spades.

'Oh, shit!' said Israel. 'I don't like the look of this, Ted! What are the police doing here?'

'The same thing we're doing here,' whispered Ted. 'Come on, we need to get out of here,' and so they wriggled along on their bellies beside the hedge, as quietly as they could, away from the police, taking a much longer, snaking, circuitous route through fields of wheat towards the travellers and their burning tyres.

Eventually, having successfully evaded the police, and down towards the bottom of the hill, safely hidden in among some trees, they were close enough to observe.

'Travellers in their natural environment,' whispered Israel, putting on his best David-Attenborough-observing-the-gorillas voice.

'Sshh!' said Ted.

Men and women, stripped to the waist, were leaping over fires. Someone was playing bongos, and people were dancing barefoot, and there were jugglers, and fire-eaters, and people were being tattooed, and there was a child dancing around in a luminous skeleton suit, while other people lay around on the ground, wrapped in rugs, passing bottles and joints. And there, among them, sprawled out, were Stones and Bree, locked in a – 'Sweet Jesus!' said Ted – an intimate embrace. And behind them, parked at the top of the hill, among the camper vans, old coaches, horseboxes and ambulances, there was the mobile library, resplendent, glowing in the firelight, in all its repainted glory, its Eye of Horus keeping watch over proceedings.

'Got 'em!' said Ted.

'Keep your voice down!' said Israel.

'The dirty lying thieving bastards!' continued Ted. 'Look at 'em. Totally scunnered, the lot of them. Bloody bunch of scoots.'

'So what do we do now?' said Israel.

'We're going to wait here until they're all well away from the van,' said Ted.

'And then what?'

'We're going to steal her back.'

'Steal her?' whispered Israel. 'That's—'

'How else d'ye think we're going to get her?'

'Well, couldn't we just go and talk to them first?' said Israel. 'And then we could maybe talk to the police, and explain what's happened and—'

'It'll all be happy ever after?' said Ted.

'I'm sure the police would help us.'

'Aye, well, I've never met a policeman before who wanted to help me, and I very much doubt I'm going to meet one now.'

'Well, I don't know about that,' said Israel, 'the

police can be . . .' – and then he recalled a number of recent incidents in Tumdrum, including his being accused of robbery and the kidnap of Mr Dixon, of Dixon and Pickering's department store, for example – 'a little unpredictable,' he admitted. 'But stealing the van back is quite a risky strategy, isn't it?'

'A risky strategy?' said Ted. 'It's justice, ye eejit. What is it you people say?'

'Which people?'

'You.'

'Vegetarian Jewish librarians from north London?'

'Ach, no! "An eye for an eye."'

'"A tooth for a tooth"?'

'Aye.'

'"A hand for a hand"?'

'Exactly.'

'"A foot for a foot"?'

'There you are.'

'Exodus, you mean?'

'Rebritution,' said Ted.

'*Retribution*,' corrected Israel.

'That's right,' said Ted. 'That's what you lot believe, isn't it?'

'Your use of the term "you lot" is not entirely helpful, I must say,' whispered Israel. 'And I think you'll find that in Jewish law, in fact—'

'Ach, well, all I mean is, they stole the van from us, and so we're perfectly entitled to steal her back.'

'Well, that may sound perfectly reasonable,' said Israel, mouthing the words rather than speaking them, 'but I hardly think it would stand up as an argument in a court of law.'

'We're not in a court of law, you eejit! In case you hadn't noticed, we're in a bloody field in the middle of bloody nowhere!'

'Yes, that's right,' whispered Israel, 'and how would you suggest we go about getting the van back, seeing as the obvious obstacles in our way in this bloody field in the middle of bloody nowhere include several hundred travellers, and at least the same number of riot police? Huh?'

'I don't rightly know at the moment,' said Ted. 'I'm thinking. First thing we need to do is lure them away from the van.'

'Well, that's not difficult, is it?' said Israel. 'Four fifty-eight a.m.'

'What?'

'Is the time of sunrise, didn't the steward say? They'll all be up and worshipping the sun then, or something. That'll certainly distract them.'

'Brilliant,' said Ted, patting Israel hard on the back – too hard. Israel almost fell over. 'Brilliant! Ye know what, that's the only sensible thing you've said all day.'

'Thank you,' gasped Israel.

'That'll do us rightly. So all we need to do is keep watch, wait for them to start the auld slaughtering of the sheep and the goats—'

'I don't think they slaughter sheep and goats on the solstice, Ted.'

'Or whatever it is they do, and then we slip in and take the van. We'll take it in turns to keep watch. Right. You bed down there. I'll take the first shift.'

'Bed down where?'

'There.' Ted pointed at the ground.

'On the ground?'

'Aye.'

'I'm not sleeping there.'

'Well, unless you brought a wee blow-up feather bed with you, that'll be exactly where you're sleeping.'

'Couldn't I go back to the car?'

'Of course you can't go back to the car,' said Ted.

'Why not?'

'Because we're on reconnaissance. We've got to keep a lookout.'

'Well met by moonlight!' came a voice then, and suddenly, from out of nowhere, Israel's mother was squatting down in among the trees with them. She was wearing a highly visible bright red Gore-Tex jacket – which matched, worryingly, the colour of her lipstick – and a pair of long brown boots, with heels, with velvet trousers tucked into the top.

'Jesus Christ, woman!' gasped Ted. 'You scared the crap out of me there!'

'Sorry, boys,' she whispered.

'Mother! What are you doing here?'

'I could hardly let you two handle it yourselves, could I?'

'How did you get here?'

'Ari gave me a lift down. In his Mercedes,' she added significantly.

'But how did you find us?'

'You said Stonehenge. Travellers. It's not that difficult, is it? We used to do an annual treasure hunt for the PTA when you were at school. Do you remember? That was much more difficult. People used to get lost on Hampstead Heath. They're not exactly hidden away here, are they? So, what's the crack?'

'You're an abstrakerous old so-and-so when you want to be, aren't ye, Mrs Armstrong?' said Ted admiringly.

'Am I?'

'Ye are.'

'Is that a bad thing?'

'I didn't say that.'

'Good.'

'All right, you two,' said Israel. 'Enough already. They're up to something else there now.'

The travellers seemed to be preparing for some kind of ritual involving poles and sticks.

'It's quite a nice little set-up they've got there, actually, isn't it?' whispered Israel's mother.

'Bloody headers,' said Ted.

'What are they doing?' asked Israel. 'Is it some sort of pagan ritual?'

'It looks to me like they're preparing to do limbo-dancing,' said Israel's mother.

'Ah!' said Israel. 'You're right.'

'They're all on drugs, sure,' said Ted.

'How can you tell?' said Israel's mother. 'I've often wondered.'

'Aye, well . . . I have spent a bit of time smoking dope meself, like.'

'Really?' said Israel's mother.

'Aye.'

'What?' said Israel.

'I am surprised to hear that,' said Israel's mother. 'Man like yourself, Ted.'

'Well.'

'And when you say a lot of time, you mean what? Days? Weeks?'

'Years, actually.'

'Years?'

'Aye. In Australia.'

'What the hell were you doing smoking dope in Australia for years?' said Israel.

'Better than painkillers,' said Ted, gazing off into the distance. 'Sometimes a man needs to forget.'

'Right.'

'I'd lost the run of meself entirely,' said Ted.

'I did smoke a funny cigarette once,' said Israel's mother. 'At a party, it was. In Crouch End, I think. Somewhere like that.'

'All right, let's not get into a game of truth or dare here, Mother, shall we, please.'

'You are a dark horse, Ted,' said Israel's mother, snuggling up close to him in the dark.

'Oh, God. I'm going to have a lie down here,' said Israel. 'You two keep quiet, all right? Wake me up when something interesting happens.'

Israel's sleep, when it came – muddy, twiggy, to the sound of Ted and his mother whispering, and distant bongos – was utterly wretched.

First, he dreamt he was wandering through the streets of Tumdrum with a seven-flamed candelabrum, with people trying to blow it out. Then he dreamt he was outside a locked door, and there were people inside, laughing. And then he dreamt of Gloria.

Vivid, terrible dreams of Gloria. He was somewhere waiting for her. He called out to her, but just as he caught her she reached the front door of their flat. He grabbed her by the arm and swung her around. And it wasn't her. It was another woman. And she stood still, this other woman, terrified, looking at him. It wasn't Gloria. She had her mobile phone raised to her mouth. And she started to scream at him. 'I'm so sorry,' he was saying, in his dream. 'I thought you were . . .' The woman was yelling at him. 'I'm calling the police,' she was screaming. He was running through the streets.

They were not pleasant dreams.

He woke with Ted poking him sharply in the ribs. His throat was parched. He was sweating and shivering. His body hurt all over.

'Wake up! This is us!' said Ted.

'This was me,' said Israel, wiping away dry mud from his face.

Even though he was awake, what happened next seemed to take place in dream-time rather than in reality: the whole thing was complete chaos, lit by a weird, looming blue and pink dawn light.

'This is like a film by Peter Greenaway,' he mumbled.

'Peter O'Toole,' said Ted. '*Zulu Dawn.*'

'*Mary Poppins,*' said Israel's mother. 'The bit at the fair.'

The travellers had formed themselves into a series of concentric circles. They stood holding hands in silence. Some kind of totem had been erected in the middle of the field, with brightly coloured ribbons pinned to it. They began circling the totem, chanting. They closed their eyes. The chanting grew louder. The sun was rising.

'What are they saying?' whispered Israel's mother.

'I couldn't care less,' said Ted. 'But I reckon this is our chance. Come on. Israel, any trouble, anyone approaches ye, ye land a quick right under the ribcage, and then a left behind the right ear, and they'll go down.'

'What?'

'A wee short un under the ribcage and then a left round the butt of the ear!'

'I'm not punching anybody,' said Israel.

'Well, let them punch you then. See how you like that,' said Israel's mother.

They stepped quickly from the cover of the trees, and Ted began shambling up alongside the hedge, Israel's mother following, up the hill, towards the van.

'Ted!' gasped Israel, behind him. 'Wait!'

'Come on, Fatboy Slim,' said Ted. 'Let's go.'

Somehow, stumbling, hugging the hedge, they made it to the van without being seen by the travellers, who remained absorbed in worship.

Ted had the keys. They clambered inside.

'Home!' said Ted.

'Hello, van,' said Israel.

'So this is the van?' said Israel's mother. 'It's quite cosy, isn't it?'

'Ah!' said Ted, opening up the glove compartment. 'Me Sudoku. Good.'

'Now what?' said Israel.

At that moment the sun rose decisively above the treetops, yellow light flooding the scene before them – the travellers circling and chanting – and the sound of the chanting was joined by the sound of distant drumming.

'What's that?' said Israel.

'I don't know.'

Israel ran to the back of the van and peered out.

It was the police, advancing in a line, banging their riot shields.

'Shit! Ted! I don't like the look of this, Ted.'

'What?'

'It's the police! I think the police are on to us, Ted.'

'They're not on to us. They're after these crazies. Just stay calm, we'll be fine.'

As Ted spoke, the police began beating on the sides of the vans with their truncheons.

'Ted!' said Israel's mother, who seemed frightened for the first time. 'This isn't good, Ted.'

'Sshh! Just stay down. We need to pick our moment.'

'For what?' said Israel. 'Ted? Pick our moment for what?'

The police had reached the mobile library and began banging on its sides – the sound like earth being piled upon a coffin – and then they passed on by, and then, when he could safely see the backs of the police officers moving down the hill towards the travellers, Ted turned on the ignition, slammed the van into reverse, and in one movement managed to pull the van out of its tight spot, and started gunning up across the field.

'Oh, shit!' said Israel. 'Ted! What are you doing?'

'We're going home!' said Ted.

'Yee-ha!' said Israel's mother.

'Ted! Stop!'

'I'm not stopping!'

'This is fun!' cried Israel's mother.

'Look! Stop! I'm serious! Stop! Up ahead there. There's a ditch! The police have dug a ditch! That's why they had all the—'

'We'll be fine,' said Ted.

'Ted, we're not going to be fine. We're going to die!'

'Shut up!' yelled Ted. 'And put your bloody seat-belt on. We need to take this at speed!'

'Oh, God!'

Israel fumbled with his seatbelt as Ted steered the van as close to the hedge as possible, so that at least two wheels were still – just – on solid ground when they hit the ditch.

'Brace yerselves!'

The van went down – and down – on Israel's side, knocking Israel, mid-seatbelt-fastening, forwards against the windscreen and sideways against the door.

'Aaaghhh!'

But somehow it came up again – 'All right?' said Ted. 'Fine,' moaned Israel. 'Never better!' said Israel's mother – and now they were heading for the gate. Two policemen started dragging it closed.

'Oh, my God! Ted, no! No! Ted, we're never going to make it through that. We're going to die!'

'We're not going to die. They drove it through, we must be able to drive it out.'

'Yeah, but, Ted, they weren't . . .'

Israel's mother was staring, transfixed, in the wing mirror. 'There are people chasing us,' she said.

'Who?'

'Half-naked men and women!'

'The travellers, Ted!'

'Good.'

'And the police!'

'Even better.'

They were hurtling towards the gate.

'Ted! They're going to shut the gate on us.'

'Hippies!' yelled Ted.

They're not hippies!' shouted Israel. 'They're the police!'

'They're all the same!' yelled Ted as they reached the gate, the police still struggling to drag it closed.

They just made it through, and onto the road. Ted wrenched the van left.

'Oh, God, that was close,' said Israel.

'Aye,' said Ted. 'We're all right now.'

'That was great!' said Israel's mother.

There was the sound of a police siren behind them.

'Oh, shit!' said Israel. 'Ted!'

'You take the wheel,' said Ted.

'What?' screamed Israel.

'You take the wheel.'

'Why?'

'I'm going to sort the peelers out.'

'What are you going to do? Don't shoot at them!'

'Of course I'm not going to shoot at them! I've not got a gun!'

'Good!'

Ted got up out of the driver's seat, and Israel slid across, while Ted went to the back of the van with Israel's mother and began opening the disabled access door.

'Ted!' yelled Israel. 'What the hell are you doing?'

'We're going to give the hippies their furniture back!'

'What?'

The door came open and Ted and Israel's mother were throwing stuff out of the back: rugs, appliquéd cushions, scented candles and, with a final heave, the frayed sofa, which fell – thunk! – and effectively blocked the road.

They drove on, as inconspicuously as they could, out of Amesbury, away from Stonehenge, sticking to B-roads.

'Now where?' said Israel.

'I don't know,' said Ted.

'Well, you've come this far. How far to your Mobile Meet?' said Israel's mother.

CHAPTER 15

Britain's premier – and only – convention of
mobile librarians, organised by the Chartered
Institute of Information and Library
Professionals, was taking place in a disused
airfield. The event was the opposite of the gathering at Stonehenge, just a few hours' drive away.
There was here no worshipping of the Earth
Mother by people with strange names wearing
eccentric clothes. Instead, here were men and
women called Ken and Barbara, in sensible shoes
and cardigans, standing around drinking tea and
coffee from flasks, and admiring each other's
vehicles, which had been polished and preened
and primped in preparation. There were about
fifty mobile library vans in attendance, parked in
neat rows. And in the last row, at the end of the
row, was the mobile library from Tumdrum.

Ted and Israel, and Israel's mother, had missed
most of the day's seminars and lectures – on Public
Library Service Standards, and the Disability
Discrimination Act, and New Developments in
Livery, and they barely had time to visit the coach-
fitting companies and their million-pound display

vans, which had upper floors, and on-board toilets and kitchen areas, and mini-cinemas. They had time only to grab a few brochures and then hurry to the main Nissen hut to eat egg sandwiches and wait for the awarding of the prizes.

Ted and Israel did not, needless to say, win the prize for State of the Art Vehicle. Or the prize for Best Livery. Or indeed the Drivers Challenge, presented in memory of Noah Stanley, although Ted felt pretty confident that if he'd been there in time he'd have stood a good chance. The prize for Concours D'Elégance went to a van from Bexley with a Maisie the Mouse painted on the side.

'I owe you,' huffed Ted. 'One thousand—'

'I think we'll call it quits,' said Israel.

'And now,' announced the judge, who was a man wearing a suit that he'd had so long it was fashionable, 'we come to the most hotly contested prize, as always, at the Meet. The Delegates' Choice. I think you'll agree, we've had a great turnout this year, and as always there have been so many different vans that are all so distinctive. But the ballot papers are in, they have been counted, and I can tell you that we have this year an unprecedented unanimous decision by you, the delegates. I think we can all agree that none of us has ever seen a mobile library quite like it. So, for originality, ingenuity, inventiveness, sheer fun and wit, the prize this year is awarded to . . . "The Odyssey", or should I call it "The Warehouse of

Divine Jewels"? To our brothers from across the water in Northern Ireland, Ted Carson and Israel Armstrong, and their magnificent mobile library from Tumdrum.'

As they walked forward to collect the prize the doors to the Nissen hut burst open and in walked Stones and Bree, closely followed by a dozen armed police officers.

CHAPTER 16

The police decided that in the circumstances Israel and Ted could be released without charge, and Ted in return decided not to press charges against Stones and Bree. Israel's mother decided she could maybe do with some more adventure in her life, and that it was time to spread her wings a little.

And Israel had made his decision also: he was going to go and surprise Gloria. Five days after arriving in England, five days without seeing her, five days in pursuit of the van. Now, he was going in pursuit of her. He was going to the flat; to their flat.

He'd brought flowers. And chocolates. He was going to do it right.

He caught the bus. There was the little park opposite the flat. He went to sit in the park. To prepare himself. You could see the park from their window. He would sometimes watch people come and go in and out of the park. Parents with little children – the swings, the roundabouts – how sometimes they'd be arguing or angry. And there was a man he used to see every day, always wearing a suit; the man, not much older than himself, obviously got home every day and said, 'I'll take the children', and he'd go to the park, and he'd be absorbed in playing with his children: the sight of it, day in, day out; week in, week out. It became part of Israel's routine, coming home from the Bargain Bookstore at Lakeside, waiting for Gloria, watching the man watching his children. And then one day he wasn't there. He must have moved, or moved on.

There was no one in the park today. It was a beautiful London summer's evening. He sat on the bench. If Gloria arrived he'd be able to see her. He could see their window.

He waited. And he waited.

But he couldn't sit waiting for ever.

The little patch of front lawn and the flower-beds at the front of the flats; Mrs Graham, one of the old women on the ground floor, she kept it nice. Gloria had never liked her; she said she was smelly and weird; she called her Grumps. But Israel quite liked her; she reminded him of his grand-mother: she was balding; she chain-smoked, her hair vivid with nicotine; and she would occasion-ally post furious letters of complaint – too much noise, people leaving the main door on the snib – addressed to 'OCCUPANTS!'. She was harmless.

He stood on the doorstep and could feel himself shivering and shaking with nerves. He was excited also, as though having recently won something, or been awarded a prize. He'd washed his hair specially, and shaved. He was wearing his smartest clothes: fresh cords.

He was ready. He'd returned.

Maybe it was a mistake, though, him coming. There was a great weight of the unspoken between them now. Why hadn't she rung? Why hadn't she written? Why hadn't she visited? What was he going to say? He held a hand out in front of him – he was shaking. Not like a leaf exactly. More like a jelly on the plate. He felt sick. He'd had all his Nurofen.

The old entry system to the flats. The porcelain bell buttons.

Should he stay, or should he go?

He'd come this far.

He was determined that they weren't going to argue. They just needed to talk.

The cool touch of the bell on his fingers.

No reply.

He rang again.

Nothing.

He checked in his pocket for the keys.

Took a deep breath.

Let himself in.

They'd had it fixed, the main entry door – it used to jam halfway. The communal hallway was completely plain, magnolia, blue-grey carpets, the mirror. He glanced at himself in the mirror, wrinkled his brow, adjusted his glasses. His face was comic: there was nothing he could do about it; he always looked as though he weren't able to take himself entirely seriously, as though he were not entirely in control of his expressions. At best, he thought, you might describe it as charm. At worst . . . He tried to look sophisticated. He tried to look smart. But he couldn't. He was permanently dishevelled. Too big, too awkward. Not somehow . . . right. But, if he tried, he could carry it off. Shoulders back, head up – if it worked for Gérard Depardieu . . .

Going up the stairs, it felt like he'd never been away. He could remember the day they'd moved in together, how they'd talked for months about moving in together, and then eventually it had just seemed like the right thing to do, and so they did: they'd got the deposit together somehow – mostly a loan from Gloria's father, nice man, wealthy, charming, *bastard* – and then hired a van for the day, and Israel had picked up his stuff from his mother's house, and Gloria collected her stuff from her house-share, and they'd done it. That was it. It seemed so simple, looking back. All the future ahead of them. Names on the doorbell. Israel and Gloria, Adam and Eve.

Up the last flight, and he looked at the walls, at the scuff marks where they'd carried up his old desk, and everything else; every stick of their furniture he'd carried up these stairs. Their bed: going to buy their bed together. IKEA. And Gloria insisting on buying the best mattress they could afford, and it was so heavy they'd had to ask their neighbours to help them up the stairs. Heaving their way up the stairs, and in through the door and into the bedroom. The fresh mattressy smell of it. The smell of their lives together. He could remember himself tingling with anticipation.

He came to the front door. He thought it would be better to knock, just in case.

He knocked.

And knocked again.

Perhaps he'd made a mistake in coming. Had he made a mistake in coming? He couldn't decide.

He put his eye to the little spyglass.

And then, at last, without further further ado, Israel Armstrong took out his key, put it in the lock, turned, pushed, and walked in.

Finally, he was home.

'Hello? Gloria? Hello? It's only me.'

The flat swallowed his words.

No one was home.

Gloria wasn't there.

The hallway looked different. He couldn't decide at first what it was – not much. It was just . . . different. It wasn't as if she'd redecorated or anything. A complete rearrangement would have been easier to understand: but this, this felt more like . . . It wasn't a riposte. It was more like a subtle undermining. It was the posters. They'd never agreed on the posters. He didn't like Klimt. She didn't like Klee. He had that Matisse. She had a Georgia O'Keeffe. They hadn't agreed on a lot of little things. But it didn't really matter, stuff like that. He didn't like *Friends*. She didn't like *Seinfeld*. She loved *The West Wing*. He loved *The Sopranos*. It didn't matter. That's just who they were. Israel and Gloria. Gloria and Israel.

His posters had gone.

And the other things: a carved wooden bowl that his mother had given them, for salad, which Gloria had never liked, which they'd used for keys and loose change, gone; the pile of newspapers and magazines which he used to stack by the phone, gone; the old galvanised-steel USA mail box with the red flag, which he kept by the door for umbrellas, gone. Gloria had stamped her mark upon the place, simply by erasing his. And it was *her* place. For legal purposes, when they moved in, Gloria had insisted that she sign the contracts for the flat; it made sense; Israel at the time wasn't earning much money. His name was on no piece of paper. He did not officially exist.

On into the main room, the living room.

He'd decorated this room when they moved in. From top to bottom. Stripped the paper. Put up fresh lining paper. Badly. Repapered. Big job. The radiators: he could remember pretending that he knew how to bleed the radiators, to impress Gloria, and how he'd attempted to take the first one off the wall, and not only did he find a stash of crinkly old porn mags stuffed down behind it, but he then discovered to his horror that the radiator itself had rusted to its brackets and the whole wall came away, bracket and radiator attached, and it turned out that his leaching had been rather less than successful because the carpet was soaked with stagnant water, and he just about managed to re-fix the brackets back on using some Polyfilla but then he couldn't seem to get the radiator fitted back on and attached to the pipe, and there was water dripping not only from the radiator but also from the pipe, and . . . Everything. He'd done everything here. He'd made it his own; *they'd* made it *their* own.

But now . . . His books. She'd moved his books. His books had been cleared from the top row of shelves, the IKEA shelves, and in their place were photographs. None of him. Photographs of Gloria and her family. Black and white photographs – a family in black and white photographs; that's the kind of family they were – in modern frames. And Gloria's law books. The kind of book that cost £500. His books – paperbacks, books that cost about £5.99, maximum – were now jumbled and double-stacked on the bottom shelves, down behind the sofa.

He knelt down, pushed away the sofa, looked at his books, stood up.

Took a deep breath.

Into the kitchen. The little baby Gaggia in the corner: his machine. The top-of-the-range blender: hers. It was cleaner than he remembered, the kitchen.

The whole flat seemed to have been deep-cleaned.

Cleaned of him.

And finally the bedroom. Candles in the bedroom. New duvet cover – white. Gloria had a thing about Egyptian cotton. And the pillows had been re-distributed, presumably so that Gloria was sleeping in the middle of the bed. His presence had been overruled. His space had been colonised. He checked the wardrobe. Where were his clothes? Since arriving in Tumdrum he'd been wearing cast-off clothes, like a scarecrow or a younger brother. His clothes had gone. He looked under the bed. He had no idea where she might have put his clothes.

He went back into the living room. Sat down on the sofa. The sofa he had carried up the stairs.

He was definitely going to maintain his dignity.

It was fine.

Everything was going to be absolutely fine.

He tried to do some deep breathing – he'd read about deep breathing exercises in a book from the mobile library, *Breathe to Live, Live to Breathe*, by an American with a foreign name and he'd tried the exercises a few times, when they were parked up in lay-bys; they made him sleepy, but now, when he needed to, he found he couldn't do it. His breathing was . . .

He felt himself shaking again, and he began to feel long dormant emotions, terrible forces, welling up within him. He didn't know exactly what they were: rage, passion, lust for destruction. It was as though . . . He couldn't explain it. It felt like he had suddenly fallen into a whirlpool. Him, he – Israel Armstrong, mild-mannered, vegetarian, Jewish librarian – was drowning. And he had to fight for his life.

He suddenly got up and started to ransack – that was the only word for it – *ransack* the flat, looking for clues. Clues of something.

Of another man's occupation?

Possibly.

Possibly it was that.

Maybe that's what he was looking for. Maybe he knew. Maybe he'd known all along.

He searched through the cupboards. The wardrobe they'd carried up the stairs together. The chest of drawers that Gloria had inherited from an aunt; he searched under the bed; in every drawer. Nothing. There was no sign anywhere, no trace. But then wouldn't they deliberately hide the evidence? They? Them?

He was shaking so violently now he could barely contain himself. He thought he was going to explode. He realised he could never be satisfied ever again and he found himself yelling out loud, 'I will never be satisfied.'

Then there was the vase. By the bed. A vase that Gloria's mother had given them when they'd moved in together. He'd always hated that vase. White vase. He picked it up. It was full of stagnant water. He held it – felt it, the weight of it – in his hand.

And he went to the bathroom and poured out the water. Then returned to the bedroom, stood by the bed, felt it, held it – and threw it, very deliberately, very hard against the wall on Gloria's side of the bed. It dented the wall – plasterboard walls. The vase shattered.

And that seemed to do it. That broke the spell.

He was overcome then with guilt and shame, and he fell down onto his knees and began quietly sobbing.

He cried, and he cried – deep, satisfying, pointless, lonely, self-pitying tears – and then he picked himself up, went to the bathroom, wiped his eyes, took some toilet roll and returned to the bedroom.

And he carefully picked up every scrap and splinter of the vase.

He wasn't angry with Gloria. He wasn't disappointed with Gloria.

He was angry and disappointed in himself.

He was stupid.

Totally stupid.

It was late. He lay down on the bed.

That night the ceiling, half lit by the streetlights through the curtains, became the screen for Israel's nightmares. He saw himself with Ted, in the van, travelling for ever. Travelling with no hope of arrival or rest. Pointlessness. Humiliations. Gloria with other men. Ted with his mother.

He was stupid.

Totally stupid.

It could never have worked between them. They were mismatched. Gloria's family: they had money. They were 'accomplished' – that was it. There was no higher term of praise in Gloria's family for someone they admired: 'accomplished'. Which meant money, really. He remembered Gloria's mother had once used the phrase 'inferior people'. He was an inferior person. Worse: he was neither one thing nor the other. He was neither inferior nor superior. He was just middling. He imagined himself riding in the van, down the middle of a long road, and then suddenly braking sharply, and the van beginning to keel over. The feeling of the van falling over.

He fell into a deep sleep.

And when he awoke it was morning.

And there was still no sign of Gloria.

The sun was streaming in, bright and pale. He got up, went to the kitchen. Went to the fridge. Ate a couple of crackers spread with cream cheese. Took a slug of white wine from an opened bottle. There was no other food in the house.

Gloria must have been eating out.

The flat felt cold and unlived in.

He didn't know what to do. He thought about leaving a note. That wasn't right. He went back to the bedroom. He looked again at the pile of books on the table beside the bed.

Law books.

Hardback history.

And there, on the top, was a copy of *Postmodern Allegories?* His friend Danny's book.

It must have been the copy he'd sent Israel.

It was probably the copy he'd sent him.

'Ah!'

It felt as though someone had inserted a knife into his foot. He rocked back onto the bed, and brought his foot round – a piece of the vase was embedded in there. He'd missed a bit. When he pulled it out, there was a little blister, a bleb of blood. A drop of blood on the white cotton sheet.

He lay down in a stupor, a kind of hungover

dullness descending upon him, weighing him down, a deep weariness overcoming him.

He was filled with loathing for his life. Not only away in Tumdrum, but also here in London. He no longer had a life in London. You have your life where you're living.

Everything seemed pointless and meaningless.

He thought he might perhaps spend a few days in bed, waiting for Gloria to return. Waiting to see what happened.

Knowing nothing would happen.

The phone rang. He was convinced it was Gloria. He jumped out of bed, ran to the hallway, grabbed the phone before the answerphone message began.

'Hello?' he said. 'Hello?'

The person at the other end of the phone hung up.

Israel dialled number recall.

It was Gloria's parents.

He frantically dialled, unthinking, the phone rang, someone picked up, and Israel said, 'Hello, Gloria? Can I speak to Gloria please?'

And it was Gloria's father saying, 'Who's calling?'

And Israel said, 'It's me, Israel, . . . Gloria's . . .'

And he detected a slight pause, voices in the background.

'I'll just check if she's here, Israel.'

And Mr Kahn said, 'She's not here at the moment, Israel.'

And finally, Israel knew.

It was over.

CHAPTER 17

They were driving back through England in silence.

Driving through England meant nothing. Driving through England felt to Israel like driving through his own loss and ignorance. He understood nothing about England. In Israel's mind, calling himself an Englishman meant taking no notice of what it meant to be English. His identity as an Englishman was non-existent. Yet he had no other national identity: he was hardly European. And he certainly wasn't Irish. He was, notionally, Jewish, but he had effectively reduced all his allegiances down to himself. And now, without Gloria, he was not even a couple. He was an example only of himself. There was nothing to be elaborated or extrapolated from him: he was Israel Armstrong, and that was all.

'Ye're thinking very loudly,' said Ted. 'Ye want to stop yer blertin' there. I can't hear me own ears here.'

'What?'

'Something on yer mind?'

'Mmm.'

'Ye're thinking about?'

'The future,' said Israel.

'What about it?'

'I despair of the future.'

'Well, it speaks very highly of you,' said Ted.

'Let's go home,' said Israel.

'You are home,' said Ted.

'Not any more,' said Israel.

'I don't know what ye're coming back for. Ye'll be resigning anyway, when we get back, eh?'

'I guess.'

'Shall we stop off at a service station for a coffee and something to eat?' said Israel's mother. 'Watford Gap?'

ACKNOWLEDGEMENTS

For previous acknowledgements see *The Truth About Babies* (Granta Books, 2002), *Ring Road* (4th Estate, 2004), *The Mobile Library: The Case of the Missing Books* (Harper Perennial, 2006), and *The Mobile Library: Mr Dixon Disappears* (Harper Perennial, 2006). These stand, with exceptions. In addition I would like to thank the following. (The previous terms and conditions apply: some of them are dead; most of them are strangers; the famous are not friends; none of them bears any responsibility.)

Mark Adair, Agnostic Mountain Gospel Choir, Lisa Allardice, Mark Amory, Rosie Apponyi, Matthew Anderson, Clare Asquith, Tove Bakke, Brendan Barrington, Oonagh Barronwell, Nicholas A. Basbanes, Carmel Beaney, Tal Ben-Shahar, E.V. Bernini, Andrew Black, Terence Blacker, Shona Blair, Jean Bleakney, Stephen Bleakney, Humphrey Bogart, Walter Bonatti, Sam Bowman, Owen Bowcott, Maureen Boyle, Fran Brearton, Oliver Broderick, Charlie Brown, Claire Burgoyne, James M. Cain, Garrett Carr,

Ruth Carr, Ciaran Carson, Daragh Carville, Gavin Carville, Helen Cathcart, Martina Chapman, Lorraine Clarke, Tom Clarke, Faye Clowe, Julian Cope, E.V. Corbett, Victoria Coulson, William Crawley, Edmund Crispin, Robert Crosby, Amanda Cross, Daniel Cullen, Pauline Currie, Cahal Dalat, Robina Dam, Teresa Davey, Emily Dedakis, Jonathan Derbyshire, The Destroyers, Hannah Devlin, Maria Dickenson, Lizzie Dipple, Philip Dodd, Garbhan Downey, Maria Doyle, Linda Drain, Sarah Durand, Terry Eagleton, Joe Eszterhas, Pauline Evans, Paul Farley, Leontia Flynn, Leigh Forgie, Anne-Marie Fyfe, Miriam Gamble, Becky Gardiner, Elaine Gaston, James Geary, Carlo Gebler, Kieran Gilmore, Ray Givans, Alison Gordon, Rebecca Gower, Dominic Graham, Ken Gregory, Michelle Griffin, Lisa Guidarini, The Hackensaw Boys, Salwa Hamid, Rabbi Hayim Halevy Donin, P.J. Hart, Andrew Harvey, Maria Hatchell, Gerry Hellawell, Dr Henry, Katherine Herring, Laurence Heyworth, Reginald Hill, Jonathan Hodgers, Christine Hooper, Caoilinn Hughes, Patrick Hughes, Michael Innes, Kenneth Irvine, Richard Irvine, Chris Jackson, Paul Jeffcutt, Oliver Jeffers, Rory Jeffers, Peter Johnston, H.R.F. Keating, Michael Keating, Lisa Keogh, Dave Kinghan, Lizzy Kingston, Matt Kirkham, Emily Krump, Dan Le Sac (and Scroobious Pip), Dan Leith, Amy-Rachel Lindsay, Leon Litvack, Edna Longley, Michael Longley, Lemas Lovas,

Ross MacDonald, Paul Maddern, Maureen Maher, Bernard Malamud, David Marcus, John McAllister, Mrs McAvoy, Niall McCabe, Cormac McCarthy, Eugene McCusker, Rachel McDowell, Philip McGowan, Jayne McKee, Colin McKeown, Olwyn McKinney, Chloe McLenaghan, Fionola Meredith, Robbie Meredith, Richard Milbank, Sinead Morrissey, Oliver Mort, Barbara Morton, Marie-Louise Muir, Jane Murdoch, Fionnuala O'Connell, Hugh Oddling-Smee, Malachi O'Doherty, Philip Oltermann, Christopher Owens, Boom Pam, Otto Penzler, Andrew Pepper, Charmain Porter, Nicci Praca, Gail Prentice, Ellery Queen, Antonia Quirke, Joan Rahilly, Lucy Ramsey, Tom Ramussen, David Rice, Asche Rider, Gareth Robinson, Chrissie Russell, David Russell, Noel Russell, W.L. Saunders, Maureen Scott, Michael Scott, Helena Scullion, Matt Seaton, Maire Shannon, Michael Shannon, Bernard Share, Chris Sherry, David Smylie, Damian Smyth, Diane Spratt, Elaine Stockman, C.J. Stone, Pat Taylor, James Thompson, John Thompson, Sara Tibbs, Susan Tomaselli, David Torrans, Eoghan Walls, Emma Ward, Caroline Walsh, Joseph Wambaugh, Laurence Wareing, Donald Westlake, Emma Whiteside, Vi Whitehead, Paul Wild, Paul Willetts, Alex Wylie, Rachel Younger.